Judith Cook was born and brought up in Manchester. She began her career as a journalist for the *Guardian* and went on to become a freelance writer, winning awards for investigative journalism and having several highly acclaimed works of fiction and non-fiction published. She is a part-time lecturer in Elizabethan and Jacobean theatre at Exeter University. Judith Cook lives in the fishing port of Newlyn, Cornwall, with her partner and two cats.

The first entry in the Casebook by Dr Simon Forman, *Death of a Lady's Maid*, is also available from Headline.

Praise for Judith Cook's work:

'Ms Cook sets her scene well and gives a fine feeling of what the atmosphere of the time might have been like. I enjoyed this one very much'   *Irish Times*

'Judith Cook brings her investigative journalist skills usefully to bear . . . along with a rattling good grip on the plot'   *Guardian*

'Cook roots her exciting and readable novel firmly in the world of the playhouses'   *Financial Times*

'A good, pacy read . . . Cook is keen on fine historical detail and has obviously mastered her subject'
                                                    Evening Standard

'A well-balanced thriller . . . intelligent and entertaining'
                                                                    TLS

Also by Judith Cook

The Slicing Edge of Death
To Brave Every Danger
Death of a Lady's Maid
Blood on the Borders

Murder at
the Rose

Judith Cook

HEADLINE

First published in 1998
by HEADLINE BOOK PUBLISHING

First published in paperback in 1998
by HEADLINE BOOK PUBLISHING

10 9 8 7 6 5 4 3 2

ISBN 0 7472 5609 8

Printed and bound in Great Britain by
Clays Ltd, St Ives plc

HEADLINE BOOK PUBLISHING
A division of Hodder Headline PLC
338 Euston Road
London NW1 3BH

To Ric Rutson
For his invaluable assistance with Word 6!

ACKNOWLEDGEMENTS

My most heartfelt acknowledgement is to the late Dr A. L. Rowse who edited the diaries and casebook of the real Dr Simon Forman and presented him in such a sympathetic light. Also to the Shakespeare Centre library in Stratford-upon-Avon for their invaluable assistance, and Southam public library for information on the drovers' roads. Reference books used include *Henslowe's Diaries* (*the* source book on Elizabethan theatre), edited by R. A. Foakes and R. T. Rickert and published by Cambridge University press in 1961; *John Hall and his Patients* edited by Joan Lane and published by the Shakespeare Birthplace Trust in 1996; *Culpeper's Complete Herbal* (Wordsworth Edition 1995) and *Shakespeare's Stratford* by Edgar Fripp, published by Oxford University Press in 1926. The remedies referred to are those used by Simon Forman himself, by Dr John Hall (Shakespeare's son-in-law) and recommended by Culpeper. Astrological information comes from Simon Forman's own diaries and casenotes and a sixteenth-century treatise *A Compendious Description of Natural Astrology Never to be Handled Before* by John Indagine which, so far as I am aware, has never been published since and which was kindly lent to me by its owner.

Chapter 1

The Old Wife's Tale

Promptly at twelve noon William Miller, the Rose Theatre's bookman, went into the tiring house at the back of the playhouse to make sure all the actors were present for the afternoon's performance. He counted heads, checking them against the cast list in his hand, and noted that Charles Spencer and Thomas Pope were still missing. Even as he registered the fact Pope arrived, somewhat breathless, explaining that he had taken his young son over to Blackfriars and that they'd been forced to return by London Bridge, there being so many people competing for the services of the boatmen.

He immediately went and collected his costume for the role of Sacramant the Sorcerer off one of the two wooden rails used for that purpose and swiftly changed into it, before sitting down and joining his colleagues at the trestle table along one of the walls on which were a series of mirrors, placed at regular intervals. He peered into one of them, grimaced, then combed his hair and reached for the powder and rouge pot. As he did so the trumpeter, high on the platform almost level with the roof of the theatre, blew the first fanfare to proclaim that the afternoon's performance would commence in an hour's time.

The young actor who was sitting next to Pope, busily painting his face a ghastly greenish-white, was obviously annoyed at Spencer's late arrival. His name was John Lane and he was playing a ghost with the unlikely name of Jack, which could lead to some confusion as he was usually known as 'Jack' himself. 'I don't know what's got into him,' he grumbled. 'We've neither of us played these parts before and we were supposed to go through our lines in the last scene with George there before the performance, just to make

1

sure.' He motioned towards a man of about thirty who was leaning against the opposite wall, a cup of wine in his hand. George Peele, the author of the play about to be performed, was rarely seen without such a cup and had the complexion to prove it.

He seemed sober enough now however. 'No need to worry yet, Jack, there's still plenty of time,' he replied, calmly.

The sound of hasty footsteps heralded the arrival of the missing actor, a good-looking, fair young man. He apologised profusely as he came in through the door, producing a small bottle from his pocket which he flourished at the actors. 'My throat's been giving me some trouble, so I went to ask Dr Forman if he could give me a draught for it but he was busy with someone else and I had to wait.'

'Your throat didn't seem to worry you last night,' countered Jack Lane. 'You spent hours talking to those two young women in the Anchor Tavern. Persuading them you were irresistible, I suppose.'

'Jealous, are you?' asked Spencer brightly as he took his costume off the rack.

'Of a rattlepate like you? I'd as lief be jealous of a cheapjack at a fair.'

'For heaven's sake, both of you, stop bickering,' broke in the bookman. 'You've enough to do before the show as it is. When you're all in costume and made up, the master carpenter and I want all of you under the stage to go through the three special sequences again so that you all know exactly what you're doing. Most especially,' he continued, raising his voice as the babble of conversation resumed, 'all those involved with the apprentices playing in the Demon Furies scene, the "heads in the well" scene and, most of all, at the end when Jack the Ghost returns to his grave. You all clear about that?'

There was a general chorus of assent. The bookman left the tiring room and the actors continued with their preparations, one of the older men assisting the three young boys playing the girls' roles as they struggled into their farthingales. Three wigs, carefully prepared by the wigmaster for their use, stood on short poles on a table. The elderly actor was also dressed as a woman, as he was playing the role of the Old Wife.

At this point a man who had been concealed by a rack of costumes leaned forward on the stool on which he had been sitting. He had a ferret face and small, light blue eyes. 'It's going to take more than new stage machinery to put life into this afternoon's piece,' he remarked, looking round the room to see the effect of his remark.

'Is that so?' responded Peele. 'And what might you be doing here, Nathan Parsons? I thought you were definitely *persona non grata* at the Rose since you were dismissed from the company. And if your opinion of my play's so low, why bother to come and see it?'

Parsons smiled unpleasantly. 'Let's just say I've nothing better to do this afternoon. As to my being *persona non grata* here, I wonder what mischief-maker told you that?'

Peele was about to respond in kind when Tom Pope, very much the senior actor among those present, rose to his feet. 'Be quiet, both of you,' he told them. 'You've no business backstage here, Parsons, as well you know, since you're no longer a member of the company. So get along with you before I fetch Henslowe himself to boot you out. As for you, George, you've done your part by writing the new material into the script. I suggest you go and find yourself a seat in the theatre while there's plenty of choice. Now, the rest of you, are you all ready?'

'Almost,' said one of the boy actors who was having trouble with his wig. He finally secured it with several more large pins and the actors trooped out of the door, Lane and Spencer still muttering to each other, and descended the steps which took them below the high stage to where the bookman and the master carpenter were waiting for them.

The sound of the first trumpet fanfare had been heard quite clearly in the home of Dr Simon Forman whose house, close to the water steps, was only some ten minutes' walk from the Rose. It was the cause of much excitement in the kitchen for the doctor was taking his household servants, John and Anna Bradedge, to the play that afternoon. They had therefore dined early and Anna had made elaborate arrangements for her small son, Simon (called after the godfather who had helped bring him into the world) to be looked after by the fourteen-year-old daughter of a neighbour. She was wearing her best gown of olive-green velvet for the occasion, for

3

her master was proposing to pay for seats in one of the galleries.

Simon Forman, clearing away his phials and rolling up his horoscope charts in his study, had rather more mixed feelings about the afternoon's entertainment but he felt he owed the Bradedges much: Anna for her excellent housekeeping, and her husband for having once saved his life. Keeping up his household had not been easy of late for, earlier in the year, thanks to pressure from a corrupt City merchant and his villainous secretary, the Royal College of Physicians had revoked his licence to practise medicine within the City of London, a move they had been only too willing to make as they had always been deeply suspicious of him.

There were a number of reasons for their mistrust. For a start his background was far from conventional. The son of a Wiltshire farm labourer who had died when he was still a child, Simon had shown great promise at the grammar school to which he had gone on a scholarship, only to discover that his class and lack of money prevented him from going on to study further. The situation was compounded by the fact that at the age of sixteen he had spent nearly a year in prison after a confrontation with a local landowner. But a period as a soldier of fortune on the Continent finally allowed him to study medicine in Italy. He returned to England to set up in practice as a physician and astrologer, fired with new ideas in both sciences, many of which were anathema to the Royal College with the result that although his qualifications were recognised almost immediately by the University of Cambridge, it had been an uphill struggle to convince the Royal physicians. Indeed it took considerable pressure from Cambridge before reluctantly and grudgingly they granted him a licence, and they had been looking ever since for an opportunity to revoke it. It had, therefore, suited them only too well to punish him now. While a great deal of effort was being made on his behalf to have him reinstated, it seemed the Royal College was in no hurry, and in the meantime he was having to survive as best he could without the fees of many of his wealthy City patients.

There was a knock at the study door and John Bradedge put his head round it. A sword scar down one cheek, acquired during army service in the Low Countries, lent him a somewhat villainous air

4

but this, along with his burly build, had often proved useful in difficult situations: he looked like a man to be reckoned with. But now he was in holiday mood.

'Do you think it's time we went, doctor? There are crowds of people making for the Rose already.'

'Yes, I think we should leave very shortly.' Simon wished he felt more enthusiastic. 'If there are as many people as you say it will take us some time to push our way through them.'

'Not to mention the long wait when we get there and are made to stand in line, one by one, to pay the gatherer on the door like a line of sheep being counted by a shepherd!' John commented.

Ten minutes later they were on their way. The weather was fine and warm for a good September had provided welcome relief after the poor, wet summer of 1591 that had preceded it. The three crossed the street, making their way past the notorious Clink (the Bankside was well off for gaols) and so to the Bankside proper and on towards the theatre, on top of which they could see the flag, bearing the symbol of the red rose, flying in the breeze.

It was due to John Bradedge that they were going to this particular performance, for he had struck up a friendship with the Rose's master carpenter who had waxed lyrical to him of the wonders of the new trapdoor which had recently been inserted into the stage. Trapdoors were, in any event, something of an innovation but this one, John had been informed, was by far the most elaborate and sophisticated example ever seen. Philip Henslowe, timber merchant, bear-warden and theatrical entrepreneur always tried to be ahead of the game in each of his many activities, and once he had decided that the Rose should have a trap then it had to be something quite spectacular.

Simon, who had little interest in such mechanical devices, had been forced to listen to endless descriptions of its construction. John had even gone so far as to draw a rough sketch of the contraption to convince his master of its marvels.

'You see how it's been constructed? These counterweights and pulleys enable it to be raised and lowered not only at will but so it can be made secure at different heights,' Simon was told. 'Whereas the previous one was merely a square hole in the middle of the stage covered by two hinged flaps – so – which could be dropped down to let the actors climb out of it up a ladder.'

'So how was it made safe then?' Simon had asked.

'When it wasn't in use it was secured by two baulks of timber which slid into joists under the stage. This way is much better.'

Simon had flatly refused to accompany his servant to the playhouse to view its marvels at first hand but had finally gone so far as to offer to take John and Anna to a performance where they could see it in action.

John had not exaggerated the number of people also making their way to the Rose, for the summer's bad weather had meant the playhouses had been closed for much of it. As the Rose's major rival company, that of the Lord Chamberlain's Men led by Richard Burbage, were out in the country on tour, it seemed everyone had chosen that particular day to come over to the Bankside to be entertained.

Simon and his party arrived to find, as expected, a long line of impatient playgoers slowly moving towards the entrance, their tempers not improved when carriages deposited the wealthy who were immediately shown through in front of them.

'All right for some,' grumbled John Bradedge as they joined the end of the slow-moving queue, watching the noisy parties of young court gallants arriving, some accompanied by their wives or mistresses. 'And who's *she*?' he added as a manservant ushered a richly dressed, dark young woman through the crowd to the entrance where she was greeted by the gatherer with particular courtesy.

'Some rich man's whore, I imagine,' responded Simon, wondering idly who she might be.

The half-hour trumpet sounded well before they were finally inside. Simon, in spite of his straitened circumstances, had paid sixpence for each of them to ensure a good seat and a further penny for a cushion. John and Anna, who previously had only ever stood with the groundlings in the pit, were delighted to sit back and view the scene before them from their unusual vantage point.

The newly refurbished Rose was quite magnificent. Three tiers of galleries faced on to the huge stage which thrust right out into the pit. Over it was the wooden canopy, painted a deep blue and decorated with gold and silver suns, moons and stars, known, not surprisingly, as 'the heavens'. Towards the back of the stage, about ten feet above ground level, was a wooden bridge or gallery under which was the discovery space, a curtained alcove used to set up more intimate scenes while the main action was taking place. From their seats in the second tier of the galleries, the Bradedges could clearly see the new trapdoor well towards the front in the middle of the stage, something John was only too eager to point out to Simon along with another string of unwanted technical details. In the pit below them the sellers of pies, nuts and oranges jostled with lads selling bottled ale, while whores, decked out in their tatty finery, importuned possible clients for assignations after the show.

'I wonder just how many thieves and cutpurses there are milling about down there in the crowd,' John said to Anna. 'There'll be rich pickings from those who forget to hold on to their money. Don't you agree, doctor?' he continued, turning to Simon.

'There are certainly some doubtful-looking fellows – and women – hanging around,' Simon agreed, looking at the groundlings as they jostled each other for the best position from which to see the performance.

He had picked up one of the sheets offered to those able to read on which were listed the names of the actors taking part and the roles they would be playing. The play, *The Old Wife's Tale*, was not one he rated highly, considering it to be a mishmash of popular tales, cobbled together for no other reason than to pull in an undiscerning audience. The plot, if it could be dignified as such, was based around two young men who, lost in a forest, are taken in by an old crone who then proceeds to tell them her 'tale'.

Sacramant the Sorcerer has stolen a king's daughter who is being sought by her two brothers and, independently, by her suitor, a knight errant called Eumenides. During their various adventures they encounter a man who sits at a crossroads posing riddles and who inexplicably turns into a bear at night; another who is trying to find husbands for his two daughters, one ugly and one shrewish, and a magic well from which severed heads appear to give bounty or advice. The leading role is that of the villain, Sacramant, who is finally bested by Sir Eumenides aided by Jack the Ghost, the latter bringing about a happy ending in gratitude to the knight who had kindly paid for his funeral. It was clear that the piece had been chosen because it would give plenty of opportunity to show off the new trapdoor.

The quarter-hour trumpet sounded and people were still pouring in. Simon sighed. Another disadvantage of such a play was that it rarely gripped an audience as did a tragedy or a fine historical piece like Kit Marlowe's mighty *Tamburlaine*. As a result, a great deal of activity continued in the pit throughout, with the sellers of food and drink still moving around offering their wares while a steady stream of male members of the audience kept pushing their way to the back of the playhouse to relieve themselves in the buckets handily put there for the purpose. It also meant that those young bloods who enjoyed showing off by sitting on the stools at the side of the stage had plenty of opportunity to distract both performers and audience, though on this occasion it looked as if they had been successfully persuaded against doing so, presumably because of the new trapdoor. Simon consoled himself with the fact that fortunately it wasn't a very long play although stage business would no doubt pad it out.

He looked again at the cast list and was not surprised to note that the great Ned Alleyn was not appearing in this particular show, for he was known to be extremely selective as to the roles he took on. Simon ran his eye down the sheet and noted that his friend Tom Pope was playing Sacramant, while the young actor who had come to see him that morning complaining of a sore throat had been given the role of the knight errant, Sir Eumenides. It was nearly time for the play to begin. Simon looked round the galleries to the boxes at the end of each tier which were reserved for the elite. In one, flanked by a group of well-dressed young men and women, was the young woman who had been ushered into the theatre in front of them and who had now discarded her cloak and was sitting at the front of the box.

She could not be called beautiful or even conventionally pretty but she was very striking with high cheekbones, enormous dark eyes and a wealth of black hair, her appearance enhanced by her gown which was a rich dark red, embroidered with gold thread. She looked vaguely foreign and reminded Simon of women he'd seen in Italy and this, in turn, led him on to recall that in Milan and Florence he'd often seen well-regarded and talented female actors playing the women's roles in plays. However, there seemed little chance of such an innovation being introduced in London. He looked over at the dark lady and again wondered who she might be. Wealthy certainly, or at least if she was not so herself then she must have a wealthy keeper, for she did not look like the wife or daughter of either a noble house or a City merchant.

Backstage the actors took it in turns to squint through the curtains of the discovery space to see what kind of an audience they had. It looked noisy but good-humoured. They had all listened attentively to what the master carpenter had said, yet again, about the trapdoor. A stout framework had been built under a rectangular hole in the stage to enable the door itself, a piece of carpentry on the lines of a strong trestle-table top, to be raised and lowered using the pulleys and weights. There had been much discussion with shipwrights at Deptford as to its design. When not in use the door was raised level with the stage and, as previously, secured with two baulks of timber. But the new design offered far more choice than the old.

It was to be used three times during the play. On the first occasion it would be gradually lowered while the audience was watching the action on stage, then raised as quickly as possible to bring up two Demon Furies who would haul the unfortunate brothers down to Sacramant's dungeons. Next it would do duty as the well out of which the magic severed heads were to appear, held up on poles from beneath while actors standing below spoke their lines. Lastly, at the very end of the play, it became the grave into which Jack the Ghost leaped backwards after speaking his last line. Although this latter effect looked spectacular the trapdoor would, in reality, be only about three feet below stage level with a straw mattress on it to break the actor's fall.

At last the noise in the pit lessened as it became clear the performance was about to commence. There was no Prologue to this play to explain the action and instead Tom Pope, magnificently costumed as Sacramant, came through the curtain under the gallery to welcome the audience to the Rose and proclaim that they were about to see *The Old Wife's Tale* by George Peele. Simon settled back in his seat hoping it would not be as tedious as he expected it to be, while beside him the Bradedges rubbed their hands in eager anticipation. The trumpet sounded for the final time and was followed by the artificial sounds of rain and wind as Antic and Frolic, the two lost young men, appeared on stage and Antic spoke the opening lines: 'What now, fellow Frolic? What, all amort? Doth this sadness become thy madness? What, though we have lost our ways in these woods, never hang head as though thou hadst no hope to live 'til tomorrow.' The play had begun.

It went off well, the audience rocking with laughter at the Old Wife and her dithering start to her tale, then arguing loudly with each other over the meaning of the over-gnomic utterances of the man at the crossroads. Each appearance of Sacramant the Sorcerer was greeted with loud boos. As had been hoped, few noticed that the trapdoor flaps had been lowered during the exchange between the sorcerer and the brothers, though John Bradedge had clutched Simon's arm to ensure he was watching for what came next. A shout of surprise went up as two Demon Furies, accompanied by puffs of red smoke and clad in spangled red costumes with their faces painted green, raced up the ladder and apparently leaped out of nowhere to drag the brothers down with them to Sacramant's dungeon in the lower depths.

They enjoyed equally the heads in the well sequence, during which both the shrewish and the ugly daughter each went to the well in turn to draw water and instead up came a severed head which, this being a fairy tale, was able to speak to them in doggerel verse:

> 'Gently dip but not too deep, •
> For fear you make my golden beard to weep.
> Fair maiden, white and red,
> Comb me smooth and stroke my head,
> And thou shalt have some cockle-bread.'

The tale continued on its laborious way. The two brothers found their sister, Delia, though she failed to recognise them at first, being still under the spell of Sacramant. Sir Eumenides, having spent his last shillings on a funeral for Jack, an unknown pauper, was then adopted by his ghost who offered his help in getting rid of Sacramant. There was a slight problem after this had been accomplished as Jack, too, had taken a fancy to Delia even though he was dead, and so thought it only fair he should have half the lady as a reward for half the victory; but all was finally resolved satisfactorily.

When Jack had been dissuaded from taking his half of Delia back to his grave, some stage business had been devised with the brothers and Sir Eumenides to enable him to get into the right position in front of the trap. Having done so he shouted his last line: 'Farewell, world! Adieu Eumenides!' and fell backwards, apparently into nothingness, to a roar of approval from the audience.

The play proper ends with the two young men originally lost in the wood thanking the Old Wife for her tale as they all sit down to breakfast together, but on this occasion there seemed to be some delay. The audience, most of whom knew the play was nearly over, soon became restive and there were shouts demanding that the actors get a move on and enquiries as to whether or not they had all gone home.

Eventually the two actors playing the brothers returned to the stage, along with the Old Wife, and the play was concluded but the pace and vigour that had sustained the performance all afternoon had disappeared, something made clear to the cast when they assembled on stage to take their bow. The applause was only moderate and many people were already making their way out of the building. Simon, looking along the line of actors, wondered why the actor who had played Jack the Ghost was not among them. Perhaps he was feeling insulted because he thought the poor final scene had spoiled his own exit.

Simon and the Bradedges went down the steps from the gallery and began to move towards the exit, John still extolling the wonders of the trapdoor. 'Did you enjoy the play, Doctor?' asked a voice from behind him, and Simon turned to see that they were being followed by an acquaintance of his who ran a fencing school he sometimes frequented.

Simon shrugged. 'It was well enough done but I must admit I prefer something with more meat in it. Tom Pope was as good as ever though.' People were continuing to stream down from the upper galleries, including the party from the box among whom was the woman in the red dress.

The fencing master followed Simon's eyes. 'An expensive lady, that one.'

'Do you know who she is?' Simon enquired.

'Certainly, and I'm surprised you don't. She was – most likely still is – mistress to the Lord Chamberlain himself.' Simon looked again at the lady, pondering on the fact that if such was the case she must be young enough to be his lordship's granddaughter; at which point the lady caught his gaze, stopped, and smiled at him.

'Well, well,' laughed the fencing master, 'it seems you might do well there. But be warned! The Lord Chamberlain is possessive of so tasty a morsel.'

Simon had now become separated from the Bradedges and the two men continued chatting as they made their way through the rapidly thinning crowd. Suddenly he felt a hand pulling on his arm and, looking down, saw he was being claimed by one of the child apprentices, still clad in the red spangles of a Demon Fury.

'Are you Dr Forman, sir?' asked the boy, obviously in some distress.

'I am, lad,' Simon replied gently. 'Is something the matter?'

The apprentice gulped. 'Master Pope says can you come backstage right away. There's been a terrible accident. It's Jack, Jack Lane who plays the ghost. We think he's dead!'

Chapter 2

Death of a Ghost

At the end of the morning before the performance of *The Old Wife's Tale*, a large fleshy man with grizzled hair sat in his office above the timber yard close to his Rose Theatre and made the day's entries into his diary, as was his wont. It was a haphazard document, comments on the day's events being inserted between notes of money lent or paid out, costings for costumes and props and the amount taken on the door for each performance. Interspersed with all this were handy medical remedies, for it was not sufficient for Philip Henslowe that he should be London's greatest theatrical entrepreneur and was angling to become the Queen's Royal Bearward, but he also fancied himself as an amateur physician, a view of his abilities which was not shared by the members of the company of the Lord Admiral's Men.

Therefore on the page where he was to list the events of 15 September there also appeared a *cure for blocked ears: fry earthworms in goose grease, strain, and drop a little in the ear*, while *for lower-back pain, take powder of antimony inside a stewed prune . . .* This was followed by a note: *Lent unto Mr Valentine Harris, one of the grooms of Her Majesty's chamber, in ready money the sum of three pounds to be paid to me again on his return from the country, I say LENT! As witness, Harris's brother-in-law.*

Next came the date and an entry to the effect that he had that day paid Mr George Peele the sum of two pounds for his work on revising *The Old Wife's Tale*, and had also paid the final amount in settlement of the expense of hiring a barge to bring in the construction materials he had needed for the renovation of his theatre. *Jesus*, he wrote, *I must take note of these charges I have laid out about my playhouse in this year of our Lord*. He then read

13

it through, sanded it carefully, got up and went downstairs to cross the road to see for himself how his splendid new piece of stage equipment was going to perform.

He spent most of the performance concealed from the rest of the audience behind the pillar of a side box, in a mood of self-congratulation. While he was famed for the scope and breadth of the plays he put on in his theatre and the poets and dramatists he encouraged to write for him, his own tastes were simple ones and *The Old Wife's Tale* exactly fitted his mood. However he told himself he felt he'd seen enough once the magic 'heads in the well' had said their piece and, as he had more work to do, he returned to his office to complete it. He was, therefore, somewhat irritated when half an hour later he heard the sound of hurried footsteps on the wooden stairs and one of the boy actors who had played the role of a daughter burst into the room without knocking to ask him, breathlessly, if he could come at once as there had been a nasty accident.

Simon, meanwhile, looked round for the Bradedges to tell them he would be delayed in case he was summoned out to a patient, but they had evidently gone back home, presumably having seen him in conversation with a friend. The small Demon plucked at his arm once again, so without further delay he followed the boy through a door at the side of the stage and down a flight of wooden steps which led under it.

The scene that greeted him was a dramatic one. The understage area was lit as a rule by thick candles in metal holders, each with a shield also made of metal, for safety purposes, but these had now been supplemented by several torches stuck in sconces on the walls. Most of the actors, many of them still in costume, were gathered in a circle concealing the object of their interest but when they saw Simon they parted to allow him through.

Jack Lane lay half-on, half-off the trapdoor which was now resting almost level with the floor, his head turned to the side at an unnatural angle. He looked all the more bizarre as his face was still covered in his ghostly make-up while his hair had been whitened with flour. Simon knelt down beside him, opened his shirt and put his ear to his chest.

'Thank heaven you were here today,' said Tom Pope, who had

obviously been trying to keep the rest of the company in some sort of order. 'Though I don't imagine there's much you can do.'

Simon turned his attention to the actor's head, putting his hand underneath it and raising it slightly. It drooped in a sickening manner. He sat back on his heels. 'No, I'm afraid my skills don't reach to mending a broken neck. Indeed, it hardly requires a physician to tell you he's dead.' He laid the head gently back on the floor. 'Snapped as clean as a whistle. The Tyburn hangman could wish for no better.' Then he looked at his hand, which was marked with blood. 'Can someone bring a candle?'

A candle was brought and Simon took it. A portion of the understage area had been flagged in an attempt to keep out the damp so that it could be used for storing larger props; indeed, to add to the feeling of unreality a gaping wooden hell mouth stood in a corner, a thin stream of blood trickling across the floor towards it.

'Has anyone moved him at all?' asked Simon. Heads were shaken, shoulders shrugged: no one appeared prepared to admit to anything. He was about to pursue it further when the circle of actors parted again, this time for Philip Henslowe, accompanied by a tall, distinguished-looking man in his mid-thirties who carried himself with immense importance. Simon recognised him immediately as the company's leading actor, Ned Alleyn, who was not only its chief sharer but was enjoying a leisurely betrothal to Henslowe's stepdaughter, Joan. Both men looked more annoyed than upset.

'What's all this then?' barked Henslowe as they looked down on the body. 'Why are you here, Dr Forman?' He looked around the actors. 'Did one of you send for him?'

Tom Pope stepped forward. 'It so happened that Dr Forman was in the theatre this afternoon and, that being the case, we asked him if he could come and see if there was anything to be done.'

Henslowe considered this. 'I see. Well, what happened? I take it the man's dead?'

There was a general murmur of assent. Simon stood up. 'Death must have been almost instantaneous as his neck is broken.' Henslowe nodded. 'From what I remember,' Simon continued, 'he threw himself backwards into the grave almost head first, automatically turning his head sideways as if to see where he was going. This area must be a good bit lower than the actual height of the stage and that's what – about six feet high? – so he must have fallen eight feet at least. Also it looks as if he didn't fall directly on to the trapdoor but somewhat to one side of it, so that as well as falling with his head twisted, he also hit it on the flagged floor. It's hard to see in this dim light but I'd wager that even had he not broken his neck, he might well have broken his skull and the outcome would have been the same.'

'I see that,' said Tom Pope, 'but would a fall of eight feet be enough to break one's neck? A broken leg or arm, yes, but the *neck*?'

Simon looked up at the hole in the stage above him. 'He went over at quite a speed though, with force and a good deal of energy, so he would have hit both trap and floor hard. But he was unlucky in the way he fell. All things being equal, had he fallen squarely on to the wooden trap, even from that height he should have got away at worst with a broken limb or two.'

'Particularly as the mattress was there to—' Samuel Rowley, who, as master carpenter, was concerned that all the blame would fall on him, suddenly stopped in his tracks. 'The mattress! Where's the mattress that should've been on the door?'

There was an immediate outbreak of conversation as people began milling around in the dark. 'It's over here,' called out one of the actors, 'in the corner.'

'What on earth is it doing there?' bellowed Rowley.

There was a rumbling noise from Henslowe who was obviously getting restive. 'All this is very well but if there's nothing to be done then I suggest you move the poor fellow to a more suitable place, and then we try and find out what happened.'

He glared round the assembled company. 'No one has as yet bothered to inform me how he could have met his end or why. It looks to me as if someone, perhaps more than one of you, has been criminally careless. I want everybody here on stage as soon as possible and Ned . . .' He turned to the actor who had said nothing throughout, merely looking on with his usual superior air, 'Will you go round the theatre and find anyone there might be who isn't here now and tell them to go at once to the stage too. And I mean

16

anyone – the wardrobe master, the gatherer, the bookman . . .'

'I'm already here,' Miller responded grimly.

'Well, anyone else who was in the theatre this afternoon.' Then he turned to Simon. 'Since you are already here, Dr Forman, perhaps you'd be so good as to join us if you have the time.' Simon nodded and Henslowe retreated up the stairs, accompanied by his prospective son-in-law.

There was an immediate babble of noise over which Tom Pope shouted for quiet. 'You heard what he said. Two of you fetch the mattress – which we all know should have been on the trapdoor – put Jack on it and carry him up and lay him in one of the bottom galleries. Does anyone know if he has any family in London? Did he speak of a wife?'

No one seemed to know. Charles Spencer volunteered that he thought the actor had come to London originally from Gloucestershire but could not swear to it. 'As you know, he'd only been with the company a couple of months and although he was always pretty full of himself, he never said much about his past. As to a wife, if he had one then she must be safe in the country somewhere. He spoke constantly of his prowess with the women and how he rarely spent a night in his own bed. But then,' he added, truthfully, 'I never really took to him.'

Pope heard him out. 'I see. Very well. Now you all heard what Master Henslowe said. Those of you who still haven't changed out of your costumes, do so immediately, then go up on stage.'

The actors began to climb up out of the dark while the bookman oversaw the body being put on to the mattress. 'You two,' he called to two of the bigger members of the company, 'come and help these lads here, then take him up and put him in the gallery like Tom Pope said.' They did so and, with no little difficulty, heaved the mattress and its contents up the steps to stage level.

'Are you coming, Simon?' asked Tom, making to follow them.

Simon took a final look at where the body had lain, the position of the head marked by the trail of drying blood. 'He really was unlucky. But why in God's good name was this newfangled contraption not in place – and what happened to the mattress?'

'That,' responded Pope, looking grim, 'is what everyone will want to know.' The two men climbed slowly up the steps. 'The new door should have been no more than three feet below the level of the stage at most, and as to the mattress ... heaven alone knows what happened. We rehearsed it over and over again, the last time immediately before this afternoon's show. I can't imagine what went wrong.'

They arrived on stage to find Henslowe impatiently pacing up and down. He was not an easy man at the best of times but on this occasion he had a genuine excuse for his anger, for not only had an actor met his death while playing at the Rose Theatre, he also appeared to have done so through the use of a piece of new and recently installed machinery the virtues of which he and most of the company had been extolling far and wide for weeks. Within a few minutes all those involved in the production had been rounded up and were standing in relative silence before him.

'Is everyone here, Ned?' he called out to Alleyn. The actor replied that so far as he was aware everyone was. 'Very well. Where's Rowley?' The master carpenter pushed forward.

Henslowe grunted. 'Do *you* know what happened?' he asked. 'You told me repeatedly that not only was this new trapdoor a mechanical triumph, it was also perfectly safe; that all those weights and pulleys and so forth for which I paid out large sums of money would ensure it could be used in any way and at any height without trouble. Is that not so?'

Sam Rowley agreed that it was. 'I went back just now and tried it again myself and everything works exactly as it should. The trapdoor moves easily up and down on its pulleys – though of course there's no weight as there's no one on it – but throughout the show there were supposed to be two men in charge of it all the time to ensure nothing went wrong. Will Miller and I made sure this very afternoon that everyone in the acting company, not just those people who would actually be using the trap or the platform, was aware what was to happen and when. Indeed we went through it all again one last time immediately before the show.'

'Who was responsible for working the trap?' asked Alleyn. Several people replied that they were, but at different times.

The bookman intervened. 'It depended partly on who was

available, though everyone was shown how it worked. For this show these two lads here' – he motioned towards two young men employed to help with general carpentry work, the making of props and other useful tasks – 'were mainly responsible. The first time they had to lower it at the right time, help the boys playing the Furies on to it and then haul it up to stage level and wait for them to drag the brothers down. That was the most difficult one, as there was a good deal of weight and it was quite a squeeze when all four were on it but it's never given us any real trouble. Then it was raised again and the timbers slotted into place.'

'So what happened next?' broke in Henslowe, brusquely.

'After the scene change, the timbers were pulled out and the trapdoor lowered again so it became the well. That's all that happens in that scene. The actors stood under the hole in the stage and poked the heads up on the ends of long poles as they spoke the lines, while one of the apprentices worked the bellows so that white smoke was blown up on to the stage. Then the trap was raised and secured again.

'Finally, before the last scene, it was quietly lowered, the mattress put on to it to break Jack's fall and then raised to within a yard or so of stage level so that it could be seen open like a grave. Jack practised falling backwards on to it again and again, and there'd never been a problem,' he reiterated.

'Well there is one now,' snapped Henslowe. 'You two,' he said to the lads responsible for the trapdoor, 'what have you to say for yourselves? And don't try and lie your way out of trouble. If you forgot to put the trapdoor in the right place *and* with the mattress on it, then say so, because believe me if that's what did happen I'll find out.'

'But we did everything right,' replied one, much aggrieved. 'We put the mattress on to the door then raised it very slowly – everything's been greased to make it as easy as possible – and very quietly, to avoid drawing attention to it. Then we secured it exactly as Master Rowley taught us to.'

'We both tried the ropes to make sure they were wound round the double hooks of the pulley,' wailed the other, 'then we wedged them in the wooden cleats for extra safety. And those are strong as strong, we bought them from the shipyard at Deptford.'

'Why weren't you standing there waiting when Jack jumped down, then?' asked the carpenter.

'We didn't think it necessary, Sam,' said the first lad. 'We'd tried it so many times, and we wanted to see what it looked like from inside the theatre.' A thought struck him. 'Don't you remember? You said we could.' He looked round the group on the stage. 'You were all there this afternoon, you heard me ask if we could watch it from the theatre.' There was a murmur of confirmation of this fact.

'Perhaps we might also ask,' called a voice from the back, 'if it couldn't have been prevented even if your fancy trapdoor was in the wrong place.' The company turned as one to see Nathan Parsons lounging in the shadows against the back wall of the theatre. There was a general outcry.

'What are you doing here, Parsons?' shouted Tom Pope. 'I sent you about your business before the show even started. I told you you'd no right backstage now you've left the company.'

'Backstage maybe, but you could hardly prevent my paying my penny to see the show. And I'll say it again. It could have been prevented. One of you at least must have realised the door wasn't in position.'

Henslowe walked to the side of the stage and regarded Parsons as if he had emerged from under a stone. 'When I dismissed you from the company I made it quite clear that I wouldn't have you hanging round here, as you're nothing but a troublemaker. But since you are here, perhaps you'd better tell us what you mean.'

Parsons made him an ironic bow. 'Simply this. Just before Lane jumped backwards there was a whole group on stage with him: the two brothers, their sister, Delia, and, of course, Sir Eumenides. That's *you*,' he continued, pointing to Charles Spencer. 'I was standing only a few feet from the front of the stage. Lane had his back to the trap but you were almost directly in front of him facing it. You must have been able to see into it and tell if all was in place. Added to which, we all know what you thought of each other.'

Everyone looked at Charles who had gone very pale. 'But I was looking at Jack's face, not into the trap. I couldn't have told you then or now if the door was in place or not. As to disliking him, well, I admit we didn't get on very well but God's blood, man, I wouldn't have let him or anyone else risk a serious accident without trying to stop it. What do you take me for?'

Everyone began talking at once, some suggesting Parsons should leave before summary justice was meted out. Simon, who had been listening throughout, raised his arm as if to speak.

'You have something to say, Dr Forman?' asked Henslowe.

'Just one thing. Who first found Lane?'

There was a silence, and then the elderly actor who had played the Old Wife said that he had but that almost immediately others had joined him.

'And was he lying just as I saw him? Partly on the trap and partly on the floor? Or was he in a different place?' The man thought for a moment, then said he was sure Lane had been lying exactly as Simon had seen him, and this was confirmed by several others who had arrived on the scene almost at the same time.

Henslowe strode back to the middle of the stage and clapped his hands for silence. 'It seems clear that we are unlikely to get much further this afternoon. In the meantime there are things to be done. The authorities must be informed that there has been an accident and no doubt there will have to be an inquest, but once that is over, Lane must be buried in a seemly fashion. The theatre will see to that. Then it's best, for obvious reasons, that we do not play this piece again in the immediate future. When was it next to have been performed?'

'In two days' time, Master Henslowe,' said Miller, 'then again on Friday.'

'Well, we'll just have to do other things. Tom Kyd's *The Spanish Tragedy* hasn't been done for some weeks. That'll do very well. It always brings in the crowds. I take it you'd be happy about that, Ned?'

Alleyn inclined his head to give the royal assent. The role of the avenging Hieronimo (the play was subtitled *Hieronimo is Mad Again!*) was one of his favourites.

'Very well.' Henslowe looked across to the bookman. 'And for Friday?'

The bookman frowned. 'We could do *Arden of Faversham*. We

haven't done it for a while, so it will need some recasting and rehearsal, but again it's a popular piece and that can only be a good thing in the circumstances. You still know Arden's part, don't you, Tom?' he added.

'More or less,' responded the actor. 'I'll have to do some fast work on it, though.'

'Right then,' said Henslowe briskly. 'Now you may all go about your business. But that does not mean,' he continued, raising his voice as a general noise broke out, 'that does *not* mean you're free to go and gossip in the taverns and ordinaries about what happened here today. If anyone has got wind of it and asks you, then you merely say that there was an accident and leave it at that. If I find that any member of the company has disobeyed me then he will be dismissed.' He looked directly at Parsons. 'And if I hear of any malicious stories being attributed to you, Parsons, then I shall take you before a magistrate for slander. Come, Ned. We've much to discuss.' The two men left and gradually the rest of the company, now sobered and quiet, took up their belongings and began to leave the theatre.

'I must go too,' Simon told Tom Pope. 'I can't think why Henslowe asked me to stay in the first place, as there wasn't anything I could do.'

'I don't know either,' returned his friend, 'except that Philip Henslowe never does anything without a reason.'

After briefly discussing the events of the day with Ned Alleyn, Henslowe turned once again to his diary: *Today I have lost one of my company*, he wrote. *John Lane, known as Jack, fell from the stage and so broke his neck.* Then, always the businessman, he added: *Taken at the door this day four pounds, thirteen shillings.* He then tore a scrap of paper off an old inventory. *Remember*, he scrawled, *to go and visit Dr Forman on the morrow to request his services.*

Chapter 3

Invitation from an Entrepreneur

'You mark my words, it'll turn out to be some foolishness on the part of one of those players,' was John Bradedge's response when informed by his master of the events at the Rose. 'It'll be the fault of the man who's dead, or one of those supposed to see the machinery works properly. One or other was probably drunk. Perhaps both.' He was highly incensed at what he regarded as a slight on his friend's workmanship.

Simon doubted it. 'Apart from the fact that Henslowe is very strict about actors not being drunk in the theatre, I examined the body closely and there was no smell of alcohol. Nor was I aware of any of the others being the worse for it. As for being foolish or careless, the company had rehearsed with the trapdoor many times, right up until they played this afternoon. No one seems to know how it could have happened. It would seem to be just one of those unfortunate things.'

The untimely death of the ghost crossed his mind during the evening but by the next day it was forgotten, as he worked his way steadily through all those good souls who had chosen that particular morning to come to him with their woes. Among them was a tired and distracted woman, probably much younger than she looked, who brought along two small children and a grizzling baby, all of whom had sore eyes. Simon looked at them carefully, wrinkling his nose at the smell; all three seemed in need of a good wash. He then went to his shelves, selected a large bottle and carefully poured a measure from it into a smaller one. 'This is eyebright,' he told the woman, 'a good herb, especially when picked under the sign of the lion, and then distilled. Dab it on to their eyes twice a day until the soreness goes. It's quite harmless,' he added, 'indeed the same herb can be mixed with beer, sugar and fennel seed and given for a weak memory to the elderly.' The woman thanked him, searched in her pocket and finally brought out a penny.

'It's all I 'ave,' she told Simon. 'Me man's at sea and we manages as best we can.' He took the coin and thanked her, inwardly pondering on how long he'd be able to continue treating people virtually for nothing if the Royal College didn't hurry and restore his licence.

His next patient was the young wife of a nearby glover, who he had seen when her alarmed husband had called him in three weeks earlier as she had developed childbed fever after the birth of her baby. She still looked pale and tired. 'Your son thrives?' he asked her.

She smiled and said he was progressing well but that her husband had sent her as she was still suffering from occasional bouts of fever and weakness. Simon took her pulse and felt her forehead. Then he patted her on the shoulder. 'I'll give you a draught. Something gentle, I think.' He took down several jars and bottles and spent some time measuring out ingredients. Finally he came over to her with a small phial and a sweet-smelling packet. 'The first is a hartshorn julep. You can either take a few drops of it as it is, or, if you prefer it, with some white wine. I take it you are nursing your child?' She nodded. 'Then you must get as much rest as you can. I'm also giving you this mixture of herbs with which to make a compress. You must pour hot water on to them and then, when it's cold, strain the liquid into a bowl and soak a cloth in it to lay on your belly twice a day to relieve the humours.'

She thanked him and put the phial and the packet into the small bag she had brought with her but made no move to go, waiting as if there should be more. Then, as if summoning up courage, she asked if was he not going to bleed her?

Simon frowned. 'Bleed you? Why should I do that?'

She began to look distressed. 'My husband's mother says it's the only thing for a fever.'

Simon sighed in exasperation; this was something that came up again and again. 'Well tell her that Dr Forman does not hold with bleeding except in desperate circumstances. I fear one of the matters of dissent between myself and the Royal College of Physicians concerns this very subject. I can see no common sense in letting blood either from those who have recently suffered wounds, or from women newly delivered of a child, since they have both lost blood enough. Please believe me: where childbirth is concerned it is, in the words of the play I saw yesterday, just another old wives' tale – though you'd better not tell your husband's mother that!' This time she did look reassured, paid him the two shillings he asked and went on her way.

It was his custom to keep careful notes of his patients, the remedies he had prescribed and the results of the horoscopes he had cast in the casebook he had established for that purpose, and he had just settled back at his desk to begin writing up the morning's consultations when Anna knocked at his door to say that there was a gentleman to see him. 'You'd best show him in then,' he told her with a sigh, putting down his pen. A moment later she knocked again and motioned to the patient to go in.

The visitor was a man of middle age with greying hair and beard. Simon noted that he was obviously a person of some means, for in spite of the warm weather he wore a furred gown over a doublet of fine cloth. The gown was of moderate length, revealing a pair of spindly legs in grey hose. Simon greeted him and indicated that he might sit down. 'You are Master . . .?'

'Barton,' replied the man, 'Thomas Barton.' He gave a complacent smile and added, 'One of Her Majesty's Commissioners of Customs for the county of Kent.'

Simon did his best to look suitably impressed. 'And what can I do for you, Master Barton?' he enquired.

'I wish you to cast my immediate horoscope. I have recently married – my wife is considerably younger than me,' he added.

I see, thought Simon; no doubt this old fellow wants to know how soon he'll be a proud father. He busied himself taking the brief details required for an immediate casting, the gentleman's birth date and, so far as he knew it, the time of day when he was born, his place of birth and the date of his marriage. He established he was of the Sanguine humour and other immediately relevant details. 'Since all you wish to know is how your life will progress and what

25

is in store for you over the next little while, I can do this now if you're happy to wait.' Master Barton said that was indeed what he'd hoped for, and sat back in his chair and began twisting his fingers through a handsome gold chain he was wearing across his doublet. Simon unrolled his charts, spread them out on a table and made various calculations, carefully scrutinising them and then noting what he saw. It all took some time, and it was clear that his client was becoming somewhat agitated for he rose from his seat and began to pace up and down.

Finally Simon was satisfied, rolled up the charts and came over to Barton with his notes of the result. 'Well, sir, there's nothing at all untoward in your immediate future, that I can see. You're obviously comfortably circumstanced and I can see no change in your financial fortunes or in your work. Nor can I see anything in the way of real obstacles in your personal path.' He waited, expecting Barton to express satisfaction at the result. But he did no such thing.

He must have hoped I'd be able to tell him there was a baby on the way, thought Simon, and added, 'Perhaps you also wished to hear if you're soon to be a father? I can't see any child immediately but then we were not looking very far ahead. Is that what you hoped I might be able to tell you, Master Barton?'

The man looked over both shoulders, as if suspecting they were not alone, then gave him a fixed stare. 'No, Dr Forman. I thought you might tell me if I'm soon to die.'

Simon was taken aback. 'Had you said that was what you feared, then we could have dispensed with horoscopes and talked instead of what you think is ailing you. As to what you ask, then I'd never agree to cast concerning your death – or that of anyone else who might ask it of me. It is not my practice. We are all in God's hands and He calls us when He is ready. No doubt He feels it best we know neither the day nor the hour when that might be – unless, of course, we are due to be hanged. I must tell you that when I cast to see such a thing it is done solely for my own use where a very sick patient is concerned, and I only tell them of it if the result is good and I think it might help them to recover. So tell me, why do you fear sudden death?'

Barton had stopped walking up and down. He now turned and again looked hard at Simon. 'Because my wife is trying to murder me.'

An awful feeling began to creep over Simon, a dire conviction that he'd inadvertently allowed a madman into his house. It wouldn't be the first time since he'd set up in practice.

'Why should she do that?' he enquired carefully, thinking it might be best to humour the man.

'Because she already had an affection for another before we wed. I think it likely they might even have been lovers.'

Simon wiped his hand across his face. 'But plenty of young women have such passing fancies. It doesn't mean that it ever went further than looks and sighs and possibly a love note. Nor that they intend to despatch the man they eventually marry! Are you suggesting she's already made an attempt?' asked Simon, seeing that his patient remained unconvinced.

'I am.'

'How then?' asked Simon, desperately wondering how he might draw this crazed consultation to a close.

'Poisoned broth!' said Barton triumphantly, returning again to his chair and sitting down. Simon closed his eyes. 'It was but a week ago. I drank the broth and within the hour I was taken with stomach cramps and vomiting.'

That, at least, did not sound quite so mad. Perhaps after all Barton was merely a hypochondriac rather than a lunatic. 'Well, well,' said Simon in an encouraging tone, 'there's probably a good reason for that. If the broth was reheated in this warm weather then it's very likely that it had turned sour and so gave you all the symptoms you describe. It is a commonplace. Did your wife take any with you?'

Barton shook his head. 'No. I was late home and she had already dined.'

'There you are then,' said Simon. 'I can't honestly see that you've any grounds for suspecting your wife in this matter. But if you feel your nerves are agitated, then I can give you a soothing remedy.' At least that could do no harm. He looked at Barton again. Perhaps the young wife was proving too demanding in bed and it had briefly turned his wits.

Barton thought for a moment then shook his head. 'No, Dr Forman. I'll take your remedy but what I now want is an antidote against poison. I know there are such things.'

There were indeed. In one of Simon's books there was just such a magic medicine, as invented by one Signor Matthiolus, which listed among its ingredients virtually every herb, fruit and spice known to man along with half a dozen minerals and as many ground-up precious stones, the organs of a whole list of animals, including a 'stag's pizzle', and rounded off the whole with an ounce of powdered unicorn's horn. Even had he sufficient wealth and world enough and time to make up such a concoction, Simon thought it unlikely he'd be able to track down a unicorn. All he wanted to do now was get rid of the man. 'Very well,' he said, and went over to his bench and shelves and worked away in silence for a few minutes. He put leaves of dried sorrel and red sage into a mortar, then added juniper berries along with nutmeg, mace, cinnamon and peppercorns and ground them together. He then surveyed his various jars again and added a generous spoonful of mustard for good measure. He deliberately made a great business of grinding away again with the pestle, then he put the resultant powder into a packet and handed it gravely to the customs commissioner.

'That should do the trick, I think. If you suspect you are taken ill in such a way then go immediately to your bed. Wrap yourself in your bedgown and pile on the blankets. Then take this mixture in water as hot as you can stand, after which you must wrap a hot cloth around your head. That way you'll sweat out any noxious substances.'

Barton took it with the utmost seriousness, stowed the packet carefully away, then asked: 'Is there no other way of avoiding death by poison?'

Would the man never go? 'I suppose you could do as the old Persian king, Mithridates, did – take a little of the most common poisons in your food every day to make yourself proof against those who might try to slay you in that way.'

'I do not consider this to be a joking matter, Dr Forman,' responded Barton, huffily.

'It wasn't meant as a joke,' Simon assured him. 'I merely tell you what the legend says.'

Barton shook his head, then asked Simon the fee for the consultation.

'Two guineas,' replied Simon promptly, considering he'd earned every penny of it.

Barton produced a purse and paid him without demur. Simon thanked him and began ushering him firmly out of the room towards the front door. Failing anything else to say, he asked Barton if he was staying long in London. Apparently not, his was a brief visit. 'How then did you hear of me?' Simon enquired as he opened the door, telling himself that if it turned out to be anyone he knew he'd go round and beat them over the head. 'There must be many excellent physicians in the county of Kent.'

'I was told of you by the innkeeper at the Mermaid Tavern over the river,' Barton replied, 'when I told him I needed the services of a caster of horoscopes. As to good physicians in Kent, that's true and I have an excellent one of my own. But in this particular circumstance you must see that I needed to ask advice well away from home. None of this must get back to my wife.'

Barton stepped on to the path, surveying the busy scene outside. 'I brought my wife to London on our honeymoon and we visited the Bankside several times to go to the Rose Theatre. She's very fond of plays, though they've never been of much interest to me. However, there was one play – perhaps you have seen it? – called *Arden of Faversham*, which in the light of what has happened I find of particular interest because—'

'I'm afraid I must say farewell, Master Barton,' Simon broke in, cutting him short. The last thing he wanted to hear now was the man's views on the drama.

The morning was now over and, being hungry, he went to the kitchen in search of something to eat, and, as was often his practice, sat down at table with the Bradedges. Anna immediately put a plate of steaming broth in front of him and a lump of bread. He took a good mouthful. 'This is good, Anna,' he told her, 'very good. Let's just hope you're not trying to poison me!'

She looked at him in horror. John had married Anna in the Low Countries when he was serving in the army, and had brought her back to England with him after his discharge. Simon had found the two of them literally sitting on the roadside by London Bridge, almost penniless and with a child expected within days. He had taken them in as servants at first on a month's trial but they had soon proved too useful to dismiss. John looked after his master's practical needs and also undertook various missions for him when necessary, while Anna's housekeeping was everything that could be desired. But she still had some problems with the English language in general and the English sense of humour in particular. Simon hastened to reassure her.

'Forgive me, Anna, it was only a jest. It comes from having spent the last hour with a raving madman! That last man you showed in has convinced himself that his wife's trying to kill him with poisoned broth.'

'And is she?' asked John, who was fascinated by such things.

'I very much doubt it,' replied his master. 'Master Barton would seem to be one of those people who imagine demons lurking in the dark every time they blow out their bedtime candle.'

He was halfway through his broth when there came another knock at the front door. Anna put down her spoon, handed her small son to his father and got up to answer it. Simon sighed. 'Unless it's someone bleeding to death or a personal message from Her Majesty summoning me to court to give me a knighthood, tell them to come back in an hour's time when I've supped and finished my notes.'

She left the room, and fragments of conversation drifted back into the kitchen and the sound of a man's voice becoming ever more forceful. Then came footsteps and Anna reappeared again, bringing with her an uninvited guest. It was Philip Henslowe.

'Master Henslowe said he had to see you urgently and that it wouldn't wait,' she said in explanation.

Henslowe took in the scene as Simon began to attack a slab of cheese, clearly showing no signs of laying aside his lunch. 'My apologies for disturbing you in this way, Dr Forman,' he said. 'Please go on with your meal but I've little time, and I felt it necessary to see you right away.'

'Then you'd best sit down, Master Henslowe. Can we offer you anything?' His guest, it seemed, had eaten but was not averse to a cup of wine if one was available. Anna went and fetched a bottle and two cups and then began to clear away the remains of the meal while her husband, muttering that he had things to do in the yard, went out too, leaving the two men alone.

'So,' said Simon, finishing off his cheese, 'what is it that's so urgent it can't wait?'

'It's the matter of the accident to Lane.'

'A bad business,' commented Simon.

'A bad business indeed,' Henslowe agreed. 'The inquest is to be held tomorrow and there'll be no argument as to the cause of death, of course. The burial will take place afterwards in St Saviour's churchyard.'

'But what has this to do with me?' asked Simon. 'It was obvious why the man died. He fell with some force with his head at an angle and so broke his neck. If things had been different, possibly even if the mattress had still been in place below the stage, then he might have suffered only a broken leg or a few cracked ribs. But you don't need a doctor to tell you that.'

'It's not in your medical capacity that I want to consult you,' continued Henslowe. He paused. 'It's said that earlier this year you were responsible for bringing a rare villain to justice.'

'To God's justice, perhaps. He escaped the gallows.'

Henslowe waved this aside. 'It seems, therefore, that you have a gift for tracking down evildoers.'

Simon smiled. 'I wouldn't put it as high as that. It just so happened, regarding the matter to which you refer, that I was personally involved. The victim was a patient who had recently consulted me.'

Henslowe thought for a moment. 'Let me be frank with you. There is much ill feeling at present within my company. It doesn't make for good work and it leads to constant bickering and quarrelling and threats of fights.'

'Are you suggesting that this has some connection with Lane's accident?'

'I hardly think matters have gone so far, though, having said that, I must admit I simply don't know. He wasn't a very popular member of the company and as he had only a moderate talent, I'd already decided to ask him to seek employment elsewhere.'

'Is there any particular reason for this . . . bad feeling?' asked Simon.

Henslowe shrugged. 'It's been a difficult year. I hardly need to tell you that the dreadful weather this summer meant we were unable to play much of the time. On top of that, it seemed every time we were about to start again, there were cases of plague and all the theatres were closed. It's hard to keep a company together in such circumstances. As it is, many actors move regularly between the various companies, from mine to that of John and Richard Burbage, from them to the Earl of Pembroke's or Oxford's Men and so on. It's only natural, of course, because they must seek work, and unless they are of exceptional talent and are offered a share in a playhouse – like Ned Alleyn – they are on hire, as it were.'

'And how does that work?' asked Simon.

'In a number of ways. If they're much sought after but not a sharer, then they are contracted for weeks, possibly months. Others are hired by the month or week. Then there are the child apprentices who are beginning to learn the trade, and the older boys who play the women. We usually take the apprentices at ten or eleven and the older boys from twelve or thirteen until their voices break. It depends. Then there are the poet-dramatists. As you know, I've become noted for my encouragement of new writers. I think I can say,' he continued, swelling with pride, 'that no poet of note currently writing for the theatre has not started out on his career by writing for me.'

'Not least Kit Marlowe,' commented Simon.

Henslowe smiled in assent. 'Kit Marlowe writes *only* for me.'

'I still don't understand why you're telling me all this,' said Simon.

Henslowe finally came to the point. 'I want you to look into what's going on in my company to cause so much dissent, and to find out if Lane's death is in any way connected with it.'

'But I don't see how I can possibly do that. I don't know anything about theatre companies, and precious little about actors or poets.'

'How you do it I leave to you, Dr Forman.' Henslowe paused. 'I've also heard that you're in contention with the Royal College of Physicians and as a result they have temporarily revoked your licence to practise in the City. That must make matters very difficult for you, since my company members tell me you're an excellent physician. I consider myself to be something of a doctor – in an amateur capacity, of course.' He stopped short and returned to the matter in hand. 'What I am proposing, therefore, is that I pay you for your services. I realise that you can't guarantee a solution to my problem but I would at least be grateful if you'd try.'

Simon was at a loss to know what to say. It seemed the strangest request, and he had no idea how he might possibly set about it. He'd also told himself, after that previous occasion when he'd investigated a mysterious death, nearly losing his life in the process, that in future he'd leave such matters to God and the authorities. But Henslowe had shrewdly put his finger on his present dilemma: he did need the money.

'Very well then,' he said, finally. 'But only on the understanding that I can't promise anything.'

'Thank you, Dr Forman.' Henslowe reached inside his doublet and produced a fat purse. 'I am famed within theatrical circles for paying promising writers in advance for their plays if they provide me with a good plot. Happily only rarely have I been let down. My usual fee is four guineas, which is considered generous. I propose, therefore, to pay you five guineas now and a further sum later, dependent upon what transpires. Are you agreeable?' Simon said he was, and Henslowe carefully counted out five gold coins and pushed them across the table.

Then he got up. 'I must go back to my work. I've a large delivery of timber expected tomorrow morning. Naturally you have the freedom to come and go at the Rose as you wish, and I'd also suggest that you attend Lane's burial tomorrow morning and the drinking in the tavern that will, no doubt, follow it, although I shall be over myself to ensure that it's of limited duration as we're playing in the afternoon. It might be that you learn something. Don't bother to see me out,' he added, as Simon rose from his seat. 'Farewell for now – and I wish you good hunting!'

Chapter 4

Theatrical Ambitions

By the time Simon reached the churchyard the next morning a small crowd had already gathered round the hastily dug grave. As he joined them, Simon pondered on the fact that his last such venture had begun with a funeral, or rather with two. Both had had far-reaching repercussions, the first in his personal life, for it had been that of an elderly patient, an old market woman, who had confessed to him on her deathbed that she had given birth to a daughter after a brief affair with a pedlar, something she had never told her husband. Neither did the girl, who attended the burial, know that it was her mother going to her grave, for she had been brought up by her aunt as her own child. He had always had a weakness for women but Avisa Allen, the woman in question now married to a silk merchant, had affected him deeply, and he had spent much time of late unsuccessfully trying to take his interest further.

The second funeral, that of a murdered girl, far from London in the Dedham Vale had triggered off a train of events which had nearly ended in disaster, and which had led directly to his present conflict with the Royal College of Physicians. He was determined this time that whether he discovered anything or nothing, there would be no such repercussions.

Most members of the Lord Admiral's Company were present, including Henslowe and Ned Alleyn along with others Simon did not know. He did, however, recognise the two notorious playwrights, George Peele and Robert Greene, both of whom looked very much the worse for wear after what had evidently been a hard night. Peele always looked as if he had just got out of bed having slept in his clothes, while his friend and drinking companion was attired in a stained and shabby doublet in his favourite brilliant goose-turd green, added to which, to ensure nobody could possibly mistake him for anyone else, he wore his long red hair greased to a point high on his head while at the end of his beard hung a single pearl. A little way away but obviously known to them was another man of about their age, neatly dressed in grey, his clothes of an unfashionable cut, who looked distinctly untheatrical and more like some kind of clerk.

Henslowe had seen to it that for Jack Lane's burial, paid for by the theatre, he was not fobbed off with a poor curate and it was the parson himself who took the brief service and said the prayers over the dead as the coffin was lowered into the ground. But it was an odd affair. While those present had felt it incumbent upon them to attend, especially given the circumstances, Lane had not been well liked and they could not truly be said to be sad mourners, as was shown all too clearly by the fact that four stout lads had been hired to carry the coffin rather than having it shouldered by fellow actors. All in all it was a case of going through the motions, paying their respects and getting it all over with as quickly as possible.

The burial done, the group began to disperse but not before Henslowe had reminded all those involved in the afternoon's performance that he expected them to be back at the Rose by one o'clock sharp – and sober! Both he and the bookman would do their best to see to it that this was the case, and any backsliders would soon find themselves looking for other employment.

'Does that mean you?' Simon asked Tom Pope, the only face which was really familiar, as the actor came over to him.

'No, thank God. I've got enough to do recalling my role in *Arden of Faversham* as we've not put it on since the early summer. I'll go and have a pint or two of ale with the others, then it's back home to go over the words.' He paused briefly as they were joined by Charles Spencer, the young actor who Simon had last seen being more or less accused by the unpleasant Nathan Parsons of deliberately letting Jack Lane jump to his death.

He seemed to have put it behind him, for after giving a cheery greeting, he asked if Dr Forman was joining them in the tavern. Simon said he would, if briefly, and the three began to follow the rest who were determinedly making their way in the direction of the Anchor Tavern, a hostelry which the Lord Admiral's Men considered very much their own. At the churchyard gate Peele and the preposterously dressed Greene were arguing loudly as to what they should do next, Greene, as ever, loudly complaining that he had no money.

'You *never* have any money,' the third man broke in, a sentiment with which Simon heartily concurred as he had treated Greene on numerous occasions without remuneration, for everything from the rheum and sick stomachs following too much drink, to the clap. The poet was always pleading poverty.

'I'll have some shortly,' Greene told him, 'it's my play they're doing this afternoon. In the meantime we'll let you pay for us. A little scrivener like you should be proud to be seen with a couple of university wits like us.'

'Thank you, but I'll settle to stay in relative obscurity and let my work say it for me – that is if I don't find my plays stolen wholesale and claimed by someone else,' the man retorted, after which he disappeared off in the opposite direction leaving Peele and Greene still arguing as to where they might get drinks on credit.

'Who was that?' asked Simon, looking back at the retreating figure of the butt of the playwrights' cheap insults.

'Tom Kyd. He *is* a scrivener – that's how he earns his bread, and unlike most of his colleagues he lives a life of quiet respectability, but his *The Spanish Tragedy* is the most popular piece in our repertoire, more so even than *Tamburlaine*. George and Robin mock him endlessly because he didn't go to university like they did, and doesn't game or get drunk or chase women. They can't understand such a sober soul but it's just the way he is. They're also jealous of his success, of course.'

As they reached the Anchor Simon pulled Tom to one side. 'Would you excuse us a moment,' he said to Charles Spencer. 'We'll be with you shortly. There's something I need to discuss with Tom.' The young actor smiled and left them to it.

'What's this then?' asked Tom.

'Remember what you said in the theatre? That Henslowe never did anything without a reason? Well, yesterday he came to see me.'

'About Lane's death?'

37

'Indirectly.' Simon paused, wondering how much he should say. 'This is strictly between us, but he's asked me to try and find out why there's so much ill feeling in your company and whether or not it has any bearing on Lane's accident. I told him I didn't see how I could help, but somehow or other he managed to persuade me.'

'I can imagine,' Tom gave a rueful laugh. 'He's made a profession of being persuasive, in one way or another.'

'Well I'd certainly appreciate any help you can give me, although I realise only too well that it might be difficult for you. I want neither to pry nor make you tattle about your colleagues, however if at some time we could discuss the problem in general terms, I'd be most grateful, if indeed there is a problem . . .'

'Oh, there's a problem all right. Indeed there are several and I've no objection to telling you what they are, though not here and now. Why not come and have some supper with us one evening soon and we can talk it over at our leisure? I'll check what I'm doing next week and send a message to you, by which time I'll have relearned old Arden.'

'Who is Arden of Faversham then?' demanded Simon as they entered the Anchor, but Tom was already calling to a tapster to bring them some ale. Most of the actors and the others working at the Rose had arrived before them and after Tom had greeted them, they made their way over to a corner where Charles Spencer was already sitting talking animatedly to another young man of about his own age. Simon vaguely recognised him as having played one of the two young wanderers to whom the Old Wife told her tale.

'This is Dick Marsh,' said Charles by way of introduction, 'a member of our company and my good friend.' The two young men made an excellent contrast, Charles being fair-haired and grey-eyed while his friend had the black hair and blue eyes of the Celt.

Dick Marsh smiled across at Forman. 'You're Dr Forman, aren't you, sir? I saw you in the theatre after . . . after the accident.' Simon agreed that he was, and they applied themselves to their drinks. Although the tavern was fairly full of company members conversations were subdued and, as far as he could tell, dealt with topics other than the burial they had so recently attended. Had Lane been other than what he was, then no doubt there would have been something of a wake no matter how he had died, but as this was not the case it was clear that most of those present had other matters to discuss of more immediate importance. Not least the two young actors, who were now deep in a discussion of their respective roles in the company's repertoire, which varied in importance depending on the particular play they were in. The bookman and Ned Alleyn, who were largely responsible for casting, usually arranged it in such a way that the younger actors who showed real talent were given the widest possible range of parts, which often meant that one day they might well find themselves playing a dashing young hero and the next merely a foot soldier. As Charles pointed out to Simon, although he had played the knight errant in *The Old Wife's Tale*, he had only a minor role in *Arden of Faversham* while Dick, who had only been on stage at the beginning and end of the first play, had the major part of the villainous Lorenzo in Kyd's *The Spanish Tragedy*.

Simon found them an engaging couple. 'You're rivals for fame then?'

This they vigorously denied. 'We don't see it like that. At present we seem to be cast more or less equally. I've been with the Lord Admiral's Men now for a good while,' Charles told him, 'and before that, along with others in our company, with Pembroke's Men, while Dick joined us – it's over a year now, isn't it? – from Strange's Men. But we met first when we were both in a single play for the Burbages. I've been lucky to spend so much time with just the one company, but Dick's had far more experience on tour than I have.'

Tom Pope, who had been hailed by a group on the other side of the room, excused himself briefly, took his drink and went over to them. Still not really knowing what it was he needed to find out, Simon thought that at least it might be useful to discover the backgrounds from which actors were drawn, and so asked the two young men where they came from and what had drawn them to so chancy a profession.

'Norwich,' responded Charles, promptly. 'Like Robin Greene. In fact our two families know each other. My father's a lawyer and would know everyone anyway but Robin's notorious back home. It was my father who drew up the marriage settlement for that poor wife of his. He ran through her money, got her with child then left – all in a twelvemonth!' he added in explanation. 'As to why I'm an actor – I never wanted to do anything else from the time I first saw one of the travelling companies perform *Ralph Roister Doister* in an inn yard. I'd a desperate quarrel with my father over it but we finally made our peace, thanks to my mother, on the understanding that I'd not apply to him for money for at least three years but that if I'd not proved successful by the end of that time then I could go back to Norwich, be welcomed home and put to learn the law. I must admit it was often a close-run thing, but I'm still here.'

'I had no such feather-bedding,' broke in Dick, and Charles gave him a playful punch. 'I'm from Northamptonshire. My father's a parson in the parish of Byfield and the living's not a particularly good one, so as I'm the eldest I'd to leave school at thirteen as I was expected to help support my mother and sisters and the younger boys. You can't imagine what it's like to find yourself in such a position, Dr Forman.'

Simon gave him a rueful smile. 'I can, only too well. Almost exactly the same thing happened to me but my family was in direr straits than yours, for my father died when I was a child, on top of which I'd a prison sentence thrown in for crossing the local landowner.'

'How did you become a physician then?' Dick asked.

'It's too long a story to tell you now. Suffice it to say it was indirectly, through the wars in the Low Countries and study in Italy.'

'I see.' Dick looked thoughtful. 'But do you know, even now I still feel it a disadvantage to be the poor boy from the country. And there are those who never let you forget it,' he added, though he did not elaborate on this.

'You surely can't *really* still think that,' exclaimed his friend. Dick Marsh shrugged and, in answer to more prompting from Simon, embarked on a long and hilarious account of his first attempts to find work with a theatrical company in the teeth of opposition from all his relatives, the mistakes he made and the train of events that finally brought him to the Rose. Simon had not laughed so much for a very long time. As he listened, he realised that there was indeed a considerable difference between the two young actors. Charles Spencer, as he'd seen for himself, was certainly more than competent but Dick Marsh, even off stage, seemed to have something more: an indefinable quality that on stage marks out the great from the merely talented. Intrigued, Simon decided that he must, at the next opportunity, go to see him in a play in which he took a leading role.

At this point Tom Pope returned, picked up his tankard, drained it and said he was off home to wrestle with Thomas Arden. Dick Marsh quickly followed him, leaving Charles and Simon to follow on behind.

'Your friend's an amusing and quite gifted fellow,' remarked Simon as they reached the doorway.

'He is, isn't he?' Charles agreed.

'You're truly not jealous then?'

'Not at all.' He stopped and considered it for a moment. 'It's odd, since we're chasing similar roles, but I really don't think I am. Envious maybe, if I'm to be quite honest,' he continued, 'but in my heart I know that he's better than I'll ever be and that it's likely to become more obvious as time goes on. Not that I don't think I'm quite good but it's like comparing say, oh, Tom Pope with Ned Alleyn. Dick's my Ned Alleyn. Added to which he's such a good and generous person. But I also have another ambition.'

'What's that?' asked Simon, interested.

'I've dreams of being a playwright. But that's even harder because although everyone's crying out for plays, if you don't keep your ideas close you'll find someone steals them. It's already happened to me once. I thoughtlessly told a tavern full of theatre people, including that bastard Nathan Parsons, of an idea I'd had for a piece based on a story about how the great William the Conqueror fell in love with a miller's daughter. Next thing I know Burbage's company are putting on *Fair Em – the Story of William the Conqueror and the Miller's Daughter of Manchester* by Nathan Parsons. I tackled him about it but he just sneered and said it was a common tale known to all. I went to see it,' he added, 'and it was really dreadful, which made me all the angrier. However, now I've had another idea and Henslowe's going to let me know if I can go ahead with it, and this time by hook or by crook I'll see Nathan Parsons doesn't get to hear of it.' They finally emerged from the dark taproom into the sunshine and Charles stopped in his tracks: 'God's truth, speak of the devil!'

An angry scene was taking place in the street outside between none other than Nathan Parsons and a red-faced man, unknown to Simon, who had been the worse for drink when the mourners first entered the tavern. Tom Pope, who had also halted immediately outside the Anchor, called out to them to stop acting like louts and behave themselves but then, acutely aware of the time, went on his way without stopping to see if they took any heed. It was soon clear that they were not going to do so.

'Who's that?' asked Simon, pointing to the florid man who was even now drawing his rapier.

'The notorious Gabriel Tanner,' replied Charles. 'One of our company. He's not a bad actor, not even a bad man, but he can't take his drink. Two quarts of ale and he'll fight anyone. It's lucky he isn't in this afternoon's show. Do you know what it's all about?' he called to Dick Marsh, who was standing on the other side of the street.

'Lord knows! They've both been yelling about who said what about whom and when. They're as bad as each other.' At which point Tanner flourished his sword as Parsons drew his and the two men began to fight. Simon went forward to intervene but was forestalled by a gentleman with his wife and daughter who were making their way towards the nearby water steps to take a ferry. Seeing that they were unlikely to pass safely and avoid the increasingly wild lunges of the combatants, the man drew his own sword and beat down those of the other two men, shouting to them that if they didn't stop it at once he'd send for a constable and have them both locked up for causing a breach of the peace. He added that things had come to a pretty pass when a decent family couldn't walk the streets without being impeded by roaring boys and coxcombs. It had its effect. The two men grudgingly returned their swords to their sheaths and made to move off in opposite directions but not before Tanner had called out to Parsons that he needn't think this was the end of it. 'I'll get my own back, you'll see!' he threatened.

The small crowd of onlookers which always appeared out of

nowhere whenever a street fight took place began to disperse, seeing that the entertainment was over and the two young actors, having said farewell to Simon, went off to the Rose, their arms round each other's shoulders, discussing how best they might prove how well they knew their lines. An entertaining couple of lads, thought Simon. Certainly no ill feeling or smouldering resentment in evidence there. As to the two would-be duellists, he would have to try to find out whether one or the other had a genuine grievance and, if so, did it have any bearing whatsoever on the accident to Lane, or had the quarrel been brought about purely by drink? On the whole he felt it more likely to be the latter, but it was one of the many things he must take up with Tom Pope when they met over supper the following week.

On his way home he decided to call in on the apothecary with whom he had a long-standing arrangement. While he grew fresh herbs in his own garden and sought ingredients for his remedies from many sources, he made regular use of this apothecary who stocked a far more comprehensive range of herbs, spices and minerals than he could and from whom he regularly bought supplies. The two men helped each other, for the apothecary would often make up a medicine for Simon while Simon, when asked, would give him advice on prescribing in specific instances. Many people on the Bankside and indeed elsewhere could not afford either to visit or call in a physician; and there were those who, even if they could, were deeply suspicious of doctors of medicine, preferring the more homely ministrations of an apothecary. Simon entered the shop to find a customer there before him. It was Mistress Avisa Allen, and she gave him a smile which made his heart turn over.

At the time they had first met, he had also made the acquaintance of a woman so strikingly beautiful that it was possible to understand why the poets claimed that the Greeks launched a thousand ships to fetch fair Helen back from Troy. The fact that she was also ruthless, untrustworthy and quite amoral had not stopped him from accepting her invitation into her bed, even though it had come to nothing since she'd had the forethought to drug him first. But in spite of that he'd been unable to get Avisa, with her cool dark looks, out of his mind and on the few occasions they'd met since, he'd discovered that behind her quiet speech and modest manner lay both wit and a lively mind; also that they shared an interest in the efficacy of herbs, for Avisa was practised in the art of distilling medicines and did so for herself and her friends and neighbours.

She would have made an ideal wife for a doctor – except that she already had a husband. He was considerably older than her, a situation not dissimilar to that of the mad customs commissioner with his tale of young wives and poisoned broth.

Avisa broke into his reverie. 'How pleasant to see you, Dr Forman. Perhaps you can help us, if it's not too trivial a thing. My neighbour's daughter suffers from spots on the face and spends much time sitting in her room refusing to go out. I had come for fennel to distil a juice for her but our friend here recommends camphor in vinegar mixed with celandine water. Which do you think is best?'

'How old is the maid?'

'Just fourteen. The affliction is recent and came suddenly.'

'And will depart equally suddenly when she grows older, as we all know! But in the meantime, no doubt she's proving trying to her mother and so by all means give her something to put on it. As to which, on balance I'd say most probably the last one. But the real remedy is time.'

The apothecary handed Avisa the ingredients and she paid for them, then waited while Simon bought some dried herbs and a bottle of rose water. They left the shop together chatting pleasantly enough until they came to where their ways parted.

'Am I never going to be able to persuade you to see me?' Simon asked her as she made her farewells.

'You're seeing me now,' she responded gravely.

'You know very well that's not what I mean,' he insisted.

She looked into the distance. 'I've heard that you have a way with women, Dr Forman. That it's been known for you to bed with some of your patients, no doubt with their encouragement but it is obvious they are passing fancies since you remain unwed. I am no man's passing fancy – not to mention the fact that I'm also a married woman.'

'Do you think I don't know that?' he burst out in response. 'What possessed you to marry a man so much older than you?'

She turned to face him. 'Don't you think it impertinent to ask such a thing? But since you have, then very well, I can't pretend I married William for love. But out of respect has grown affection, and he's a good and kind man. He's given me a far better life than I could have expected in my position. He also trusts me. Whatever I might feel, I would be loath to break that trust. However there is one thing more, Dr Forman—'

'For heaven's sake, call me Simon!'

'Simon, then. His dearest wish is that I should give him a child but after nearly three years there is no sign of it, though nothing seems amiss in our trying to make one,' she continued, colour sweeping over her face. 'Therefore I will seek you out shortly and ask you to cast a horoscope for me to see if I am likely soon to conceive. And now I must go home. Much as I'd like to continue our talk, I am mistress of a household and must see that our apprentices and journeymen are fed.' So saying she left, and with that he had to be content.

Chapter 5

Company Problems

Tom Pope was as good as his word and three days after Lane's burial he invited Simon to supper. The actor lived with his wife, Jenny, and their two young sons in a small house on the Bankside, an uncommonly favoured property as it had an open outlook towards the river. Although the weather had remained fine, Simon could feel a new chill in the air as he walked the short distance from his own home to that of the Popes, and it was also obvious that the nights were starting to draw in. Soon it would be autumn proper, then winter, and the acting companies would be hard-pressed to play: it took a dry day, reasonable weather, an extremely tempting play and a sturdy audience to survive playgoing during the winter months. Surely, thought Simon, the time must come when at least some playhouses were roofed over against the elements.

After some thought he had decided to take John Bradedge into his confidence, not least because his servant was still muttering darkly about how unfairly his friend the carpenter was being treated, and how he felt he was being blamed for what had happened even though he'd proved there'd been nothing wrong with his workmanship. John had been most useful to Simon in the past as a means of seeking out information in places where his own enquiries would have met with suspicion. Simon told him therefore what Henslowe wanted to know.

'So encourage your friend to talk to you,' he told him. 'I promise you I won't give away any confidences. Go and mix with the actors in the taverns they frequent like the Anchor and the Green Dragon and see what you can find out, whether there are particular causes of ill feeling, people who are unpopular for whatever reason. That way we might even be able to prove that the trapdoor was moved

47

deliberately. It could be that someone wanted to make a fool of your friend or give the Rose a bad reputation.' John Bradedge visibly brightened at this, and at the thought of sitting around in alehouses as a legitimate part of his employment.

The scene that greeted him when he arrived at Tom Pope's house was a domestic one. Jenny was at the hearth seeing to a bubbling pot, while her husband, as usual, scanned lines. In a corner of the room their two small boys were kneeling on the floor playing some complicated game with counters on a marked board in company with two older lads, one of which Simon recognised as the Demon Fury who had called him to the scene of the accident at the Rose. It seemed something was distracting him, as the other players continually had to remind him when it was his turn and hurry him to move the game along.

There was much sighing and groaning when Jenny told them to stop playing and come and eat their supper, and it was only after a great deal of fuss and complaint about not being allowed to finish it that they conceded and seated themselves at the long deal table at the end of the room. 'Don't worry,' said Jenny, 'once we've eaten these boys can have one more game and then the apprentices will have to go back to their lodgings. It's a busy week for them and though they won't have it, they need their sleep. And our boys have to be up at six to go to school.' She was an attractive and unusually well-educated young woman, the daughter of a Chancery clerk in Oxford. She and Tom met when he had been a member of a company which had toured at that city and her father had taken her to see a play. The two had immediately been attracted to each other but for some time her father had been set against a marriage, considering that his daughter, whom he had taught to read and write by the time she was five and who now had more learning than many young men of her age, was wasted on a mere player. Eventually he had been persuaded and had come round to it. Happily the Popes had proved wrong the forecasts of both her anxious family and his cynical fellow actors as to the probable success of their marriage.

An hour later, after Simon had consumed a piece of excellent pigeon pie served with turnip and beans, followed by a syllabub, the young Pope boys were sent to their beds, while Tom saw the two young apprentices over the road to where they lodged with the motherly widow who regularly took in the Rose's apprentices. When he returned and Jenny had come down after hearing the boys' prayers and settling them to sleep, he brought out a bottle of canary wine and poured a cup for each of them.

'I fear young Daniel's sickening for something,' he told his wife. 'He's said hardly a word all evening and you must have seen how he picked at his food. That's the little, dark apprentice,' he said to Simon in explanation. 'He's usually quite irrepressible, never stops talking and eats like a horse. Come to think of it, he's not been himself for several days.'

'Perhaps he's upset over Jack Lane's death,' suggested Jenny. 'Possibly he admired him in the way young lads do.'

'I don't think so,' replied her husband, 'though I may be wrong. But I never thought he felt any particular liking for Lane. I'm afraid few people did. Anyway I'll keep an eye on the boy and see what happens.'

'Tom's particularly fond of Danny,' Jenny told Simon, 'because he more or less rescued him from a life of crime – or at least beggary – didn't you, love?'

'Possibly.' Tom put his arm round his wife. 'He turned up when we were on tour in Gloucestershire and hung around the company for days, begging us to take him with us when we left. He said he wanted to be a player and he certainly had tumbling skills which he was only too delighted to show off. Ned Alleyn, of course, said no, that we'd apprentices enough but young Dan wouldn't take no for an answer and when we set up again in Tewkesbury, there he was. He'd hung on to the back of one of the wagons all the way from Gloucester.'

'So my husband,' broke in Jenny, taking up the tale, 'soft-hearted as he is, talked Ned Alleyn into agreeing that they would take the child on if his parents approved, and back Tom went to Gloucester on a hired horse, the boy behind him, and tried to seek out his family.'

But his family, if so it could be called, turned out to be a tribe of tinkers living rough on the outskirts of the town who, according to local worthies, earned their living by thieving and deserved to be whipped out of the neighbourhood. 'It seems young Daniel's mother was dead,' Tom continued, 'and as to his father – who knows? He was being grudgingly reared by a sour-faced woman with a tribe of children of her own and a husband who communicated mainly with his fists. The young lad was expected to earn his bread as best he could, by tumbling if he was fortunate and thieving if he was not. So after some discussion, during which the man of the family demanded money with menaces, accusing me of stealing away the lad they'd kindly brought up now he was a breadwinner, and my threatening to go straight to the magistrates if he attempted to lay a finger on either of us, we finally came to an agreement and the boy came back to Tewkesbury with me. He's now properly apprenticed and showing great promise. But you didn't come here to hear me talk about our apprentices.'

Simon took a mouthful of the excellent wine and set down his cup. 'I meant what I said when I told you I didn't expect you to tell tales on your colleagues. It's just that I don't really know where to start, and you agreed something's amiss. Henslowe said it possibly had to do with the insecurity caused by the poor summer and too many of the actors moving between the different companies.'

Tom thought for a moment. 'That's all true to some extent, and certainly it helps if you have a company of regular actors who get on with each other and are used to playing together, but what's wrong seems to go deeper than that. Nor is it any secret that we seem to have had a continual string of troublemakers in the company. There's always rivalry, of course, and there have always been those who are prepared to stop at little to achieve some kind of success. Oh, I suppose it's just that we've had more than our fair share of late.'

'Like Lane?'

'He was annoying, and it was obvious Henslowe wanted rid of him but he was a mere irritant set against people like Nathan Parsons, for example.' Tom turned to Jenny. 'I meant to tell you, he was even involved in a street fight almost straight after Lane's funeral.'

'Who with?' she enquired, and hardly seemed surprised when he told her. 'Gabriel Tanner's always in fights, Simon.'

'So Charles Spencer told me. He says it's because he can't take his drink.'

'All the more reason for cutting back on it then,' said Tom. 'He's weak that way and can be extremely irritating but, unlike Parsons, he does have a better side when he's sober, is deeply contrite afterwards and swears he'll never drink again. He always does, of course! He's got the perfect role in *Arden of Faversham*: he plays the hired murderer, Black Will.'

'And Parsons?' asked Simon, fearing his friend would digress.

'Oh, Parsons is a different matter altogether. He's one of that poisonous breed who mire everything they touch. He's not a bad actor, which is why he gets hired, but his overweening ambition is to become as famous a poet as Kit Marlowe and see the playhouses fill with people mad to applaud his genius. Unfortunately he's got little natural talent and even less imagination, and no scruples whatsoever about stealing other people's work and passing it off as his own – which is why he was thrown out of the company. He's been trying to get his own back ever since.'

'Charles Spencer said he'd stolen an idea of his, something to do with William the Conqueror – though it sounded a most unlikely tale to me – and sold it to the Burbages.'

'That'd be *Fair Em*. The story would hardly set the Thames ablaze, and the writing was even worse but then companies are so hungry for plays they're willing to take almost anything if they think they can make it work. That's why Philip Henslowe's so unusual. He actually pays in advance to ensure a flow of scripts, although even we have our problems from time to time. But you can imagine what having someone like Nathan Parsons around does, forever eavesdropping and picking up ideas, and it's not stopped even now. We can try and prevent his hanging about backstage but there's nothing to stop him paying to come in and see a show and noting down plots and dialogue, or drinking in the taverns with company members afterwards. So that's one certain cause of discord.'

'What about straightforward actors' rivalry and so on?' asked Simon. 'There must be much competition for the best parts. Those who are passed over surely feel slighted.'

'That's always been the case, of course, but competition is more cut-throat now. Times have changed. The generation of actors before us came from a different tradition. After all, it's not yet twenty years since we were classed with rogues, vagabonds and sturdy beggars who could be whipped out of town if the local dignitaries felt so inclined. Those men served their apprenticeships tumbling at fairs and playing off the backs of carts, and were grateful if their skill earned them a square meal a day and a night's lodging. It's very different now. Most actors are like us, Simon, the first generation of the sons of artisans—'

'In my case a mere farm labourer,' Simon interrupted.

'Well, then, the first generation of boys who were not the sons of gentlemen but who were educated in the grammar schools, and so learned more than simple sums and how to sign their names. That in itself was no mean achievement and then along came this wonderful new invention – the playhouse – which meant they could play to audiences of thousands rather than forty or fifty people in an inn yard in some rural market town. So, like moths to a candle, we've all been drawn to London to seek fame and fortune. For many – and I'm one – to be recognised as a competent actor and be able to earn my living as I wish is good fortune enough, not to mention my having acquired a pretty, witty wife as well! But for others, often those with only modest talents, my lowly ambitions aren't enough. They look at those who've climbed far above the rest of us and want it for themselves.

'Parsons is a prime example. Envious of Greene and Peele simply because they're the sons of gentlemen and went to Oxford or Cambridge – I think Robin Greene claims to have been to both! – and call themselves "university wits", though they're bitterly and desperately jealous of Kit Marlowe.'

'From the little I know of him Marlowe can be more than difficult himself,' Simon put in. 'I'm told he's adder-tongued in drink, and I know he doesn't suffer fools gladly.'

'Maybe, but he really does have a great and rare talent and much else that men desire. Fame, certainly, for there can hardly be anyone in London who hasn't at least heard of his *Tamburlaine* and *Jew of Malta*, but even more, it's the world in which he now moves. Think

52

about it. A mere cobbler's son with the Walsinghams, one of the most powerful families in the land, as his patrons; the great Sir Walter Raleigh a close friend and confidant; contacts at court and in high places. And with all the arrogance that goes with it: that's what men like Parsons would kill to get.'

He looked at his wife. 'But enough of all this. That's the best I can do, Simon. You're surely busy enough with your own work, but if you can spare the time, why not come in and see us rehearse during the next day or two? That way you'll get to know everyone better, and it could be useful.' Simon agreed it might be a good idea, adding that he was by no means as busy as he might be, thanks to the Royal College.

'Tom knows it makes me sad to hear this kind of thing,' said Jenny as her husband rose to pour them more wine. 'And not all actors are like Nathan Parsons or even Gabriel Tanner.'

Simon reassured her that he knew that. 'I was particularly taken with young Charles Spencer and his friend – Dick Marsh, isn't it? They not only seemed intelligent and talented and happy to be members of an acting company, but good friends too, not rivals. In fact I was most impressed by Spencer, who not only convinced me that he had no jealousy in that direction but was generous in his praise of Marsh, who he said was a better actor than he'd ever be and seemed to mean it. I haven't yet seen him play anything of note but even from so brief a meeting I think he might well be right.'

'They're a great pair and a tonic to have around,' Tom agreed. 'And certainly Dick Marsh has the makings of a fine actor and also great charm, hasn't he, Jenny?' Jenny smiled and did not add anything to what had been said.

Simon thought for a moment. 'I don't like even to hint at this, but I suppose there can't possibly be any truth in what Parsons said on the day of the accident – that Spencer could see the trapdoor wasn't in place and let Lane fall backwards anyway? It was said there'd been ill feeling between them.'

'No,' said Jenny decisively. 'Charles would never have done such a thing.' Her husband remained silent. 'Surely you don't think that, do you Tom?' she added.

'I couldn't absolutely swear to it,' he replied with some reluctance.

'He's an emotional young man, Simon, lets his heart and tongue rule his head. He can easily lose his temper if he feels slighted, though it's over just as quickly. He still needs to grow up somewhat. Certainly Dick Marsh scores over him there, he shrugs off most things and is rarely ruffled.' He was aware he might have said too much. 'It's more than likely he couldn't have seen whether the trapdoor was there or not, and I find it hard to believe he'd actually have tampered with it. But enough of such depressing thoughts: on the whole those two lads are a tonic to have around and as for Charles . . .'

Jenny laughed and turned to Simon. 'Tom hasn't told you what's happened to Charles, Simon?' He shook his head. 'Well *I* must. Charles has fallen in love!'

'Madly, passionately, roaringly in love,' agreed her husband.

'It's rather sudden, isn't it?' commented Simon.

'Oh, where's your sense of romance, man? This is love at first sight and all of three days old. The stuff of chivalry and the troubadours. Their eyes met and . . . oh, you know the sort of thing. Or are you too old to recall it?' he added, mischievously.

Simon gave a rueful grin. 'I can recall it all right. And if I remember, you and I are much of an age. So who is this lady who's stolen the lad's heart?'

'The spoiled daughter of a goldsmith who brought her to see *Old Wife* in which our hero, you may recall, played the gallant knight errant. The next afternoon she was back for *The Labours of Hercules* solely to see him again as she'd taken such a fancy to him. This time she came with her maid and without her parents, and hung about until we were leaving the theatre whereupon she rushed up to Charles to tell him how wonderful he was – hardly fitting behaviour for a well-brought-up young girl of marriageable age. He took one look into those big blue eyes and fell right into their depths. Since when he's done little else but sit around writing sonnets to her flaxen curls and dimpled cheeks and wondering how he can be of service to his lady.'

'And how's friend Dick taken it? Or does this mark the onset of rivalry at last?'

'If Dick also favours the lady, he shows no signs of it. He merely mocks Charles's lovesickness and says he hopes he'll soon be over it like a dose of the rheum. Come to think of it, I've never seen Dick smitten in such a way. Behind that engaging manner he's very single-minded about his vocation and doesn't let anything interfere with his work. But no doubt he too will find some goddess to worship in the none too distant future.'

Tom fetched out another bottle of wine and the rest of the evening passed very pleasantly, the two men talking far into the night, long after Jenny had yawned, said that she had to be up betimes to see her sons off to school and so had taken herself to bed.

Simon awoke the next day with a bad head and a throat that felt as if it had grown fur during the night. The sky, seen through his bedroom window, was overcast and a shower of rain pattered against the glass. As he finally gathered strength to get up there was a knock at the door for the third and fourth time calling to him that he had half a dozen people sitting in his hall waiting to see him. Groaning to himself, he clambered out of bed, struggled into his clothes and made his way down, hoping he'd have time to wash his face and drink something to soothe his parched throat. The lack of light meant that it was dim in his hall and at first he did not see the man standing in the corner until, hearing Simon's footsteps on the stairs, his visitor turned towards him. It was Thomas Barton.

Simon's heart sank to his boots. What on earth could the man want now? He was soon to find out.

'No doubt you're surprised to see me again,' he said as soon as Simon reached ground level. 'But this matter will not wait.'

'Well it will have to until I've washed and broken my fast,' Simon replied, firmly. 'You're not in pain?' Barton shook his head. 'Then you can either wait here or take a walk and return in half an hour. As you see, I have others to attend to also.' Barton was less than pleased but seeing that Simon meant what he said, grudgingly took himself off.

Simon went out to the pump in the yard for water to splash over his face; the rain had stopped but it looked as if there was more to come. He then went back into the kitchen, calling to Anna to bring him some bread and a drink while he gathered his wits to deal with his patients. A short while later, and with considerable reluctance, he went back into the hall, opened the door of his study and called the first patient in.

The man introduced himself as a local merchant and admitted that there was nothing wrong with him but that he had come about his wife. That's two of them at least this morning, thought Simon, already dreading the return of Barton. I expect he's come to ask me if his wife's playing cat's cradle with a neighbour. It was indeed so. Simon took the essential details, unrolled his charts and set to work, his head still thick with fumes of canary wine. Then he did some swift calculations.

The answer did not seem to be one the man would wish to hear, for according to the stars the wife would play the whore privily although her outward show would give no hint of it. He mused for a moment as to what to say then turned to the man. 'She has it in her to play you false, sir, so it's best you see to her needs yourself. Frequently.' The man looked doubtful. 'I'll give you a draught that might help.'

'To keep her faithful?' asked the husband.

'No, man, to help you satisfy her so that she's no wish to stray!'

There followed a number of minor injuries, and then a cocky young man who announced that he was an actor with the Burbages' company and had come about a sore throat. Simon peered into his mouth. 'There seems to be little inflammation here.' The actor produced a graveyard cough. 'Nor,' Simon added, 'any noticeable rasping of the lungs.' The actor summoned up another cough. 'Very well, I'll give you a syrup of angelica and horehound. Take a dose now and then, and another before you play this afternoon.'

'I hear there's been a death at the Rose,' said the actor as Simon went over to mix the medicine. 'It's said that the newfangled trapdoor was deliberately lowered so that Jack Lane broke his neck.'

'Is it now?' responded Simon, measuring out the dosage. 'Why tell me?'

'Because it's also said that you were there and saw what happened.'

Simon turned round. 'If this is your real reason for being here you can go now. It's nothing to do with me, or you either. So far as

I know and, as you rightly say, I was there, it was a sad accident.'

The actor remained seated. 'I sometimes drank with Jack Lane. It seems he felt some of the company of the Admiral's Men had taken against him. Especially – now who was it? – Spencer, that's right. Charles Spencer. I had it from . . . no matter.'

Simon put the phial of medicine down on the table with a bang. 'Here's your throat syrup. If you come again to waste my time and peddle gossip, I'll prescribe you something that will keep you running to the close stool for the next two days!'

He walked purposefully over to the door and ushered the actor out to find that Thomas Barton had returned and was waiting impatiently outside. He motioned him in. 'So what can I do for you this time?' he asked, in a brisk no-nonsense tone.

'She's tried again. Poisoning me, that is. But this time, it wasn't broth, it was a poisoned picture.'

'God's teeth, man!' Simon exploded. 'This isn't the playhouse, nor are we in Italy with the Borgias. Poisoned pictures? You can't surely be serious?'

Barton looked affronted. 'I can assure you that it is true. It seems my wife sought out a young artist who bears me a grudge – I turned his family out of a house I own to let it to a man who could pay me more for it. She told me she wanted this young man to paint her portrait as a gift to me, and that he'd agreed to let bygones be bygones and do so.'

'Well? What's amiss with that?'

'The portrait was finished two days ago. She insisted I look at it particularly closely in order to appreciate the fine workmanship, which I did. The picture was so new it still had the smell of paint on it, or at least I thought it to be the smell of paint. But within hours I was stricken with pains in the chest. I took your antidote, as you'd advised, and so came to no harm but you see, do you not, why I've grounds for suspicion?'

'I see that your wife gave you her picture as a gift and that by chance you suffered some indisposition about the same time. But as a physician who is well versed in the properties of herbs and minerals I can assure you that there is no poison known to man which could possibly affect you merely by being painted on a picture. The famed Italian poisoners are no doubt skilful at their trade but outside the pages of romances or in the theatre, they could not possibly perform such a feat in real life. Think about it, sir. Were it possible, then your man would risk poisoning not only you but *anyone* who regarded the picture too closely.'

Barton looked unconvinced. 'You might be right on this occasion, I suppose. But I now fear she and her ex-lover will turn to other methods to get rid of me. I'm a wealthy man and she would inherit a sizeable fortune. There have been such cases known before; I read a pamphlet to that effect,' he added, seeing that Simon remained unimpressed. 'Dr Forman, would you consider coming back to Kent with me so that you might assess the situation for yourself and advise me?'

Simon sighed in exasperation. 'No, Master Barton, I would not. I have more than enough to do and am presently unable to leave London. Possibly, if I see my way clear at a later date, I will do as you ask – purely to try and set your mind at rest, for I must tell you honestly that I think you are deluding yourself. In the meantime I suggest you find someone else in whom you might confide. Your parson, perhaps?'

'I am in dispute with him over my refusal to increase my church tithe,' Barton responded shortly. 'Very well. It seems I've had a wasted journey. I bid you good day but should anything untoward happen I might well be back. And one more thing,' he added. 'I have written a note of what has occurred saying that I have consulted you on this matter, and requesting that if I should die suddenly *in whatever circumstances*, you are to be informed of it. I intend leaving it with my lawyer.'

He strode out, obviously displeased. A loud knocking on the front door heralded the arrival of yet another patient. He heard Anna come out of the kitchen to let them in and show Barton out. So much suspicion, he thought. First the man with the roving wife, then the actor from a rival company trying both to spy out the land and peddle mischief, and finally an obsessed madman prating on about poisoned pictures. He slumped over his desk, his aching head in his hands.

Chapter 6

Fair Iseult

John Bradedge wasted no time in doing as Simon had asked, and went down to see his friend Sam Rowley at the time he judged the afternoon's performance would be over. Although an inveterate grumbler he rather enjoyed these excursions into information-gathering, and in this instance he had the added incentive that his efforts might finally help clear his friend of the charge that a man had died possibly as a result of his careless workmanship. He found Rowley in his workshop close by the theatre working on a massive imitation cauldron, big enough to hold a man, made of canvas stretched over a wooden frame. The two men had not met since the disastrous day at the Rose and John was quick to commiserate with him.

Sam Rowley thanked him but shook his head when John asked if it was now accepted that there had been nothing wrong with the trap. 'I reckon most people believe the trap was well made,' he told John, 'but there are those who are only too happy to try and put the blame on me. In spite of what Henslowe said about not gossiping, it's obviously got about because I met Burbage's carpenter on London Bridge yesterday and he asked me about it. Their trap at the Theatre's quite an old one and they were thinking of replacing it with something better. Though he *did* believe me when I said that I couldn't see how I could possibly have been at fault. Look,' he said, putting down the saw he was using, 'you're a practical fellow. Let me show you.'

He led John in through the door of the Rose as the last of the actors were leaving after the performance, and down under the stage to the trap which was now in place and flush with the boards surrounding it. Its new ropes and weights hung down below and

Sam showed John the large cleats which ensured the ropes were quite secure, whatever the position of the trap.

'So it must have been carelessness,' he told him. 'The two lads who were working the trap were in a hurry to see how the last scene looked and one of them must somehow have failed to secure the ropes properly so that it fell back down instead of staying up where it should be.'

John looked up at the trap and down at the square of flags beneath and to the right of it. 'But surely if it had fallen down someone would have heard something? The door would have hit the floor and the ropes would have run out through the pulleys. I remember what a noise that kind of thing made on the ships I went back and forth in to the Low Countries.'

Sam thought about this. 'That's a point. No one said they'd heard anything, though most of the cast would have been backstage waiting for their entrances. But it's a good point. I'll ask around and see if anyone did hear anything untoward.'

'Could it have been done deliberately?' John persisted. 'Is it possible the trap was put in position just as your lads said, and with the mattress on, but that someone came and gently let it down to ground level, without a sound, and took the mattress off for good measure?'

'If someone did then there's an evil person loose among us, either within the company or one who knows our work well. I wonder . . .' he stopped. 'That poisonous Nathan Parsons was in the theatre that day *and* backstage earlier. Whether he'd have had the opportunity – oh, I'm grasping at straws. They're not like ordinary folk, players. There's so much spite and petty jealousy and falling out. I suppose almost any of them *could* have done it.' Then he shook his head. 'No. I reckon it's down to simple carelessness.'

John left him to go back and finish his cauldron, then went and ensconced himself firmly in the Anchor with a quart of ale before him. There were a number of actors already there and John greeted those he knew slightly, ordered some bread and cheese and sat back prepared to say little and listen much.

'They're a funny lot,' he told his master later. 'They take all their dressing up and prancing about deadly serious. And gossip! They're like a bunch of women sitting out together with their spinning wheels on a fine day.' But some of the gossip had been interesting. The name of Nathan Parsons had cropped up a number of times and, what was more, linked on several occasions with that of John Lane.

'They were thick as thieves at one time, they say. It seems they knew each other before Lane joined the company, and until Parsons was kicked out they spent a lot of time together. Lane reckoned Parsons as a writer of plays – or a "poet" as they like to call themselves – though he seems to have been the only one who did. But then something happened and the two must have fallen out because all of a sudden they were spitting at each other like alley cats every time they met.

'None of them have any time for Parsons; he seems to have got across almost everybody. They say he's also quarrelled with someone called Spencer and that Spencer, whoever he is, had been at odds with Lane and so on – round and round it goes. I don't know whether that's of any use to you,' he concluded.

'Neither do I,' admitted Simon, 'but I'm desperate for anything that might help throw some light on what's been going on. And your suggestion as to how the trapdoor might deliberately have been lowered to the floor is of even more interest. So keep your ear to the ground and see what else you can find out. In the meantime I'll send a note round to Henslowe telling him what you've told me about the trapdoor, and I'll also see if I can discover if anyone knew where Parsons was during the performance and if he watched the play throughout. He was certainly there at the end to make his presence felt.'

Over the next day or so Simon found himself with enough to do on his own account, not so much from those folk seeking his medical skills as from others who wanted him to cast their horoscopes which was time-consuming but at least paid well. After writing up the notes of his most recent clients, he glanced back through his book. Real oddities such as Thomas Barton with his poisoned picture and desire for an antidote were, fortunately, rare. The mind was a strange thing, mused Simon. Barton, convinced that his young wife sought his death, had somehow managed to string together a number of unconnected and innocent events and then weave them into a murderous conspiracy. Seen from Barton's skewed perception it was all quite logical, whereas to the outsider it was but a fantastic delusion.

Fortunately, however, most of those seeking to have their horoscopes cast wanted answers to more mundane questions. Easiest were those who wanted to know if a proposed journey or business venture would turn out well. Next came the men, mostly (but not all) young, who asked if he could forecast when or if they would be rich and the women, also mostly (but not all) young, who were seeking husbands and wanted to know how long they might have to wait until someone rich, handsome and lusty turned up. Close on their heels came those who had already made their choice, the married who, like the merchant he had seen the previous day, now wanted to know if their respective partners were still faithful to them.

But among the most regular requests were those from wives. They were almost equally divided into two categories. The first were those desperate to bear a child, wanting to know if they would ever be successful and to beg for medicines that might cure their barren state. The second, at the other extreme, were the young single girls or wives whose husbands had been long away from home who desperately wanted to know if they were right in suspecting that they were unwontedly with child and if so, if he would give them a remedy for it.

These he dreaded for he knew he was bound to refuse what they sought. There were, he knew, numerous potions used by old women made from a wide variety of ingredients such as dried bishopsweed, fennel seeds, dittany, centaury, capers, Cretan asphodel, the 'intemperate gum' styrax and hot turpentine, a combination of any of which would be likely to provoke vomiting and the flux and so possibly produce the required effect but he had never been prepared to prescribe any abortifacient. Even had he not been set against it on moral grounds, the possibility that he might be hanged for so doing, should he be found out, was sufficient deterrent.

He had put his casebook away and was tidying up his shelves

when Anna put her head round the door to say that a lady wished to see him, before showing in a most unexpected visitor: it was the Italian-looking young woman who had attracted his attention at the performance of *The Old Wife's Tale*. She was more soberly dressed on this occasion, in a plain but well-cut russet gown over which she wore a fine velvet cloak, but she was instantly recognisable. She smiled at him as he greeted her, sat down in the chair he proffered and slipped the cloak from her shoulders. Her hair, the blue-black of Italian or Spanish women, was a mass of wiry curls, her eyes among the darkest he'd ever seen. She gave him a brilliant smile revealing even white teeth, and announced herself as Emilia Bassano. Ah, he thought, so she hails from Italy. Yet she had no trace of an accent.

'I trained as a physician in Italy,' he said, expecting this to prompt her into saying where she came from.

'It was my father's country,' she replied, 'but I've never been there. I was born here in London. My father was a musician at the court of King Henry. He was only seventeen when he came to England from Florence. I was born late in his life.'

Simon nodded. 'I see. Well, Mistress Bassano, what can I do for you?'

'I would like to know if I am with child or soon likely to be.'

Oh dear, sighed Simon, yet another. Now, does she wish to be or is she fearful that she is? Would his answer prove good news or bad? He cast the horoscope for her simple request, which she watched with great interest. 'Well?' she said. 'What have you to tell me?'

'You've given me no indication as to what you hope the outcome might be, but I can see no child in the immediate future although the stars tell me it won't be all that long delayed. Is that what you wished to hear?'

She smiled in obvious relief. 'I'm most grateful to you, Dr Forman, that's what I hoped you'd say. At least I'm free for the time being.'

'But I must tell you, I think it is only for the time being. I see one, possibly two children coming to you in due course. Was there any particular reason for your coming to see me now? Have you symptoms that make you think you might be with child? Irregular courses? Sickness early in the day? No reading of a horoscope can be infallible.'

'No. But it's a matter of continual concern to me. Given my circumstances, I've not the slightest wish to conceive.'

He could hardly be other than intrigued. According to his informant at the Rose, she was mistress to Henry Carey, Lord Hunsdon, Lord Chamberlain and cousin to the Queen. Indeed there were those who said his relationship to Her Majesty was even closer, that of half-brother, for his mother was Mary Boleyn and she had been the old king's mistress before he ever set eyes on her sister, Anne. After he had tired of Mary he had married her off to Carey's father to whom she had swiftly borne a son – some said too swiftly for it to have been her husband's. But whether cousin or half-brother to Her Majesty, he was one of the most powerful men in the land.

'And what are your circumstances?' he asked, unable to resist the temptation to find out more about this self-assured dark lady.

'My protector is the Lord Chamberlain himself,' she replied with some pride. 'I'm his official mistress. Does that shock you?'

'I'm rarely shocked by what I hear in this room, Mistress Bassano. There are few human weaknesses or revelations I haven't heard over the years.'

This seemed to amuse her. 'I was fourteen years old when I was left an orphan. My older sister had married well but all I could hope for was a poor marriage or going into service. I wanted neither. So I gave the matter some thought and decided I'd but two things in my favour: I was clever, and also a skilled musician. Later I realised I had also a third – an ability to give pleasure to men.'

Simon found it fascinating that she did not seem to count her striking looks as an advantage. 'I was lucky, for I went into the household of the Countess of Kent,' she continued, 'and she took me to court, where my skill on the virginals drew much attention to me, which is when I learned my other skills. I had little trouble being kept in gowns and pretty finery and was soon able to leave my lady's service for service of another kind. Some of my lovers were men of title and fortune but none so high as my Lord Chamberlain, and when he suggested we came to a permanent arrangement, who was I to refuse? As matters stand I have my own apartments, fine clothes and jewellery and I'm accepted almost everywhere, even by Her Majesty not only because of her fondness for her cousin but also because she enjoys my playing to her on the virginals or the lute. I live the life of a fine lady, Dr Forman, but should I conceive a child then I will swiftly be found a husband and so lose it all. That's been the nature of the bargain I made with Henry these last five years.'

'If your relations with Carey have lasted as long as that, then you're fortunate not to have had a child long before now.'

She looked him in the eyes and smiled. 'Henry is now well into his sixties and is still a fit man, but he cannot, let's say, *apply* himself like a young lover in spite of all my skill! Though in other ways he can outdo a man half his age. As you probably know, he was a brave soldier.'

'Indeed. He fought the Scots, did he not, and was once a warden on the Borders.'

'Have you met him then?'

'No, Mistress Bassano. But it fell to me to treat his son Robert during the wars in the Low Countries. And later he came to me again to see if he should have success with an argosy he was venturing to the East. I told him he would, and so it turned out. Well, bear in mind what I've told you. No child, perhaps, as yet but one not long in coming.'

She rose and drew up her cloak. 'Thank you again, then, Dr Forman. And your fee?' He asked her for a guinea which she gave him from a bulging purse.

'Why did you come to me?' he asked as he showed her out, recalling how he'd asked the wretched Thomas Barton the same thing.

She gave him a look of frank sensuality. 'Because I've heard much of you, and because of the way you looked at me at the Rose last week. You should come and see the Lord Chamberlain's Men now that they're back at the Theatre. Ned Alleyn is a fine actor in the grand manner but young Richard Burbage has a far wider range. And we have some good poets writing for us too.'

'Perhaps I will,' he said.

65

She turned and took his hand in hers. 'Oh but you must. I will look out for you, and if I don't see you within the next little while I'll send you word when I'll be there. Affairs of state keep his lordship busy. I don't spend all my days – or nights – at his side.'

That was all very well, he thought, after she'd gone, but what about the task in hand? The next morning he took up Tom Pope's suggestion that he should go to the Rose and watch the Lord Admiral's Men in rehearsal. Although the sun shone, a chill wind blew upriver with the incoming tide. It was cold in the theatre too, and the actors were walking up and down the stage trying to keep warm. The play was Marlowe's *Jew of Malta*, and Simon was disappointed to see that its famous author did not appear to be present but at least he had an opportunity to see Ned Alleyn playing the Jew.

The newly finished cauldron, in which his character would be boiled alive at the denouement of the play, stood gleaming in a corner. As Simon arrived an argument was taking place about where it should be put, as the original idea had been for it to be set on the trapdoor with only its top half showing above the stage, thus giving the lads the opportunity of puffing smoke up from underneath it. The carpenter was arguing for all he was worth that there was absolutely nothing wrong with the trapdoor mechanism, while the actors informed him that that might well be the case but until it was known for sure what had happened, and that there could not be another such accident, they'd stay on stage thank you very much. This was settled when Ned Alleyn swept in, was told of the dispute and informed the carpenter coldly that as it would be he who would be playing the Jew in most performances and would therefore have to stand in the cauldron and boil, he was not going to risk his life on the trap.

Simon found watching the actors work fascinating and whatever personal problems might be besetting the company there was no sign – disagreement over the use of the trap apart – of any bad feeling among those rehearsing under the watchful eye of William Miller.

Halfway through the morning the actors were given a break and Simon noted how Charles and Dick immediately sought each other out, one bringing out two apples which they munched contentedly, sitting side by side on a wooden form. He waved to Tom Pope, who came over and sat beside him in the seat he had taken up in the lower gallery facing the stage. 'It's a fine piece, isn't it?' he said. 'Plenty of good parts for everyone, especially Ned of course. There are those who find it shocking but they all love it when he falls into the cauldron at the end, and it looks as if it really is boiling. So how about you? Any luck?'

'Nothing worth the telling,' Simon admitted and added that he was thinking of telling Henslowe he was getting nowhere.

'Oh, leave it for a while yet,' Tom responded. 'He'll soon let you know if he thinks you're wasting his money.'

'I suppose so. One thing, though: is there any way of knowing if Parsons was really in the pit during the play?'

'You're thinking that way too, are you? The only person who might know is the gatherer. I'll ask him at the end of the morning when we've finished. You can stay 'til then? Oh, and by the way, I do have one piece of news for you. We're soon to start rehearsing Charles's play.'

'What's it about?' asked Simon.

'I'll leave him to tell you himself.'

The rehearsal continued and Simon watched with awe as the cauldron was set up in front of a low brazier in which there lay a glowing bed of coals. These were then damped down to provide smoke which could be blown around the cauldron by an apprentice energetically working a pair of bellows – not as effective, perhaps, as it might have been set on the trap but good enough. Finally the rehearsal ended to everyone's satisfaction, even that of Alleyn, who at one stage had rounded on the apprentice for producing so much smoke he'd been unable to see what he was doing. The actors made their way across the pit in twos and threes, and eventually Tom appeared with the gatherer, a burly man whose previous profession as a wrestler stood him in good stead with difficult members of the audience or those who tried to slip in without paying.

'Harry here says he did see Parsons in the pit, near the front of the stage as he said he was,' Tom told him after introductions had been made.

'But I can't swear he was there all the time,' added the gatherer. 'As you know the theatre was pretty full and one of my jobs is to try and keep an eye out for cutpurses. It could be that Parsons managed to slip away for a few minutes, but yes, I did see him standing up by the stage most of the time, and I'm almost sure he was there at the end when Jack Lane fell into the grave. That's all I can tell you. If I could tell you more, I would. Can't stand the bastard.'

Simon thanked him and he and Tom made their way out of the theatre. As they were doing so, the sound of hurried footsteps came from behind. It was Charles Spencer.

'I can't stop,' he said, 'I'm rushing home. I've work to do.'

'What are you playing next then?' asked Simon, stopping behind and waving Tom off home, knowing well what the answer would be.

'Oh, it's not a *part* I'm working on,' returned the young actor, visibly swelling with importance. 'It's a play. I'm finally going to write a play. Henslowe didn't much care for the idea I put to him a couple of weeks ago but then suddenly a brilliant new notion struck me, so I went to see him again last night and told him about it and this time he liked it. He's given me three guineas to go away and write it. Isn't that splendid?' Simon agreed it was, and asked if he could be trusted with the subject matter of the piece.

'So long as you promise not to tell anyone. Dick knows, of course,' he added, 'but that's all right. He'd never say anything. And no doubt Henslowe's told Ned Alleyn, for he'll be playing one of the three main characters. I feel absolutely *inspired*!' Obviously the goldsmith's daughter was to thank for this, thought Simon as Charles continued without pause for breath. 'It's about the love of the knight Sir Tristram for the fair Iseult. You know the story? How Tristram was sent to Brittany by his uncle, King Mark, to fetch Iseult back to be the King's bride and how the two, unbeknown, drank a love potion and were swept away by passion and how King Mark finds out and it all ends in tragedy. I wanted to call it *Fair Iseult* but Henslowe says it must be *The Tragical History of King Mark of Cornwall*, since plays about kings seem to be all the rage.'

Simon congratulated him and asked what had given him the idea.

A look of adoration crossed Charles's face. 'You see,' he confided, 'I've met a real-life Iseult. A girl to die for!'

'I hope not,' said Simon, doing his best to suppress his amusement.

'Well, perhaps not literally, but certainly the next best thing. It's her, this angel, who's inspired me to write the play. Henslowe's only given me two weeks in which to do it, and then if he and Ned Alleyn and Will Miller think it good enough, we'll rehearse it and it'll be played at the Rose. And my Audrey will be able to come and see it. Think of that!' He was obviously in a world of his own. 'I wonder if they'll think I'm good enough to play Tristram, or whether it will go to Dick? As for Fair Iseult – oh, if only they'd let girls become actors! There's not one of our boys who could possibly be made to look beautiful enough for my Iseult.'

Oh the naivety of young love, thought Simon, as he walked back home. It was highly unlikely a shrewd goldsmith would countenance an indigent actor as a husband for his pearl of great price – if she really was as pretty as Charles said – though possibly he'd be more likely to consider it if the young man was prepared to go back to Norwich and become a lawyer. Except that by the time he qualified, no doubt both of them would have long since looked elsewhere.

Chapter 7

Uproar at the Theatre

By the end of the first week in October, Simon felt he had discovered as much as he was ever likely to without arousing the suspicions of the entire company of the Lord Admiral's Men. It had proved, as he explained to Henslowe who was sitting in his office working on his accounts, an almost impossible task for an outsider.

'You see,' he told the entrepreneur, 'I could think of no good reason for hanging around the theatre or the taverns too often asking questions. As you probably know already, there's a general feeling that Nathan Parsons had something to do with the accident of John Lane. I was told they'd recently quarrelled after having been particularly friendly. Your gatherer agreed that he had been standing near the stage for much of the performance that day but couldn't swear that he'd never moved from that spot since he'd plenty of other things to take his attention. But whether it could ever be proved that Parsons tampered with the trapdoor mechanism, I very much doubt.

'Also,' he continued with real reluctance, 'it seems that young Charles Spencer was on particularly bad terms with Lane. Tom Pope, who's fond of the lad, tells me that he has a tendency, when aroused, to act first and think afterwards. But if that's the case then it would surely be more likely that he would punch someone on the nose than go to elaborate lengths to cause an accident, as that would need to be carefully thought out beforehand. But I felt it was something you should take into consideration.

'As to other reasons for ill feeling, they appear somewhat diffuse and seem mainly to do with company rivalries and, in the case of the writers, of their plots or even their playscripts being stolen and sold to other companies. It seems Nathan Parsons is also accused of having done that on a number of occasions.' It occurred to him as he said it that Charles had complained bitterly about Parsons stealing an idea he'd had, but decided not to pursue the point, continuing: 'So in my own opinion, for what it's worth, Parsons is not only the most likely suspect for tampering with the trapdoor but was, and possibly still is, at the root of most of it. I'm sorry I haven't got any further,' he added.

Henslowe remained for a while deep in thought, then he looked up. 'I thought it might be a difficult task but thank you for what you've done, Dr Forman. I'll see if there's any possibility of taking it further. In fact I will seek out Parsons and inform him that he is suspected, in the hope that it might do some good and stop anything else untoward happening in the future, to which end it must be ensured that he is never again allowed into the Rose. All we can do now is put it all behind us, try and behave as if nothing is amiss and continue with our season of plays. However, I would like to think I might be able to call on you again should I find it necessary. I will also, if you feel it might be helpful, write to the Royal College of Physicians on your behalf. Presumably the more people prepared to do so the better.'

After Simon left Henslowe turned to his diary, dipped his pen in his ink pot and wrote:

> Received at the door for play of *The Spanish Tragedy* thirty-four shillings and for *King Harry Fifth* fifteen shillings and sixpence. Bought for the company a white satin woman's doublet and a black tinsel veil for twenty shillings and a black velvet jerkin and a pair of silver hose for thirteen shillings and five pence. Note that I paid to Charles Spencer the sum of three pounds for a play of *King Mark of Cornwall*. Needs must from now on his conduct be noted if he is to remain with the company. Today Dr Forman told me that Nathan Parsons continues to make mischief and might well have caused our sad trouble. I must see to this. Paid to Dr Forman, I say paid, the sum of one guinea.

Simon ran down the wooden steps from Henslowe's office,

pocketing the further guinea Henslowe had given him and feeling he'd had enough of the theatre for the time being, although he intended to go to see *King Mark* if he had time and if it ever reached the stage.

It was at the beginning of the following week that a smartly dressed servant knocked at his door with a personal letter for him sealed with a curious seal picturing naked nymphs sporting on the backs of dolphins. Emilia Bassano had kept her word. Would he like to accompany her, she wrote, to a performance at the Theatre in Finsbury Fields the following day? The play was a comic piece about two sets of twins, one of each pair being separated from his brother, until all meet up years later when they are mistaken for each other, causing much confusion all round. *It is*, she wrote, *by a young man not long up from the country who has also written for Philip Henslowe. I think he shows much promise – but come and see for yourself.* If he was worried about the proprieties, she would of course be bringing her maid and a party of friends as well. When he arrived at the Theatre he was to ask for the Lord Hunsdon's party and he would be shown straight in.

As Simon crossed London Bridge the next day on his way to Finsbury Fields he wondered why he was always such a fool where women were concerned. Had she been willing, then there was no doubt he would have found solace enough in Avisa Allen but consummation in that quarter seemed as far off as ever. But what in heaven's name was he doing involving himself with the Lord Chamberlain's mistress? There was little doubt she enjoyed a flirtation – possibly even more than that – but how would his presence with her at so public an event be explained to his lordship, should knowledge of it reach his ears? He was hardly likely to take it well.

He need not have worried. Emilia, as she had told him she would, had brought half a dozen other people with her as well as her personal maid, and Simon was swiftly introduced to a number of young men of the court, dressed in the height of fashion, and two other young women with whom they seemed on intimate terms. There was also a box containing a delicious array of small pies, fruit and sweets made of marchpane. Their seats were to the side of the second gallery, screened off from the rest of the audience. A table had been placed at the back on which were several bottles of wine and a set of glasses. The lady obviously liked her comforts. She was dressed this time in a gold-coloured gown, a necklace of amber wound round her throat. As the actors came on stage to begin the performance she motioned to Simon to sit beside her and to bring his wine with him. 'That's the author of the piece,' she informed him, pointing to a dark-haired man of middle height who was playing one of the citizens of Ephesus. 'He's called William Shakespeare and he's also an actor.'

Simon had to agree, *The Comedy of Errors* was extremely enjoyable but throughout he was aware of Emilia's knee pressing against his own and her fingers lingering on his as she offered him sweetmeats. At the end of the performance, as the audience applauded the actors, she leaned and whispered in his ear that my lord was away to the Queen at Nonesuch soon and that she might well send to him again so that they might get to know each other better and in a less public place.

He squired her outside to where her carriage was waiting and saw her and her female companions into it. A groom was holding the horses for the gentlemen who would escort them safely home. He thanked Emilia formally and she drove off without another word. He was just about to leave, telling himself he must not, he really *must not*, take up Emilia's invitation should she send one, when a lad thrust a handbill at him. He pushed it into his pocket as he walked back home and it was not until he undressed for bed that he remembered it. It was a roughly printed sheet drawing the attention of playgoers to a forthcoming new production on the fifteenth of October: *The True Tale of Sir Tristram and the Tragic Iseult by Nathan Parsons*. Simon's heart sank. Here, surely, was a recipe for trouble.

Charles Spencer had spent the last week writing all day and half the night, excused, apart from a couple of performances, from having to play any part of substance until he had delivered his script. He had shown Acts One and Two to Henslowe and the bookman and it had been decided that, with the days growing shorter and the weather colder, rehearsals should start at once while he continued work on Acts Three and Four. Since that was the case, he had to shelve his dream of playing Sir Tristram, at least for the time being, and the role went as he had expected to Dick Marsh. The best-looking of the lads was chosen for Fair Iseult and Ned Alleyn himself would play King Mark for the first few performances, which would guarantee a respectable audience, after which Tom Pope would take over the role, as Kit Marlowe had nearly finished another play and Alleyn always played his great protagonists.

He'd hoped that Henslowe might have been prepared to pay out for new costumes at least for the principals but in this he was to be disappointed. The wardrobe master was told to look out what he had in store and reported that suitable costumes for King Mark and his knights, including Sir Tristram, could be refurbished from those last worn in the old play of *King Harry the Fifth* while there were women's gowns and to spare from both *Crack Me This Nut* and *Barnardo and Phiametta*.

It was on the morning of the day Simon had his assignation with Emilia that Charles completed Act Three and the bookman handed out to each actor his part written out on a roll, complete with its cues, after which he read the new Act out in full from his master copy so that they would know when they had to enter, what they were doing and where their own speeches fitted in with those of everyone else. It was a cumbersome way of doing things but making a copy of the entire play for each actor was impossible, and it also helped save the full text from being stolen as the master copies were kept locked in a heavy oak chest, to which only the bookman and Philip Henslowe himself held the keys.

The actors then began to run through the whole of Acts One and Two to ensure that they were firmly fixed in their heads before they started learning the last two Acts, which they had been told they had to do by the end of the week at the latest. Learning lines was a constant nightmare as so many plays had to be held in repertory at once, on top of which any player could suddenly find he had to play something other than the part he had been playing quite happily for years.

Some had more of a knack for fast learning than others but all was going well until it came to a small scene between Sir Tristram and his page, who was played by young Daniel Lee. The boy was usually quick to learn both his cues and his lines but on this occasion he kept missing both. For a long time Dick was patient with him, waiting while the boy struggled to remember what came next but eventually even his patience began to wear thin, and he was about to say so when the bookman forestalled him.

'What's the matter with you, boy? Are you sick?' Daniel miserably shook his head and said that he was not. 'Why then have you not learned your lines? They're not many. If there's one thing I can't abide it's lazy boys. Very well,' he continued as Daniel looked close to tears, 'we'll move to the next scene and you,' he pointed a finger at the boy, 'will go down under the stage and stay there until you can come out and say every speech to me without a single mistake.'

There must be something badly wrong, thought Charles, for Daniel was usually conscientious and eager to please. He felt so concerned that some twenty minutes later he thought he would go and find out how the boy was getting on. To his surprise, as he went down the steps to go under the stage, he could hear subdued voices, one of them a man's, the other that of the boy. Daniel had lit two candles in order to be able to see his script and he and Nathan Parsons were caught in a pool of light like actors in the discovery space.

'Believe me, I mean it!' Parsons was saying, and although he was keeping his voice down it was clearly menacing: 'You'll not act here or anywhere else. You'll be turned loose to thieve on the streets and end on the gallows as your father before you.'

'But I don't know what to do,' the boy responded, breaking into tears. 'What was done was wrong and—'

Parsons picked him up by the collar and shook him until his teeth rattled. 'Then let this be a lesson to you,' he snarled and, raising his hand, boxed the boy's ears. In an instant Charles was across the floor and on to him and the two men fell to the ground. Daniel, his eyes wide with fear, ran up the stairs calling for help, shouting out to the actors on the stage. Oblivious to everything going on overhead, Parsons rolled on top of Charles and banged his head on the floor, while the young actor tried to retaliate by punching him in the eye. Within minutes footsteps sounded on the stairs and Miller, Pope, Alleyn and half a dozen other actors appeared and the two men were pulled apart.

'What's the meaning of this?' roared Alleyn, in the voice he usually reserved for Tamburlaine the Great. 'God's blood, must be Rose be turned into the bear pit? You've been told by Master Henslowe that you are forbidden entry to the Rose. Who let him in?' There was no response. He turned back to Parsons 'If you're ever – ever – seen here again, I'll personally take you before a magistrate and have you bound over. As for you, Spencer, haven't you enough to do that you must brawl in such a way? Is time hanging heavy on your hands? I must warn you that your conduct too is under review. We can do without hotheads in the company.'

The two got to their feet, Charles bleeding slightly from the back of his head, Parsons with a rapidly blackening eye.

'All I did was to come down to see how Daniel was getting on with his lines,' Charles began, feeling he was being unfairly accused, 'and found this – this – *dunghill rat* here beating him. I intervened, that's all.'

'Is that true, Dan?' asked Tom. The boy nodded. 'Why was he threatening you?' The boy looked from Parsons to Pope, clearly distressed. Then he shrugged and shook his head as if he did not know. Tom turned to Alleyn. 'I think this needs discussing later, Ned,' he said. 'In the meantime I suggest Daniel sits in the theatre proper to learn his lines, where we can all see him. And that Parsons is thrown out.'

'Have you anything to say for yourself, Parsons?' demanded Alleyn.

Parsons shook his head. 'Nothing worth wasting words on.'

Alleyn looked round. 'Is the gatherer in the theatre? If so, ask him to come here straight away.' Within minutes the burly doorman had joined them and, firmly seizing Parsons by the neck of his doublet, pushed him roughly up the stairs and almost dragged him across the pit to the theatre entrance. As they reached it, Parsons turned and yelled, 'I'll laugh last, you wait and see! *The Tragical History of King Mark*, is it? It will be! Oh, I assure you, it will be!'

The actors resumed their rehearsal, although much of the energy had gone out of it. One of the lads fetched a bowl of water to wash Charles's cut head but the wound was not thought sufficiently severe to merit a trip to the physician, though another boy was sent to Henslowe for one of his remedies for wounds; fortunately an innocuous one on this occasion made from butter, sugarloaf and woundwort. It had not been a good morning, and Charles felt deeply depressed as he left the theatre with Dick Marsh, his head pounding. Everything had been going so well, too.

At that moment an acquaintance hailed him in the street and handed him a playbill for Lord Chamberlain's Men at the Theatre, bearing the legend that the Burbages' company were about to present *The True Tale of Sir Tristram and the Fair Iseult by Nathan Parsons*. Charles stood rooted to the spot, scarcely able to believe his eyes.

'He's taken my play! The aborted son of a witch has stolen my play!'

'You don't know that,' soothed Dick. 'It could be coincidence, though I realise that's not very likely. But it can't possibly be your whole play, it's not even finished. It'll be like last time, he'll have just taken your idea, which is infuriating but not the end of the world. You know as well as I do that there are many different plays going the rounds on the same subject matter.'

'Perhaps so,' fumed Charles, 'but I'll be there at the first performance and if there's a single sentence of my play in his script I'll kill him!'

He repeated his threat to Simon the following morning. His head had ached badly all night and that, coupled with spots of blood on his pillow, argued that he should after all seek some professional advice.

'What was all the trouble about?' Simon enquired as he deftly cleaned the wound, and Henslowe's patent remedy away, with a lotion of his own.

'We still don't know. Young Daniel won't say why Parsons tried to attack him, probably because he's afraid of him. Ouch!' he concluded as Simon probed the cut.

'There doesn't seem to be anything to worry about. I'll put something on to dry it up and give you a draught for your aching head. I'd take it quietly though, if I were you.'

He made up a salve in a pot and a potion in a phial and handed them to the young actor. Charles thanked him, then, with some trepidation, asked Simon if he might possibly be able to do him a favour. 'It's this. I told you Parsons had stolen an idea I'd had for a play once,' he began. Simon groaned to himself. So Charles now knew the bad news. He wondered what was to come next – that the young knight errant required his services as a second in a duel?

'Well, it looks as if he's done it again but this time it's much worse.' He brought out a copy of the handbill Simon had already seen. 'Look at that! A play by Parsons about Tristram and Iseult. It can't be coincidence. I trust your judgement to be impartial. Will you come with me to see if again he's stolen mine? I can show you the first two Acts so we'll both know soon enough if he has.'

Simon's heart sank. 'What about taking someone from the company, they'd surely know more about it?'

'If the weather's good enough they'll almost all be playing; anyway I trust you to tell me the truth. I still have some of the play to finish but I'm more or less excused from acting until the end of next week, so I can take the afternoon off to go over to the Theatre. My play must be done now as we're soon to go out on tour and by the time we get back it'll be winter, and Henslowe will want only the most well-known and popular pieces to go on then.'

On that mid-October day the weather was still fine enough for both the Theatre and the Rose to offer performances, although sitting or standing around exposed to the elements for anything up to three hours could still be a chilly business, and the people in the line moving slowly through the entrance of the Theatre were warmly wrapped. Charles had turned down Simon's suggestion that they buy a seat in the gallery 'because I want to stand in the pit, right close up against the stage, to make sure I hear every word and this is an old playhouse – often you can't hear or see as well from the galleries'.

Simon was hoping that his excitable young companion might have other matters to help distract him, for he had confided to him during their long walk to Finsbury Fields that he had an assignation that very evening with his Audrey. She had taken into her confidence a young married friend whose husband was away visiting relatives, and the friend had agreed to host a supper party for four, Dick Marsh making up the fourth. Simon was sure that at any other time the prospect of such a delight would have taken precedence over everything else in Charles's calendar; it was highly unfortunate that the assignation had been arranged for that particular day.

Once inside the Theatre Charles pushed his way through the groundlings and planted himself foursquare in front of the stage. At least he had the satisfaction of noting as the last trumpet sounded that the Theatre was only half full. Gradually the general noise subsided as the time came for the play to commence and a group of actors trooped on. There was no spoken Prologue. Instead either Parsons or Richard Burbage had decided to offer the audience a brief dumbshow explaining what was to come, for the benefit of those unable to read or who knew little or nothing of tales of chivalry. Charles stood silent as the actor playing King Mark mimed sending Sir Tristram (played by Richard Burbage) off to France but began to be restive as Tristram and Iseult drank from the silver goblet, gazed into each other's eyes, then fell into each other's arms. 'Give it a chance,' whispered Simon, as the dumbshow ended and the actors made their exit. 'The story's the same whoever tells it.'

Finally the play proper began and King Mark walked back on with his courtiers and chamberlain, sat on his throne and declaimed his opening lines:

> 'Go Chamberlain, and call my nephew here
> So I can bid the gallant lad farewell.
> The wind's set fair, he must away to France
> To fetch me home my bride. They say the lady is the
> Fairest of her sex. Her beauty, matchless.'

What the chamberlain replied before he left the stage Simon was unable to hear, since Charles had pulled his play rolls out of his doublet and was hissing in his ear, 'It's all here. You've read it, you must know. It *is* my play!' This provoked those standing around him to tell him to *Snek up!* as the chamberlain returned with Sir Tristram. There was a round of applause which Burbage acknowledged, turning to the King who continued:

> 'Dear nephew, dear to me as any son,
> Our prayers are with you as you board your ship.
> You now have all that's needful for your journey?'

Simon, aware of Charles muttering and rattling pieces of paper, began to wonder how he might manage to extricate them both from a situation which could only get worse. Meanwhile Sir Tristram was answering the King:

> 'Uncle, I have. And give you grateful thanks.
> For you have sent me forth as if a prince . . .'

What else Burbage had to say was left unsaid as Charles, unable to take any more, pushed through the line of people standing in front of him until he reached as near the front of the stage as he could and still be seen by those above him. 'Shame!' he bawled at the top of his voice. 'Shame on you, you bastard!'

King Mark and Tristram stopped in their tracks. Both had been in the theatre long enough to have experienced all kinds of interruptions but this one could hardly be ignored. Those standing nearest to Charles and Simon were rapidly becoming angry, one enquiring why a drunken madman appeared to have been let in to spoil everyone's enjoyment.

'Listen to me, everyone!' shouted Charles. 'That's my play you're watching. I wrote it, not Nathan Parsons. He's stolen my play!' There was a hubbub of noise from the crowd. Burbage, concerned to keep the play going, strode to the front of the stage.

'If you feel you have a grievance, young man, then come and see me about it afterwards. You've no business attempting to wreck the performance. Be quiet now, or I'll have you turned out.' He peered closer at Charles. 'You're an actor too, aren't you? From the Lord Admiral's Men? What would Ned Alleyn say if one of our company came over to the Rose and did the same thing there?' The noise from the audience was rising in volume by the minute. Burbage looked down on the groundlings, then raised his hand for silence.

'My apologies to you all. We will now continue.'

For the next half-hour or so the performance went on without interruption, with Charles muttering a continual counterpoint of complaint to Simon which finally rose to outright fury as Tristram and Iseult drank the love potion from the cup and plighted their troth, a scene during which Iseult spoke what Charles had considered to be his best piece of writing. It was clearly his work, as he could recite the words in unison with the young boy actor playing the tragic heroine. It was then that Nathan Parsons himself came on stage in his role as the captain of the ship which was to take Iseult to Cornwall.

Simon did his best to hang on to his enraged companion but Charles broke free. He pushed his way through the crowd until he reached the side of the stage where steps led up from the pit, and would have climbed them had not a couple of stout playgoers prevented him. 'So you've the brazen neck to show your face, have you, Parsons?' he called out over their heads. 'It's not enough that you've stolen my play, you prancing turd!'

'Get him out!' roared Burbage. Half a dozen willing volunteers stepped forward to be joined almost immediately by two of the Theatre's backstage men, and the crowd in the pit parted as Charles was half-dragged, half-carried towards the doors at the back of the theatre. Simon was close behind, acutely aware that the actor was damaging his own case by his behaviour. The groundlings kept up an angry buzz until Charles was thrown into the street, at which point he wrenched himself free again and turned towards the stage. 'I'll kill you for this, Nathan Parsons!' he yelled. 'As God's my witness, I'll kill you for this!'

It was all Simon could do to restrain him from trying to get back inside the Theatre once they were outside with the doors firmly shut. Concerned at what mad antics he might get up to next, he took him by the arm and led him into the nearest hostelry, sat him down, told him to keep quiet and called the tapster to bring them some ale. 'All right,' he told the infuriated young man, 'so Parsons has almost without doubt stolen your script, though it would surely have been more sensible to hear the whole play out so that you could be quite certain. You say yourself you haven't quite finished

yours, so some of this play at least must be Parson's or some other
writer's.'

'But I *am* quite sure,' raged Charles as the tapster set down their
ale, 'it's word for word what I've got written down here. You've
seen for yourself. I'll drink this, then I'm going back in there again.'

Simon caught his arm. 'You certainly are not! It's not done you
any good at all to make such an exhibition of yourself – you've
played right into Parsons's hands. He must be cock-a-hoop. Richard
Burbage was right. What in the name of all that's holy would you feel
like if someone came in as you've done and completely ruined your
own performance? From what I've heard of John and Richard Burbage
they're eminently reasonable men. Calm down, and then first thing
tomorrow morning, when you're coherent, go and tell the bookman,
Ned Alleyn and some of the more senior actors what's happened and
ask them what, if anything, can be done about it. Perhaps a meeting
could be arranged between members of your company and the
Burbages at which you could show them your original script. It wasn't
their fault Parsons foisted your play on them as his own.

'But doing anything at all in your current frame of mind can
only lead to trouble. And,' he added, as Charles looked mutinous,
'surely you haven't forgotten your love tryst with your own fair
Iseult? You're unlikely to get such a good opportunity again. Put
this out of your mind until tomorrow and play the lover yourself.
She'll hardly want to spend the evening listening to you ranting on
about stolen plays!'

It did seem by the time they crossed London Bridge again that
Charles was beginning to see reason, and the two parted amicably
enough as they reached the south side of the river. As Simon returned
home after what had been one of the most embarrassing afternoons
of his life, he was at least thankful that the furious poet hadn't
asked him his opinion of his opus, as from what he'd read and
heard of it he could not with honesty say the play was worth the
stealing. There was no life, no fire in the writing. Would there, he
mused, ever be anyone else to match Marlowe's poetry, which stayed
in the mind long after the play was done? What were those words
of Tamburlaine's?

83

> I hold the Fates bound fast in iron chains,
> And with my hand turn Fortune's wheel about;
> And sooner shall the sun fall from his sphere
> Than Tamburlaine be slain or overcome.

Now there, indeed, was a king.

Chapter 8

Cry Murder!

Simon was unlikely ever to forget that night, and the morning that was to follow it. He arrived home from Finsbury Fields to be handed a heavily scented letter by a smirking John Bradedge, who informed him that the same oily fellow had delivered it who had brought its predecessor, also sealed with the dolphin seal. He waved his servant away, went into his study and opened the missive. It was, as he had guessed, from Emilia Bassano. My Lord of Hunsdon had, as expected, she wrote, gone to see the Queen at Nonesuch Palace and she was therefore at liberty. If he would care to accept her invitation to be privately entertained that evening then her direction was given below. She suggested he might come about nine o'clock, and that he should look for a small doorway at the side of the house where she would station her maid to let him in. A mere scratch at the door would suffice.

Truth to tell, he would have preferred another evening for such dalliance for the afternoon's events had left him weary and also, to be quite honest, he would have preferred another lady. But Avisa Allen remained unattainable, such opportunities did not frequently come his way and Emilia was extremely attractive. So it was that he took himself over the river, this time by ferry, and made his way towards the Strand and his lordship's house wondering uneasily what might happen should the Lord Chamberlain ever find out or, even worse, return unexpectedly. He duly tapped gently on the small door which was half concealed under an archway and was immediately shown up a flight of stairs and into a pleasant chamber by a young maidservant who curtsied to him, informing him that he was expected by the mistress.

Emilia greeted him with such overt enthusiasm that it was clear she at least appeared to have no qualms about betraying her protector in such a fashion, which led him to think this could not be the first time she'd strayed.

The maid waited on them while they ate a light repast, then discreetly left them to themselves. Once alone, Emilia came round to sit beside him. 'Lord Hunsdon . . .' he began as she commenced nibbling his ear.

'Oh, Henry's safe away for at least another two days. There's nothing to fear. Because of his own particular situation there are locks between my apartments and his so that he cannot be disturbed when he visits me and we cannot be surprised. And all the entrances are most discreet.' Simon was not entirely convinced but the lady was becoming steadily more amorous and his resistance in such circumstances had always been weak. He soon gave up the fight and followed Emilia into her bedchamber where, after assisting her to take off all her clothes, he climbed into her bed.

He woke before dawn the next morning after one of the most energetic nights he had ever spent and broke into a cold sweat as he recollected where he was: in the bed of the mistress of Queen Elizabeth's nearest relative. Without more ado, he dressed as rapidly as he could and in answer to a sleepy query from Emilia as to what he was doing and why didn't he come back to bed, claimed he had urgent business and so made for the door to the outside world. Once at the river, he paced up and down impatiently as he waited for it to be light enough to find a wherryman to row him back home. It had been a curious interlude. Emilia had been quite uninhibited in her lovemaking but he'd felt throughout that there was no emotion behind it, that she had taken her pleasure as if . . . as if she were a *man* in the same circumstances. It was a disturbing thought.

He arrived back at his house and let himself in. He felt tired out and fit for nothing but it hardly seemed worth while going to bed. He made his way out to the backyard, drew a pail of water from the pump, doused his head in it and went into his study to write up a horoscope for a client who would be calling in for it later in the day. He wondered how young Charles had fared with his fair Iseult. It was unlikely the goldsmith's daughter would have let matters go as far as Emilia, for even if she was, as Tom Pope had told him, little more than a pretty face, she would be shrewd enough to know that virginity fetches a high price on the marriage market, especially when laced with gold.

Rehearsals usually began at the Rose within an hour or so of first light, thus giving the actors time to break their fast and, where applicable, shake off the effects of whatever it was they had been doing the previous night. Various people, however, would arrive earlier such as William Miller the bookman, to see to the putting out of any play rolls that might be needed and to check that the stage was set correctly for whatever was to be rehearsed that particular morning. Soon he was joined by the apprentices and stagehands whose task it was to clear up and tidy away any detritus that had been missed after the previous afternoon's performance, and also to collect any props that might be required from the chests under the stage where they were kept locked away for safe keeping.

Miller had been called in by Henslowe the previous evening to discuss with him and Alleyn the proposed tour. November was never a good time to play in London and in previous years the company had toured for about a month, their regular circuit being Southam, Coventry, Worcester, Tewkesbury and Gloucester, possibly with a few days in Oxford on the way home if there was time and there had been sufficient audiences to cover the expenses of the tour and to pay the wages. It was, however, a risk, as had been proved only too clearly on one dreadful occasion when the weather had been so bad and audiences so poor that they had had to sell half the costumes and most of their personal possessions in order to scrape up enough money to get themselves back to London. But with some reservations Miller agreed it was not a bad idea, for two reasons: first, that the events surrounding the use of the trapdoor would hopefully be forgotten while they were away, and second because now at least some of the venues they played in on tour were large houses or covered spaces where they were protected against the weather.

The bookman was not in a good mood that morning. Gossip travels fast in theatre circles, and during his conversation with Henslowe he had learned what had happened at the Theatre earlier in the day, for a friend of Alleyn's had come hotfoot straight to the Rose to tell the actor that one of his company, who he understood was called Charles Spencer, had interrupted Burbage's performance by claiming that the play being presented was his and that Nathan Parsons had somehow stolen his script. This matter too had been discussed. They had all expected Charles to return at once to the Rose to explain himself but he had not done so, and Henslowe had sent word round to Miller that morning ordering him to send the actor up to see him immediately he came in for rehearsal. 'And unless he has a good case to make I truly think his services should be dispensed with,' Henslowe had threatened. 'There are plenty of young actors looking for work.'

Miller walked to the front of the stage, then turned and looked round to check that all was well. He was surprised to notice that the curtain of the discovery space was drawn across its alcove, as he had felt sure it had been left open the previous evening. He was about to go and investigate himself when one of the stagehands appeared from beneath the stage carrying a box of props.

'Draw that curtain, will you?' he called out to him.

The man set down his burden and went over to the discovery space. He had his hand on the curtain when something caught his attention and he looked down. 'Wine must have been spilled here,' he called back, 'looks like wine, anyway, or it could be paint.' With that he drew back the curtain with a flourish, then stepped back aghast.

The area inside the space had been set for the scene where Iseult, overcome by love and guilt, has fallen ill and taken to her bed, and a narrow couch had been placed at an angle towards the back of it so that the tragic queen was visible to the whole audience. But now it bore another occupant. Lying on it, as if in state, was Nathan Parsons. He looked quite peaceful, his hands crossed over his chest. The blood appeared to come from underneath him and had trickled down over the side of the couch and under the curtain, to form the small pool outside. The would-be dramatist of renown would now never hear a theatre resound to the acclamation of thousands, nor would he ever poach any more plays. Nathan Parsons was dead indeed.

'Merciful heaven!' exclaimed the stagehand as Miller ran over to join him. 'Is he dead?' he asked, as Miller gingerly laid a hand on Parsons's head.

'Cold as charity,' replied the bookman, straightening up. 'He's dead all right, God save us.' He thought for a minute. 'Run to Dr Forman's house and see if he can come over here straight away – yes, I know there's nothing he can do for Parsons but perhaps he can suggest how best to proceed. And Master Henslowe must be told at once. Call in on him on your way. Oh, and we must tell the constable and – thank heaven,' he said with relief, 'here come the actors. Off you go, be as quick as you can,' he called after the stagehand as he rushed away.

The noise of voices came from the theatre entrance as the actors began to enter in a steady stream. They seemed somewhat taken aback by the precipitate exit of the stagehand who pushed through them as if there was a fire, but most were so deep in conversation that at first they took little notice of Miller, assuming he was checking that all was properly set up in the discovery space. Then one of the older men realised there was something wrong, and called out to ask what was the matter.

'You'd better all come up here,' replied Miller, grimly. 'You'll not believe what you're going to see.'

Slowly the actors made their way up on stage to the discovery space, looked at the scene before them and stood appalled. 'Yes, he *is* dead,' announced Miller before anyone asked, 'and I've sent young James to fetch Dr Forman.'

'Isn't it rather late to call in a physician?' queried Dick Marsh with a shudder.

'I thought it might be useful. Dr Forman has something of a reputation for looking into violent death.'

Ned Alleyn looked particularly grave. 'Has anyone gone to tell Philip?' Will explained that James would call in on his way to fetch the doctor. Alleyn turned to the assembled actors. 'Are we all present?' he asked. They looked at each other and concluded that all were there except for Charles Spencer. A look of intense annoyance crossed Alleyn's face. 'Possibly he felt he daren't be seen here after yesterday's disgraceful episode at the Theatre. Philip is intensely displeased, and is waiting to tell him so, not to mention—'

'I think that's something to be dealt with later,' broke in Tom Pope. 'Here and now we are before a dreadful situation. We'll wait for Dr Forman and Master Henslowe and then obviously we must send for the constable. It's as well we're not playing today. Has anyone touched Parsons?' Miller shook his head and said that everything had been left exactly as he'd found it.

Young James had had no luck when he called in on the Henslowe household, for the entrepreneur was out on some business unconnected with the theatre but his stepdaughter, Joan, Alleyn's prospective bride, was a sensible and practical young woman and she listened to what he had to say without either swooning or bursting into hysterical tears. Then she told him that she was sure her stepfather would want him to fetch Dr Forman but that she thought they ought to leave sending for the constable until Master Henslowe returned. She did not expect him to be long, and he would go over to the Rose straight away.

Simon meanwhile, wearying of endlessly being asked the same questions, had turned to copying out some advice on prospective marriage partners from an ancient treatise *On Astrological Judgement*:

When under the sign of Libra, if the Moon upon a Criticall day apply to a Malevolent, you'll say this is but a scurvy sign and I am half of your opinion, yet it is a good time to be wife and that you may see which of them is strongest, the Moon or the Malevolent; if the Moon be strongest, she'll make a handsome shift with him, if she be weak then you know the old proverb, 'the weakest go to the walls' and if sick is like to be forced to make more use of a winding sheet than a feather bed, but if the Moon upon a Criticall day be with the bodies of Sol, Mars or Saturn, any which of them *he* is withall, then he be Lord of the Eighth House and away trots life to seek out a new habitation for she is weary of her old House.

* * *

He was pondering as to what exactly this Delphic advice meant and if he could make use of it, when there was an urgent battering at his door. He went himself to find an agitated young man standing outside. 'At the Rose,' he gasped, trying to get his breath, 'dead. He's on the couch, dead. Will Miller says you're to come at once.'

'Get your wind back, man; who's dead? What do you want me for?'

'Nathan Parsons. When Will opened up the theatre he found him there on stage – dead. He's asked for you to come at once and Master Henslowe and I've just been round for him but he's out and won't be back yet awhile, and so he doesn't know, but they don't know what to do, whether to send for the constable or—'

'Very well, I'll come with you at once,' said Simon, picking up his cloak. He called for John Bradedge, telling him, as he appeared from the backyard, that he thought it best he should come with him.

'What's to do then?' asked his servant. 'What a noise! You'd think someone's been murdered.'

'You might well be right,' responded Simon grimly, then, to the stagehand, 'Very well lad, we'd best be off, and on the way you can tell us as clearly as you can what's afoot.'

They hurried through the crowded alleys of the Bankside as the stagehand described how he'd seen a small pool of what he'd thought was paint coming from under the curtain of the discovery space; 'That's the big alcove at the back with a curtain in front where we can set scenes while others are happening on stage.' Both he and Will Miller were convinced that when they'd left the Rose the previous day the curtain had been drawn back, as they had set the bedchamber scene ready for rehearsal the following morning. 'So Will asked me to pull the curtain back and when I did there was Parsons stretched out on Iseult's bed as if in a play. Even his hands were crossed on his chest as if he'd already been laid out.'

When asked how Parsons had died he shook his head. 'No one wanted to touch him but I reckon he must have been knifed or had a sword thrust through him, since there was blood on the floor.'

On arriving at the Rose Simon went straight to the stage, leaving

John Bradedge in the pit where most of the actors were now standing talking among themselves in hushed tones. There was still no sign of Charles Spencer. He went over to the body and looked at it carefully. 'Fetch me some water and a cloth, will you?' he asked. 'I'll have to see what's happened and it's likely to be a messy business. You agree I should do so?' he asked Alleyn who, in the absence of Henslowe, was the obvious person to apply to. The actor nodded and said that now Simon had arrived, he would go and see if Henslowe had returned and that in the meantime Tom Pope should take charge.

Simon gently uncrossed Parsons's arms and opened his doublet fully. 'No wound at the front. Let's look at the back.' He put his hand under Parsons's back and lifted up the stiffening body, grimacing as he felt sticky blood on his hand. He then laid it back down, rolled it over on its side and raised the bloodstained doublet and shirt.

'He's been stabbed all right. And with a poniard or even more likely a stiletto. I should say that a dagger would have caused far more blood loss. Come and have a look, Tom. See how small the wound is. Scarcely an inch, if that. But it was a deadly blow between the ribs and straight into the heart. Whoever did this knew what he was about.'

'Stabbed in the back then?' commented Tom.

'Quite so.'

'But why should he have been laid out like that as if he were a stage corpse? Even to his eyes being closed and his arms crossed? And when could it have happened?'

'I've no answer to your first question except that whoever did it has a macabre turn of mind. As to the second, well there's not too much death stiffening otherwise I wouldn't have been able to move his arms. I reckon he was killed either late last night or in the small hours. It must have been here, as his killer could hardly have dragged his body into the theatre without it being noticed!'

'Was he killed with his own weapon?' asked Tom. 'Though I don't remember ever seeing him with a poniard or stiletto. He didn't always wear a sword but he usually had a serviceable dagger with him.' He began to look around behind and under the draped couch, then on the floor of the discovery space. 'There's no weapon here.

92

Not even his own dagger. Now that *is* odd. He never went about unarmed. Did you ever see Parsons without some kind of weapon?' he called out to the actors in the pit. There was a general murmur of dissent, one actor going so far as to say that it was because he'd put so many people out he'd needed to be armed 'more than most'.

Both Miller and the wardrobe master joined Simon and Tom then, and they too searched the discovery space without result. 'Have you any poniards or stilettos in the theatre?' asked Simon.

The wardrobe master informed him that they had but that they were usually kept locked away with the more valuable props. 'We use them in some of the plays like *The Spanish Tragedy*, usually for foreign villains as they're supposed to be nastier and more Machiavellian than ours. We have about half a dozen. Master Henslowe bought them as a bargain lot from an Italian dealer.'

'Well can you go and see if they're still all there?' asked Simon.

There was a sound of scurrying feet and Charles rushed into the pit, loudly apologising for his late arrival. He stopped short as he saw the grave group of actors gathered close to the stage. They turned as one and looked at him in silence. 'What on earth's the matter? What are you all looking at me like that for?'

'You'd best go up on stage there, Charles, and see what's to do,' said Dick, coming over to him and putting his arm round his shoulder. 'Parsons's dead. It looks as if someone's killed him. He's lying up there in the discovery space.'

Charles went white. 'Dear God – *how*?' Slowly he made his way up the steps and Simon and Tom stood aside so that he could see the body. For a long moment he said nothing. 'Who did it?' he asked eventually.

'We've no idea,' answered Tom Pope. 'I imagine there'll be no shortage of possible contenders, do you?' he asked, raising his voice so that it carried across to the rest of the company.

'You needn't look at me,' growled Gabriel Tanner. 'Very well, I didn't like the man, and I fought with him the other week when I was drunk but it'd take a sober man to set him up like that and I don't fight people when I'm sober. Nor do I stab people in the back, if that's what you're saying happened. Anyway, he'd a host of enemies.'

Charles bent over Parsons's body, then looked up, his face grey. 'Holy Mother of God, Dr Forman, after yesterday they're going to think . . .' He stopped, unable to finish the sentence as a loud noise heralded the arrival of Philip Henslowe and the return of Alleyn. Henslowe moved swiftly through the theatre and up on to the stage and surveyed the scene.

'Well, Dr Forman? What are we to make of this?' Simon told him briefly of what he had discovered. Henslowe thanked him. 'Has anyone sent for the constable?'

'We thought it best to leave that until you'd seen the situation for yourself,' Tom Pope told him. 'Now you're here we can send for him at once.'

But Henslowe was hardly listening. He was looking at Charles. 'So what's your part in this?' he asked, gripping the young man by the sleeve. 'Do you think I don't know what happened yesterday? How you conducted yourself like any roaring boy from the back alleys, shouting out to all in the Theatre that you were going to kill Parsons?'

'But that was in a fit of blind rage, believe me,' he pleaded, 'I know nothing of this. And had I intended to carry out my threat I'd have challenged Parsons to a fair fight, not crept up and stabbed him unawares. I'd never do such a thing.'

'We'll let the constable decide that,' retorted Henslowe. 'One of you go and fetch him immediately. Well, what do you want?' he asked the wardrobe master, who had just returned from under the stage.

'Dr Forman thinks Parsons was killed with a poniard or stiletto and asked if we kept such things in the theatre. I said we did, and went to check the box in which we keep the stilettos you bought from the Italian merchant. There's one missing. There's only five there now.'

'Were there six last night?' asked Simon.

The wardrobe master looked unhappy. 'I don't know. I suppose we've all got careless. I can't remember when I last checked after a rehearsal. Sometimes actors forget and go home with stage weapons at their belt, or they get left lying around the theatre and are put away in the wrong place.'

The actors were still deciding who should fetch the local constable when it appeared they were to be forestalled, for even as one of the actors turned to go, the local constable appeared flanked by two robust members of the watch. The actors looked on in amazement as he made his way to the middle of the pit and looked up at the stage, wondering how he had arrived without being called upon. The man was soon to explain the mystery.

'Is Master Henslowe present?' he called out. Henslowe stepped forward.

The constable walked towards him, oblivious of the implications of the scene before him. 'I am looking for two of your company, namely Gabriel Tanner and Charles Spencer.' Then, with much ceremony, he unrolled a scroll of paper and put on his most official voice. 'I have a complaint laid against you, Gabriel Tanner, that some two weeks or so ago you accosted one Nathan Parsons in the street and did set on him and fight with him.'

'*He* fought with *me*,' retorted Gabriel. 'And anyway I was drunk. I'll fight anyone when I'm drunk. And surely, if he'd wanted to lay a complaint against me he'd have done it long ago. Why wait all this time?'

'I have no idea,' responded the constable. 'All I know is that Master Parsons has laid information that you threatened him and therefore I must take you before a magistrate to be bound over to keep the peace. If you have anything to say in your defence then you can do so, and it will be for him to decide what to do about it.' He thought for a moment. 'Possibly he has decided to make a complaint against you to add to another he made yesterday against Charles Spencer. Is he here?'

The silence became profound. 'Charles is up there on stage,' said Dick Marsh.

The constable made his portentous way towards the steps. His sight was not of the best and he had been unable to see what was happening on the stage, coupled with which he tried to continue reading from his scroll. As he reached the top he paused for breath, then launched into his next announcement. 'I also have a complaint against you, Charles Spencer, that some six days ago you also fought with Nathan Parsons in this very theatre, and that yesterday you threatened in the presence of all those attending a play at the Theatre playhouse in Finsbury Fields that you would take his life. I have therefore also to bring you before a magistrate for this offence. So grave a threat may well merit more than a binding over and . . . God's blood!' he gasped, stopping short at the scene before him. 'What's this?'

'We were about to send for you, Constable,' said Henslowe. 'The man lying there dead, stabbed through the heart, is that very Nathan Parsons. And this here is Charles Spencer.'

It was at this point that Charles finally turned away from the body. He had, unwittingly, put his hand on Parsons's shirt as he'd bent to see the wound and it was sticky with blood. 'Yes, I'm Charles Spencer, Constable,' he said as the awfulness of his position hit him.

'And with blood on your hands, I see,' returned the constable.

'But I only just got here. Everyone will tell you that. I was late!'

The constable was unmoved. 'As you know, I was already sent to bring you to a magistrate for threatening only yesterday to kill Nathan Parsons. And now I find you here with his body, your hands stained with his blood. Charles Spencer, I am arresting you on the grounds that I suspect you of this man's murder and you must come with us to the magistrate without delay. There's little doubt he'll have you in gaol and—'

'But I didn't do it!' shouted Charles. 'I never touched him. I know I made all sorts of stupid threats but I never even saw him after leaving the Theatre yesterday. I told you, I only just got here and there are plenty of people who'll vouch for where I've been and what I've been doing.'

'Then you'd best hope they will,' responded the constable dourly. 'In the meantime you're coming with me.' He motioned to the two members of the watch as Charles made his way down the steps. 'Dick, Tom, Simon – can't any of you do something?' he pleaded.

Tom Pope looked at Henslowe. 'I'd best go with the lad and see what happens, don't you think? I can't believe he'd anything to do with this.' Simon motioned to John Bradedge who had been watching the goings-on without, most unusually for him, saying a word. 'Go with Tom, will you John? I'd like to know too.'

Henslowe looked far from happy. 'Very well,' he said to Tom, 'but come back as soon as you know the outcome.' The watchmen hustled Charles out of the theatre, the constable following behind. He appeared to have forgotten all about Gabriel Tanner.

'So,' boomed Henslowe as they left, 'yet *more* trouble. Why, one asks, are we singled out so for disaster?' No one answered. 'We must send to the coroner to tell him what has happened and ask where Parsons's body must be taken for the inquest. Somebody see to it straight away.' Then he bethought himself of another pressing matter. 'There seems little point in continuing with *King Mark* in the circumstances, which means changing our programme yet again. I suggest either *Crack Me This Nut* or, if you think we should have a play about a king, then what about that written by the actor who's gone off to work for the Burbages – *The Tragical History of King Henry VI*? Yes,' he continued, 'that will do very well.'

There was a subdued murmur of conversation and Henslowe clapped his hands for quiet. 'And one more thing. We had already decided that the company should do its usual midlands' tour in November. I now propose that this starts earlier. You will leave for Southam at the end of the week.' He then descended smartly from the stage, leaving Will Miller and the wardrobe master in charge of the corpse.

'It seems Parsons has finally got what he always wanted,' said Miller with grim humour. 'To be centre stage.'

Chapter 9

A Girl to Die For

Before Henslowe left the theatre he called Simon over to him. 'This really is beyond everything, Dr Forman. Do you believe Spencer killed Parsons? I'm told you were with him at the Theatre yesterday and heard him threaten to do so. It wouldn't be the first time I've had a hothead in the company, though never before with such appalling consequences. Street fights, duels even – yes. But deliberate murder – and this must be deliberate since whoever did it took the trouble to display the corpse in such a way – that's quite outside my experience.'

'I don't know the boy well enough to swear that he'd be absolutely incapable of killing Parsons; extreme fury can drive people to extraordinary lengths,' Simon responded with some care, 'and we've already discussed the fact that he can be over-emotional and act without thought but going on what I've seen of him, as well as my own instincts, I think it highly unlikely he would do such a thing as this.

'After his intervention at the Theatre and his being thrown out, I took him on one side and lectured him on the foolishness of his actions and how he'd not helped his cause at all, in fact quite the reverse. I told him he must apply to you and to senior members of the company and explain his grievance, and that the sensible thing would surely be for there to be a meeting with the Burbages to get to the bottom of the matter. We then walked back to the Bankside together and when we parted he appeared to have calmed down considerably.' He considered mentioning Charles's evening assignation but then decided against it, for no doubt Dick Marsh would if he had not done so already since it meant that Charles had been fully occupied the previous evening. 'Dick Marsh probably knows him best,' he added. 'They're close friends and share lodgings; why not ask him?'

Henslowe looked across to the actors who were still gathered in a group in the pit. With the prospect of an almost immediate major tour there was now plenty to do, especially if they had to revive yet another play. 'Some of you help the stagehands to move the body off the stage,' he called to them, 'and make it ready to be taken to wherever the coroner decides. Then the stage must be cleaned and everything cleared away. You must be ready to leave as soon as the inquest has been held, which will be either tomorrow or the day after. Hopefully by the time you come back this business too will have been almost forgotten. In the meantime I see no point in giving any more performances. Have you anything to say to them, Bookman?'

'I want you all back here this afternoon to go over *Henry VI* and to discuss what we'll tour,' said Miller. 'All of you. Is that understood? There's no time to be lost.'

Still subdued, the actors began making their way out of the theatre, Dick Marsh among them, and Henslowe started to follow. 'Wouldn't it be worth talking to Marsh?' Simon reminded him as the young actor disappeared out through the entrance.

Henslowe swore, a rare event. 'Go after him will you, Dr Forman, and fetch him back and say I want to see him at once.'

Dick had not gone far and was standing just outside the Rose talking to one of the other actors, and he readily re-entered the theatre with Simon. Henslowe came immediately to the point, demanding to know if he thought Charles capable of such a murder. Simon had expected him to come at once to his friend's defence, as no doubt Charles would have done had the situation been the other way round, and swear that Charles was incapable of such a thing. But somewhat to his surprise Dick gave a more qualified response.

'He was absolutely furious about what happened, I've never seen him so enraged, and that was even before he went off to the Theatre and made his threat. It's hard to know what any of us are capable of driven to extremes, and Charles had become obsessed by his play. But he's never been involved in anything really serious all the time I've known him. The odd quarrel certainly, but it usually blows over. Nor,' he added, warming to his theme, 'is he someone who gets violent in drink. His attack on Parsons the other day was the first time I've ever known him resort to fists.'

'I'd have thought it more likely he'd have challenged Parsons to a duel if he'd been determined to carry out his threat,' commented Simon, to which Dick agreed. The actor looked quite shaken, which was hardly surprising, thought Simon, close as the two were.

'Well, I don't know what to think,' said Henslowe. 'What I am sure of is that it's going to plunge us into trouble again – a second crowner's 'quest within a matter of weeks, with the possibility that one of our own company will be put on trial for a killing.' He turned to Simon. 'Is it possible Spencer could be responsible for both deaths, Lane's and Parsons's? You did mention him once in connection with Lane's death, and it seems he was on bad terms with both.'

'You didn't say that, did you?' Dick burst out. 'Surely not!'

'I said, if you remember, Master Henslowe, that I'd been told Spencer had a short fuse and was prone to fits of temper but that I thought it unlikely he had anything to do with Lane's death, not least because he had little or no opportunity to tamper with the trapdoor.'

'Perhaps someone else was responsible for both deaths,' suggested Dick.

From somewhere outside a clock struck the hour. 'I've been here long enough,' said Henslowe abruptly. 'I am in the middle of an important transaction concerning timber and now Ned, Miller and I must see to the setting up of the tour. As for Spencer, we'll soon know the outcome of his being brought up before the magistrate, though I don't doubt it will be gaol at least for the time being. This really is a very, very bad business. Can I take it I may count on your services again, Dr Forman?'

'I'll help you all I can, Master Henslowe, though I'm as much in the dark as anyone else but as things are, I honestly don't think Spencer killed Parsons whatever it might look like. Perhaps whoever did it chose that particular time as they knew about the threats he'd made. And I suppose it is possible that Lane's death wasn't an accident and that his killer also struck down Parsons.'

All three left the theatre together. 'You'll do your best for Charles, won't you?' Dick pleaded as Henslowe went back to his office. Simon assured him that he would and went on his own way. As he walked back to his house he realised that it was only just past noon, although he felt as if he'd been up for two days. A night spent attempting to satisfy Emilia's voracious sexual appetite followed by a morning of murder and mayhem had taken its toll in no uncertain terms.

He was tired and felt the need of rest and for once he hoped there wouldn't be anyone waiting to see him, but as is the way of these things he opened his door to be told by Anna that a number of people had called. She left promising to return, and informed Simon that there was a mother and child being comforted in the kitchen, the child having spilled hot water on its arm.

'And I'm here too,' boomed a voice from a dark corner of the hall. Simon's heart sank as he saw it was Robin Greene. 'And it's urgent!' he insisted.

'Hardly as urgent as a child in pain,' retorted Simon. 'You'll have to stay where you are until I've seen to that first, or call back later.' He went into the kitchen to find the child, still tearful but no longer howling, sitting on its mother's knee exchanging incomprehensible words with Anna's eighteen-month-old son. He gently raised the little girl's arm, which caused the child to cry out again.

'I only had my back turned for a minute,' the distressed mother told him, 'but somehow she managed to pull the pot towards her and some of the broth spilled over.' Simon reassured her that the scald looked worse than it was and went and found a salve to put on it. He also handed the woman a tiny phial. 'That's poppy syrup. I've already weakened it a little with water. Put just a few drops – and no more – into some water and give it to your child so that she will sleep. Sleep's the best remedy I can prescribe.' She thanked him and he showed her out, then turned with a heavy sigh to Robin Greene.

'You'd best come into my room,' he said, 'but I'll tell you now I've little time or patience to spare this morning, nor am I in the mood for giving free treatment.' To his surprise, Greene produced a small purse from his pocket. 'I have money, Simon. Emma insisted I pay you properly this time.' Emma was Greene's long-suffering mistress. He lived in the house she had been left by a former lover, the comic actor Tarleton, and although he liked to play the gentleman he was quite prepared to let her whore for him when necessary. No doubt she'd earned the money he offered in just such a way. She was also, by her own standards, an honest woman, and liked to pay her debts.

'Very well. So what is it this time? The clap again?' He had only recently treated Greene for that condition.

'It seems to have come back,' the poet admitted. 'But I also have a fever that won't go away.' Seen in the light he certainly looked far from well.

Simon sighed. 'Well I suppose there's little point in repeating yet again that if you will drink like a fish, stay up half the night and whore around then you'll continue to get ill. However, let's have a look at you.' Greene's clap had indeed returned and this time Simon changed the treatment, making up a mixture of two drugs from the Indies, guaiacum and sarsaparilla, which he was to drink three times a day. Then he felt the poet's forehead and his pulse. 'You would seem to have a quotidian fever as a result of a hot liver. Hardly surprising in your case. I'll make you up a draught of cardus benedictus to take by mouth and a pot of oil of wormwood and mastic to apply warm to your right side as a poultice.' He stood back and surveyed his patient. 'This time, Robin, I agree. You are a sick man. How old are you?'

'Thirty-two next summer.'

'For God's sake, do as I say then if you want to live to be thirty-three! That'll cost you four shillings; the clap remedy alone costs me the best part of a florin. Then be off with you, I'm dead on my feet.'

Greene gave him the money without a word, for once looking less than his usual bombastic self. 'Emma's with child,' he said shortly. 'Whether mine or not, who knows? But it's making her sickly. Life's a bastard!' He turned to go, then a thought struck him. 'What's made you so short-tempered? You nearly bit my head off when you saw me.'

Simon hesitated as to whether or not to tell him of the happenings at the Rose, and decided he might as well since no doubt it would soon be all round the Bankside. 'There's been a murder at the Rose. When they came to open up the theatre this morning they found the body of Nathan Parsons on stage. He'd been stabbed.'

Greene whistled. 'Well, there's a thing. They'll have real problems finding out who finally did the deed, he'd so many enemies. My friend George Peele for one; he had no love for Parsons, though I doubt he'd take his dislike that far. Too idle.'

'The constable's taken away Charles Spencer. The young fool caused a disturbance at the Theatre yesterday claiming Parsons's new play was his own and shouting out for all to hear that he intended to kill him.'

'And did he?' enquired Greene, whose own reputation in that quarter was by no means spotless. 'Parsons, steal the play I mean. And the other, come to that.'

'I don't think so. But he's the obvious person to suspect. And yes, Parsons almost certainly did steal his play. I'd seen the script myself and it seemed very like it.'

For once Greene reacted with sobriety. 'Well, we all stay stupid things in wrath, myself included. And as for Kit Marlowe, if he'd actually fought with all those he'd threatened with death over the last few years the streets would be paved with corpses. I don't think you can put this one down to him, though, I'm not sure Kit even knew Parsons.

'But it's true, Nathan really did have plenty of people wanting to get their own back on him and some with more stomach for it than young Spencer, I'd have thought.'

Simon showed him to the door. 'Keep your ear to the ground, if you will. You move in circles where you might well hear something.'

'Disreputable ones, you mean?' countered Greene with a wry laugh. 'Very well, I'll enquire around. It might be nothing to do with plays or players but an unsettled gambling debt or a quarrel over a whore.' Simon thanked him, surprised that for once Greene had actually said something sensible. He was also more alarmed than he had admitted at the state of the poet's health.

Meanwhile, back in his own office, Henslowe finished his

negotiations with the timber merchant and turned as usual to writing his diary.

It is decided that the company shall go out into the country for approx. one month. There will now be no play of *King Mark*. Today was Nathan Parsons, actor, discovered dead in the Rose Theatre, stabbed through the heart. Charles Spencer of the company was taken before the magistrate.

He then added, since Tom Pope had just returned with the news:

And has been ordered to the Clink on a charge of murder. Jesu, what next!

Shortly after Robert Greene had departed John Bradedge brought the same news back to Simon. 'You could hardly expect anything else, could you?' he told his master. 'It turned out that what he said at the playhouse yesterday and the trouble it caused was all over London, being as hundreds of people heard him, and the magistrate, Sir somebody-or-other Grafton, knew all about it. He didn't waste no time. "Spencer," he said, really nasty, "you were to be brought here for fighting with this man, Nathan Parsons, and for threatening in a public place to kill him. And now it seems the man's been stabbed to death. Have you anything to say?" '

'Well the lad says he didn't do it, didn't know anything about it, but you could see old Sir Whatnot didn't believe him. "That's enough," he said, "I don't want to hear any more. Charles Spencer," he went on, "we're not long into the sessions and I'll see you come up before a judge soon, very soon. I must tell you that I've no time for the playhouses, which in my opinion are breeding grounds for crime and introduce the populace to things it's better they shouldn't know about; and as for common players, it was better when they were classed with beggars and vagabonds and whipped out of town. I trust you'll be made an example of. You'd best be prepared for Tyburn. Take him down to the Clink!" And that's what they did. Don't tell me you're going to get mixed up in all this,' he finished.

'I don't know there's much I can do but I'm loath to see an

innocent lad go to the gallows. I'll go over to the Clink later and see if they'll let me see him. In the meantime you too keep your ears open – there'll be plenty of talk about it, and it could be you hear of others who had reason to murder Parsons. Robin Greene spoke of creditors, debts to gaming houses and whores – but then he would, I suppose. It's the world he knows best.'

'I'll see what I can do. Oh,' he exclaimed, putting his hand in his pocket, 'I'm sorry, Doctor, I nearly forgot. Anna just asked me to give you this. It came about noon.' He handed Simon a letter. 'It doesn't stink of scent nor have naked women on the seal.'

He went out and Simon carefully broke the seal. It looked vaguely official. It was: the seal was that of the commissioners for customs and the letter was from Thomas Barton. Simon opened the sheet of paper and groaned.

Doctor Forman, wrote Barton

I told you I would inform you if another attempt was made on my life. It has come sooner than even I expected. Last Thursday on my way to Ashford where the road crosses a ford, I was set upon by two villains. Had there not been a party of horsemen coming behind who heard my shouts for help, I am sure I would have been murdered there and then but when the villains saw the horsemen approaching, they cut my purse and fled. I am greatly shocked by this experience, sufficient to take to my bed. Once I am restored, however, I shall visit you again in London in the hope that this time I can persuade you to come back to Kent with me. I will also bring details of my wife, in order that you might discover her wickedness by casting her horoscope. Yours, Thomas Barton.

God's breath! swore Simon to himself; first poisoned broth and poisoned pictures, now an attempted assassination, no doubt at some river crossing notorious for footpads waiting for unwary travellers. Dear Lord, deliver me from a visitation by Thomas Barton, he prayed with real feeling.

Then he felt cold. If Barton could continue to link events together in such a way as to accuse his wife, how much more could the same kind of logic condemn Charles Spencer and with far more reason? It was then that he remembered the conversation he had with the two young actors after Lane's funeral. Surely Spencer had said his father was a Norwich lawyer, prompting Marsh to tell him how fortunate he had been compared to himself, a poor parson's son? Plainly word must be sent to Spencer senior to advise him of his son's predicament.

This boosted Simon's spirits sufficiently to send him along to the nearby Clink gaol to see if he might see Charles Spencer. He was known to the chief warders of most of the local gaols, since from time to time he was called in if a prisoner had sufficient money to send out for a medical man. There was little to choose between any of them with regard to filth and the conditions in which prisoners were kept, although he thought the Clink marginally better than Newgate. He found the chief warder in a reasonable frame of mind. Tom Pope had returned earlier with some money collected from Spencer's colleagues, enough for him to be put in a room of his own for the time being and to buy him some food.

The room, however, was grim enough even so: small, dirty and very dark. Charles was sitting dismally in a corner on a rough stool, and Simon noted that at least the money had also seen to it that he was not shackled.

'I didn't do it, Dr Forman,' he began at once. 'I'll swear on anything you'd like to put before me, on every chapter of the Bible if you want me to. But I didn't do it.'

'Well then,' Simon replied, 'we'd best find out who did. But first, wouldn't it be as well to let your father know? He's a lawyer, isn't he? Did he train at Lincoln's Inn?' Charles nodded. 'Then he must know people in the law in London still who might prove helpful.'

Charles looked horrified. 'I don't want him to know anything about this if it's at all possible. I can't face bringing so much disgrace on my family.'

'It'll be a bigger disgrace if you end your days at Tyburn because you did nothing,' Simon retorted. 'At least let me send to tell him what's happened. I'll make it clear that none of us think you did it and that you stand wrongly accused. No, I insist,' he continued as

Charles appeared to be about to disagree again, 'and now we must get down to business. Tell me exactly what you did after we parted on the Bankside yesterday. Everything you can think of.'

Charles thought for a few moments. 'Well, at first I was going to rush into Henslowe and tell him what had happened but then I thought I'd leave it until the next morning. I wasn't feeling very brave about what I'd done by that time,' he admitted. 'Then, let's see . . . I went to the Anchor to see if there was anyone there who might be sympathetic, like Tom, but none of the actors were about. So I went round to Tom's but there was no one home. He must have been out somewhere with Jenny and the boys.'

'Didn't you go and look for Dick and tell him what had happened?' asked Simon.

'I told him later. I knew he'd some business of his own to see to after the afternoon's performance, so we'd arranged to meet at the house of Audrey's friend at nine o'clock in the evening but on my way back to our lodgings I met up with him anyway and told him then. He said I was a fool and an idiot and I had to agree. By that time I was late anyway, so he went on ahead and I washed and changed into my best doublet and hose and went straight to the house of Audrey's friend, Mistress Mary Goodman. She lives in Fish Street, near the great hall of the Watermen's Company. By the time I arrived they were wondering what had happened to me and were about to start supper.'

'And you had a good evening?'

'Ye-es.' Charles sounded doubtful. 'I suppose I hoped for too much. I mean I could hardly expect Audrey to have . . .' He trailed off, leaving his obvious train of thought unfinished. 'I didn't care for her friend all that much either. She made a dead set at Dick, though, which surprised me as Audrey said she was devoted to her husband and had only set up the supper for her benefit.'

He had however managed something of a tête-à-tête with his beloved and she had let him kiss her, though no more than that. The four had stayed together until around midnight but when he'd hopefully suggested staying the night, in a separate chamber of course, Audrey became agitated, saying her father would be sending a servant first thing in the morning to fetch her home and she was frightened someone might see them together. So, after more passionate protestations of undying love, he had finally left.

'With Dick?'

'Oh yes. Though Mistress Mary was very pressing that he should stay! We walked back to our lodgings and drowned our sorrows in a bottle of wine. Then I went to bed and fell asleep straight away. I left Dick learning lines by candlelight.'

'And he was there when you woke?'

'Of course. Why shouldn't he be?'

Indeed, thought Simon, and it ought to stand Charles in good stead that he and his friend had been together throughout the time when Parsons was killed; except that most judges held the same views on actors as the magistrate who had put him in gaol, and might simply not be prepared to believe fervent testimony from so close a friend to the effect that it was impossible in the circumstances for the accused to have committed the crime. But this still left Audrey and Mistress Goodman, both respectable young women from City families, who would be able to vouch for Charles at least until midnight.

'You'd best give me the direction of Mistress Mary,' said Simon, 'and your Audrey. I'll approach your Iseult most discreetly, I promise you, but it may well be needful for her to swear you were at her friend's house with her that night until late. The more people we can get to say you could not have killed Parsons the better.'

Charles was scandalised. 'But you can't possibly do that! You can't involve either of the women, especially Audrey.'

'Look,' said Simon, exasperatedly, 'this is no time for niceties. The young woman can merely say she held a late and perhaps rather indiscreet supper party. If she's as coming on as you say then surely she can convince her husband that you were both friends of Audrey's, and that while it might have been a rather foolish thing to do, she wanted to please her best friend and was persuaded there was no harm in it. Better still, I really do think I should talk to Audrey. If she feels for you as strongly as you do for her then she'll hardly refuse to help you in such dire circumstances. If she was devious enough to set up an assignation with you, she must be able to find some way of doing this without involving her fond parents.'

'No, no!' exclaimed Charles wildly, 'no, I couldn't put her at so much risk. I can't chance her reputation or what her father might do if he discovered she'd been meeting me in secret. No, Dr Forman, you mustn't go near either of the girls.'

'For Jesu's sake, Charles, you aren't playing a role in some romance!' shouted Simon, rising to his feet. 'You're not riding out like some knight in shining armour with your lady's scarf on your lance to save her honour, nor are you Sir Tristram of Cornwall counting the world well lost for love. Some time in the next weeks you will come up for trial. It will suit everyone, the judge, the magistrate, the constable, the authorities – even, God help us, possibly Henslowe – that you should be found guilty as that means a tidy end to the affair. If that happens, then failing some last-minute reprieve, you will be taken to Tyburn and hanged. Man, you stand in mortal peril of death on the gallows!'

But Charles remained obstinate. He would not, he could not, involve his Iseult in any way, even if it meant his life was forfeit. As Simon left, beside himself with frustration, he recalled the young actor's words spoken almost in jest only weeks earlier: *A girl to die for*. It was, he thought sombrely, likely to be only too true.

Chapter 10

A Testing Time

The next day Simon, as good as his word, sat down and wrote as promised to Charles Spencer's father but, having done so, he wondered how on earth he was going to ensure his letter would reach him in Norwich. Then he recalled that Robert Greene was able to get messages to and from his parents and estranged wife (mostly demands for money), and that Charles had said the two families knew each other. So he walked round to Emma Ball's little house to see if he could find him. Emma opened the door to him and told him, unsurprisingly, that the rambling poet was out, but could she help? She was a small, auburn-haired woman who looked older than her years and would have been pretty had she not looked so tired and worn down. Simon had a good deal of time for Emma, and felt life should have had more to offer her than a highwayman for a brother and a debauched poet as a lover.

If he would like to give her the letter, she told him, she'd ask Robin about it as soon as he returned. He still had links with his home city, and knew a number of merchants and old friends of the Greene family who visited London fairly regularly. 'If it's urgent,' she added, 'possibly he'll know of some carrier or groom who's riding that way and can take it for you. Don't worry, I'll see he does it!'

'It's urgent all right,' he told her, 'it's not too much to say a man's life might depend on it,' and he explained the circumstances.

'Robin told me about the killing,' she replied, 'and you say you think this poor young man didn't do it?'

'I'm as sure as I can be that he didn't.'

Emma sighed. 'Innocence is no proof against hanging. When my brother Jack and I were orphaned and running wild on the streets,

111

stealing to keep alive, we saw plenty of poor folk hanged either for very little or for what they hadn't done. They must know Nathan Parsons was notorious for making himself enemies but I suppose it'll be easier for them to ignore that and hang the wrong man!'

He handed her the letter and thanked her and she gave him a tired smile. She looked very pale. 'Robin tells me you are with child,' he said. 'How is it with you?'

She shrugged. 'I've ceased weeping over it since there's nothing to be done. But what kind of a life is it going to have? As to how I feel – very sickly.'

Simon looked at her with sympathy. 'I'll bring you a remedy to help with that, and if you feel I can do anything to ease you at any time, you know where I am.'

On his way back home he ran into Tom Pope who, he said, had been trying to seek him out. 'I've just come from the crowner's 'quest,' he told Simon. 'It was all over in minutes, unanimous verdict of wilful murder with the coroner adding his pennyworth to the effect that he understood a man had already been accused of it and was due to come up before a judge during the current sessions. Oh, and that death was caused by a stab wound to the heart from a weapon such as a poniard or stiletto. I thought you'd want to know, and I also wondered if you'd been able to see Charles yet.' Simon told him that indeed he had, and of the depressing outcome of it.

'The young fool,' Tom expostulated. 'If he persists in this mad, romantic frame of mind, I doubt he can be saved. Indeed I fear he'll be rushed into court to be made an example of before we return from tour. Which reminds me, will you keep an eye on Jenny for me? I know she's full of common sense and most practical but I always worry when I'm away. We never enjoy being separated.'

'Of course.' The request gave Simon an idea. 'Do you think Jenny might have more luck than I had at trying to make Charles see sense? He's fond of her, and possibly a woman he likes might prove more persuasive. If she's agreeable then of course I'd go with her to the Clink.'

'That's a good idea.' Tom looked across to his little house. 'Since I've found you, I'll go back home. I'll ask her now, but I'm sure she'll agree.'

'When do you leave?' asked Simon.

'Tomorrow morning. It's been a desperate rush.'

'Then I'd best try and see Dick Marsh before you go, and tell him what the situation is if he doesn't already know it. Perhaps he could write out a statement for me to the effect that the two of them were together all evening and all night and that he'll stand witness to his friend. Presumably there'd be sufficient warning to get a message to you if he was needed in court. If the furthest afield you're going is Worcester, it shouldn't take him more than a couple of days to get back if he can hire a horse.'

But it seemed there was a problem. Dick and another actor, Luke East, had already left London as they had volunteered to go on ahead of the main party to make arrangements for lodgings and to find the best place in Southam where they could set up. If time allowed, they were also going on to Coventry to ask the landlord of the Wall Tavern if they could play in his yard even though they were several weeks earlier than usual. 'Because we do have more time we're also thinking of playing in Stratford-upon-Avon and Evesham as well, and it seems the Lucy family of Charlecote Park has sent a message to Henslowe asking us to give a special private performance.

'If we'd thought of it sooner I'm sure he'd have been only too happy to do as you suggest: he's very upset, very quiet – not his usual self. But as it is he's somewhere between London and Oxford by now. As to a horse, then the company has already hired two for them. Well, I'll away to my packing. I'm also responsible for the apprentices, so I have to see to their needs as well.'

'How's young Daniel?' Simon asked.

'More cheerful since Parsons's demise but still not back to his old self. No doubt the excitement of the tour will cure that, though now he's worrying about running into members of his family in Gloucester, though I imagine they've probably moved on long ago.'

They were about to part when Tom swore and struck himself on the forehead. 'Discussing Charles put it out of my head. I don't know if this has any relevance to anything but when the gatherer and stagehands went into the Rose this morning to start clearing up and packing, they found a stranger there before them. He was

113

reticent about how he got in but it wouldn't have been too difficult for someone to do so as the door was open most of yesterday afternoon and he could have slipped in unnoticed and hidden in the theatre.'

'Did he say what he wanted?'

'That lump-headed gatherer didn't even ask! He just yelled at him for trespassing, then threw him out. From what we could make out the man wasn't your usual cutpurse or vagabond but fairly well dressed and well spoken. The gatherer's a fool. The man should have been taken to Henslowe to explain himself: now we'll never know who he was or what he wanted. Oh, and the other thing. The sixth stiletto turned up – it seems one of the hired actors had wrapped it up in his costume and forgotten all about it, and no there was no sign of blood on it, or that it had recently been cleaned.'

The next morning three great carts rumbled across London Bridge bearing the actors, the bookman and the big baskets of costume and props. The actors had to be their own stagehands and carpenters on tour, and the whole venture was a tiring business as they had to set up in so many different places for such a short time. Tom, sitting in the first cart with a sleepy Daniel leaning against his shoulder, prayed that Dick and Luke would have ensured they had somewhere suitable to play and decent lodgings in both Southam and Coventry.

Simon, feeling there was little he could do for the time being but wait, applied himself to his own concerns. To his delight, two days later Avisa Allen came to consult him. She had come, she told him, not on her own account but on that of her husband, who was loath to consult doctors. He was suffering from pains in the joints and an intermittent fever, both of which were having a lowering effect on him, added to which he was also depressed for another and more worrying reason. 'Did you know William's a Catholic?' she asked Simon. 'A "recusant" as they call him, or rather us, for I too was baptised in the Old Faith.'

'I had no idea,' said Simon but, as he said it, he suddenly recalled how her real mother had asked on her deathbed for a priest and of her need for confession and absolution and how, in her extremity, she had turned to him and told him of the love child she had born without her husband's knowledge. Presumably she and the sister

114

who had brought Avisa up had been Catholics, though neither continued to practise as such.

Mistaking his silence for concern, Avisa added that he need have no fear. She attended church every Sunday and no one was the wiser. 'I agree with what the Queen said many years ago, that there should be no looking into windows in men's souls and I don't believe that God will punish me for which church I go to. But it's different for William. His conscience won't allow him to attend church, and you know what the penalties are for attending a secret Mass! He already owes a hundred pound in fines and though he says he is not fearful of what might happen to us, I think deep down he does and the worry makes him unhappy. Times have changed for the worse for us since Mary Stuart was executed and the Spaniards launched their Armada.'

'Well, whether his sickness is of body or mind or both, it would be better if he came and consulted me himself,' stated Simon. 'Try and persuade him to do so, but in the meantime, what is it you want me to do?'

She had come, she told him, to ask if he would cast William's horoscope, first in the hope that it might show what was ailing him, and second, to see if he could foresee if he would be in trouble with the law. 'Perhaps then if I could convince him of your skills I might be able to persuade him to come here himself,' Avisa remarked.

'And do you want me to cast for you also? You told me you wanted to know if you might soon conceive a child.'

'Very well,' she said with some reluctance, 'though it was not my intention today.'

She handed him a note of the birth dates of herself and her husband and the time of day and the place where they were born, and he noted that William Allen was a good twenty years older than his wife. They discussed the positions of the planets for some time, as well as the humours which might affect them both. 'This will take me some time to do,' Simon told her. 'Unless you are in great haste, can you return for them in two days' time? I must cast these with great care, and then I will have to draw up charts for you both and write down the results of the casting.' He took her hands in his.

115

'You know how I feel about you, Avisa. I can hardly bear to let you go now I have you under my roof.'

She gently disengaged herself. 'And you know how *I* feel, Simon, about William, about you, about the situation in which we find ourselves. Perhaps you'll see the outcome in the stars, Sir Necromancer!' she joked, trying to make light of it.

He watched her cross the road and go down to the water steps to find a wherryman to take her over the river, then he immediately unrolled his charts, spread them out on the floor and began to make feverish calculations based on the information she had given him. It took some time before he was able to return to his desk and study his findings.

He saw continuing problems ahead for William Allen, probably to do with his faith but there was nothing to suggest his illness was a matter of immediate concern, though he would still have to see the man in person properly to diagnose it. He then did what he knew he should never do, and which would certainly have brought down the rightful wrath of the Royal College of Physicians had they known of it: he returned to his charts and cast again, this time to see if William Allen was likely to die in the foreseeable future. Here he drew a blank. If that was indeed the case, then the stars steadfastly refused to reveal it.

Next and with real trepidation, he turned to Avisa. He saw a troubled path ahead for her. There was no immediate child, although it looked as if it was certain there would be at least one in the future. He tried in vain to discover if she would take a lover and, if so, if it might be him but again he learned nothing. Even more rashly, since it was not considered lucky to attempt to force an answer from the stars, he tried a cast pleading with them to reveal if she would soon be a widow, and if so, what the future might hold. This time he had an answer, one that made him wish he'd left the subject alone, for it seemed to say that Avisa would never live to be widowed, for she would die a wife in the thirty-seventh year of her age. Shaken, he refused to believe it, angrily tearing up her chart: he had offended the stars by his actions and the stars had paid him back. He would, he vowed, never break the rules again.

It was in this frame of mind that he left his study to find another letter from Emilia informing him that she was alone for the next few days if he wished to pursue their fascinating discussions. He put it aside, ruefully wondering if he was now heading rapidly for old age since hitherto he would have responded to such an offer with the greatest enthusiasm and no emotional involvement whatsoever. Over the years he had become used to invitations, from the hesitant to the overt, from women who came to him for advice – invitations which he had happily accepted on a number of occasions.

Recently a woman had asked him why he'd never married, and he'd found himself responding to her question with unreasoned anger, unwilling to tell her that during his time in Italy he had fallen deeply in love with a young Italian girl, who, against the wrath of her parents and the fear of family vengeance falling on both of them, had run away with him and become his mistress. He had planned to bring her back to England and marry her, only to find himself some months later standing helplessly by while she died in childbirth along with their son. Now, for the first time since her death, he was conscious that he was experiencing the same feelings again – and for a woman who could never be his.

He was jolted out of his reverie by a woman who caused him no such anguish. Jenny Pope came to tell him that she had received a note from Charles Spencer in the Clink. Unaware that the company had left London, he had written to Tom asking why he had heard nothing from Dick Marsh, in spite of sending notes to their lodgings. Was he ill? Or had the notes gone astray? He had been surprised not to have had a visit from his friend but it was now urgent that they talked, and would Tom tell him this and ask him, if it were possible, if he could come to the Clink that very day.

'I came at once,' she told Simon. 'Tom said to ask you if I was in need of help. He also talked of what had passed between you and Charles, and I'll certainly do all I can to persuade him to change his mind. I'm also willing to go and visit the two women on his behalf if you think it'll do any good.'

'He's as stubborn as a mule but it's worth trying. It could be that something's happened we don't know of and that's why he's sent so urgent a request. That being the case, I think we'd best go to the gaol now to discover what it is. We can also tell him that the reason he's not heard from anyone since he was put in prison is because the company has now left London, and not because he's just been abandoned.'

Jenny agreed, asking only if he could spare the time for her to call in at her house and put together a basket of food and drink for Charles. Without more ado he fetched his cloak and together they walked first to her home, then to the Clink gaol. Once again, money changed hands to enable them to have free access to the prisoner, and they were guided to his cell by a gaoler who seemed to be enjoying some private joke. 'He's still here where you left him last time, Doctor,' he said as he unlocked the door. 'Though,' he leered with relish, 'not for much longer.'

Charles greeted them with obvious relief. He was looking pale and haggard, his clothes now dirty. He thanked Jenny profusely for her basket of food and bottles of ale, 'Though I've somewhat lost my appetite.' His voice wavered. 'It's very good of you to come but why isn't Dick here? Didn't Tom get my note?'

'He'd already left London,' replied Jenny. 'Henslowe decided to close the Rose and send the company out on tour. They must be in Southam by now, and they'll be away for a good month. Tom left with the main party three days ago but Dick and Luke East were ordered to go on before them to see to the setting up in Southam.'

'I see.' Charles leaned back against the stone wall and put his head in his hands.

'What is it?' asked Simon. 'What's happened that made you write to Tom so urgently?'

Charles looked at them, his face even paler if that were possible. 'I'm to be tried in three weeks. They've decided that I'm to be made an example of; the magistrate who committed me has much influence in the courts. Oh God, I've waited every day expecting to see Dick. Why did he leave without coming to visit me?'

'It was a frantic scramble, Charles,' said Jenny, 'They had to be up and off with hardly any warning. Everything went by the board.'

'Sweet Jesu! So Dick's in Southam?'

'Only for two or three days, and then the company goes to Coventry.'

'I've *got* to see him,' cried Charles wildly. 'Whatever Henslowe says, he'll *have* to come back. He's got to tell everyone that we were together all that evening and night and that I couldn't have killed Parsons.'

'But even if he can be brought back,' said Simon, 'as I told you before, is he likely to be believed? Two close friends who work together without rivalry, share lodgings and spend much of their leisure time in each other's company are unlikely to renege on such a friendship even if one of them *has* committed a crime. All right,' he went on as Charles was about to break in, 'we'll see what can be done about getting Dick back here but now, in the name of all that's holy, you must see that you'll have to have some corroboration from the women with whom you spent that evening.'

'I'll undertake to do that for you,' said Jenny. 'It will be easier for me and cause far less comment.'

'But as I told Simon, I can't have Audrey involved in this affair.'

'And I told you then and will again that you must! If you don't change your mind you'll be dead in a month. You can protest your innocence all you like but it will fall on deaf ears. Have some thought for yourself before it's too late. There must be some way these women can support your story without either of them actually having to appear in court on your behalf.'

'If I am proved innocent, suppose Audrey will never see me again because I asked her to do this?'

'Then she is a worthless and selfish young woman and you are well rid of her,' Jenny replied firmly. 'Now if you've decided to see sense, I'll call on Mistress Mary – Goodman, isn't it? – and if possible and with the utmost discretion, on your Audrey and explain exactly what has happened and how best they might help you.'

Finally Charles was persuaded to agree but only with extreme reluctance. Simon heaved a sigh of relief. 'And when she's done so I'll go and see Henslowe and ask if I can ride out after the company and bring Dick Marsh back to London. In the meantime, so far as is possible, be of good cheer. Between us all we may yet bring you off.'

He and Jenny parted outside the prison, she assuring him that she would do her best to see both the women that afternoon, and would let him know the outcome. Simon returned to his house to be told that a gentleman was waiting to see him.

'He came shortly after you left, Doctor,' Anna informed him, 'and although I told him I'd no idea how long you would be, he insisted on staying to see you.' He sighed and thanked her, hoping that the matter was a simple one and would not take too long. His visitor was sitting in a chair in the hall and rose as Simon came to greet him. He was, Simon guessed, about forty years of age, well but not richly dressed, and possessing an air of authority.

He showed him into his study and motioned him towards a chair. 'And how can I help you, sir?'

The man sat down. 'I've come to you on the recommendation of one who might be termed a colleague, though we work many miles apart. His name is Thomas Barton.'

Oh no, thought Simon, surely he's not sent along another lunatic husband with a string of fantasies. 'You are also a customs commissioner then?' he enquired.

The man agreed that he was, 'but for the port of Gloucester, not in Kent. However I know Barton from many years back, and I wrote telling him I was coming to London and suggesting we might meet but he sent word that he was indisposed and unable to do so on this occasion. He also told me that he had consulted you on a delicate matter. This interested me, as by the time I received his reply I had also determined to seek you out on my own account, as I have been making some enquiries and understand you know something of a death at the Rose Theatre.'

'Of Nathan Parsons, you mean?' asked Simon in some surprise, wondering why a customs commissioner from far-off Gloucester should take an interest in the matter.

'No, although I've heard of it. It's common talk hereabouts. No, I speak of that of the actor Jack Lane. I'm told he met his death by falling down a trapdoor in the stage which had been either accidentally, or purposely, let down.'

A thought struck Simon. 'Are you the man who was found inside the Rose some days ago?'

His visitor nodded. 'I had been asking questions in the taverns and among players but remain dissatisfied, and so took the opportunity, the door being open, to slip into the playhouse and look for myself. Unfortunately the door was then locked and I was left in the Rose all night.'

'Before we go any further,' said Simon, 'might I know why you are so interested?'

The man stood up and began to pace the room. Then he turned and looked hard at Simon. 'My name is Lane. Matthew Lane. Jack Lane's older brother. And I'm not prepared to let this matter rest. We are not a family that accepts wrongs lightly, and we were not even informed that he was dead. I came to London from Gloucester fully expecting to see Jack.'

'Then you have every right to feel aggrieved but I can tell you that no one in the company knew anything of your brother's family. It seems he never spoke of it. If it's any consolation, he had a decent burial in St Mary's churchyard, and I can show you his grave.'

Lane thanked him but pressed on. 'So what happened, Dr Forman?'

'The part he played in the play meant he had to throw himself backwards into an open, er, grave and the trapdoor was used for that purpose. It had already been used successfully several times during the performance. When your brother came to make his spectacular exit the trap had been lowered to the ground instead of it being, as arranged, just three feet below stage level. He was also most unfortunate,' Simon continued, 'since even such a fall should not have proved fatal. It just happened that he fell in an awkward fashion and so broke his neck.'

'Was no effort made then to find out what happened?'

'Since I was a doctor and was there at the time, Master Philip Henslowe, who owns the Rose, asked me to look into it but I have to admit I came to no firm conclusion. Obviously the death of the young man was a sad happening but whether it was by accidental carelessness or deliberate intent, I'm unable to say. I did, however, tell Master Henslowe it was widely thought that a disaffected actor and dramatist, Nathan Parsons, might have had some hand in it, since he and your brother had quarrelled shortly beforehand and while it's not good to speak ill of the dead, the man was a pest and heartily disliked.'

'And now he's dead too,' said Lane, with an unpleasant smile. 'How convenient.'

'In what way?' enquired Simon.

'Only that if he too is dead – stabbed in the back I was told – and it is generally thought he might be responsible for the death of my brother, then there's no more to be said, is there? Particularly if the man was much disliked. I have continued asking questions, Dr Forman, and continue to be dissatisfied.'

'A young actor is being held for Parsons's death but I do not happen to believe he did it nor, in case it has crossed your mind, that he was in any way responsible for the death of your brother. That was not possible though he, too, was not on good terms with him.'

Lane sighed. 'That I can well believe. Jack had a gift for falling out with those around him. He was the youngest of the family and much indulged. It was expected that he would go into some useful profession since he had no shortage of brains, but he was set on becoming a player and finally left without warning, fleeing possibly from the fathers of the two girls he had left behind bearing bastard children! Speaking of which, when I was in the theatre I saw from a distance a boy I thought I recognised as a bastard of a tribe of tinkers called Lee, who camp on land nearby that of my father. Ne'er-do-wells, thieves and liars all of them. Do you know of such a one?'

'There are a number of boy apprentices and I'm not acquainted with them all,' Simon responded, uneasy at the direction the questioning was taking.

Lane nodded. 'Well, I must take my leave: no doubt you've much to attend to. Thank you for your help, Dr Forman, and, if you will tell me whereabouts it is, I'll seek out my brother's grave – there's no need for you to accompany me. But I must tell you, I shan't let this matter rest here. I shall follow and seek out the Lord Admiral's Men to see what else they can tell me. And also if the boy I saw is indeed the bastard Lee.'

He left Simon to ponder if all customs commissioners, by the very nature of their employment, were obsessive, suspicious and unbalanced. It seemed more than ever necessary that he caught up with the company himself, not least because he could warn them that they had a would-be avenger on their heels.

While Simon was still wrestling with Matthew Lane, Jenny briefly broke her fast and then set off for Fish Street, acutely aware that there was now no time to be lost. She pushed her way through the crowds of shoppers on the bridge, made a mental note to look in at the cloth merchant's shop on her way back as the boys needed new shirts, and remembered to avert her eyes from the rotting heads of felons that regularly decorated the entrance to the north end of the bridge. A brisk walk took her to Fish Street and to the house, a handsome timbered property, that Charles had described as belonging to the Goodmans. Master Goodman was obviously a warm man, thought Jenny, as she applied herself to a handsome knocker in the shape of a lion's head.

The door was opened by a middle-aged maid and in answer to her request to see the mistress of the house, was informed that if she would give her name she'd see if Mistress Goodman was at home. Within a few minutes the maid returned to say that the Mistress would see her, and she was to be taken through to her sitting room. The house was well furnished with much in the way of hangings and pictures, including a rather poor double portrait in garish colours, presumably of Master and Mistress Goodman.

The maid opened the door into the sitting room on to the original of the female half of the picture, who was sitting working half-heartedly at a tapestry frame. Next to her was a slight, flaxen-haired girl. Could she be fortunate enough, thought Jenny, to have hit two birds with one stone and this was Audrey? Surely it must be.

Mary Goodman was a full-bosomed, determined-looking young woman. Her wiry red hair was elaborately dressed and her gown was of dark blue velvet with a ruff stiffened with the fashionable yellow starch. She looked very much the mistress of the establishment. 'So, Mistress – Pope, is it? – what is it you want with me?'

Now it had come to it Jenny felt somewhat hesitant but saw no help for it than to plunge in. 'I've come on behalf of someone I believe you know, Mistress Goodman – Charles Spencer.' The lady said nothing. 'My husband Tom is also an actor with the Lord Admiral's Men.' At this a look of disdain crossed her features, while her companion made a small sound like a squeaking mouse. You'd imagine I'd said I was a tinker's wife, thought Jenny, noting the reaction.

'And what about Charles Spencer?' asked Mary in a tone which suggested she was not particularly interested in the answer.

'Possibly you don't know, but he's been arrested on a charge of murder. He comes to trial in three weeks.'

The younger woman squeaked again. She looked like a doll. Her hair was a riot of carefully constructed curls, her cheeks were rosy and dimpled and her gown was of a baby pink patterned with seed pearls. She turned on Jenny a pair of large, vacuous blue eyes and pouted her pretty lips. What an expensive toy, thought Jenny, and just about bright enough to know her own worth. Oh Charles, Charles, I'd have thought you'd have had better taste! 'We were told about it,' she said in a childish voice, 'isn't it *dweadful*. I'm Audrey Newbold, Mistress Pope,' she added by way of explanation.

Mary Goodman yawned. 'I cannot imagine what interest you think we might have in the arrest of some player.'

'But Charles Spencer isn't just *any* player, is he?' Jenny looked across to Audrey. 'He's had enough to say about you over these last weeks, singing your praises to all and sundry; even writing a play in your honour. He's accused of murdering an actor from the Burbages' company at the Theatre, a man he'd accused of stealing the play he had written for you. The man was killed on the evening he and his friend, Dick Marsh, had supper here with the two of you. Please don't insult my intelligence by saying that you did no such thing,' she continued as Mary Goodman shook her head and began to deny it, 'for I know for certain that you did,' she added, hoping she wouldn't be asked to provide proof.

'We won't *deny* it, will we, Mary?' said Audrey in her affected little-girl voice. 'Poor, poor Charles, of course I'm *vewy* sorry for him but we could get into so much trouble. You see,' she continued in a confiding tone, 'it was *vewy* wicked of us to hold such a party when Mary's husband was away and we were just two girls on our own but it *weally* was quite harmless. But you're wrong about Charles being here.'

'It's true to say he was invited,' snapped Mary. 'But he never came.'

'I was *so* upset,' added Audrey, 'and he'd been going to wead me some of his play. He said I was his inspiwation for fair Iseult.'

'Dick Marsh came as promised,' continued Mary, 'and we all waited supper on Charles but when it came to nearly ten of the clock and he still had not come, then we dined and had as merry an evening as possible in the circumstances.'

'I see.' Jenny was nonplussed. 'Well, I won't take up any more of your time.'

'I still don't see what you wanted from us,' said Mary impatiently.

'I'd hoped you might have been prepared to swear that Charles had been with you all evening, and therefore could not have been at the Rose before the small hours of the morning at the earliest.'

'Swear in *court*,' squealed Audrey, her voice rising even higher. 'In front of all those people?' she exclaimed, suddenly dropping her affected manner of speech. 'You must be mad! What would my father and mother say? They don't know anything about my . . . my friendship with Charles. And as for Mary . . .'

Mary Goodman was adamant. 'I'm not prepared to put my marriage in jeopardy for the sake of what I now realise to have been an exceptionally foolish escapade. I was quite wrong to have agreed to something which might so easily be misconstrued. Anyway, as it turns out, it wouldn't be possible anyway, since Charles Spencer never came to this house that night. And now, Mistress Pope, I think you'd better go. My husband is expected home at any time and I'd prefer he didn't find you here.'

Jenny had reached the south side of London Bridge before she realised she had completely forgotten about the cloth for the boys' shirts. Her head seethed with incoherent thoughts but one thing was certain: either the two women were lying or Charles was.

Chapter 11

Emilia

'Spencer comes up for trial in just under three weeks,' Simon told Henslowe, 'and Dick Marsh must come back to London to stand witness for his friend. He's the only person who can swear to the fact that he and Charles Spencer spent that evening having an illicit supper with two well-brought-up young women, and that afterwards they walked back together to their lodgings before spending the rest of the night asleep in the same room. They were never out of each other's sight.'

He spoke with a confidence he was far from feeling, for he had been greatly shaken by the women's firm denial that Charles had ever visited them that night. Like Jenny, he had not known what to make of it, although after a great deal of discussion they both thought the most likely reason was the simplest: the girls were terrified that their indiscreet supper party would be discovered. Presumably they had heard of Charles's arrest, panicked, and to ensure they were not linked with him in any way, had devised the story told to Jenny; though perhaps it was truer to say that Mary Goodman had devised it, since in Jenny's estimation Audrey was the kind of girl for whom serious thought was an alien concept.

But Simon was now haunted by the real possibility that they might after all have been telling the truth and that Charles really had not gone to the supper party. But if so, where had he been all evening? And why tell such an outright lie to those trying to help him, especially as he was so desperate for his friend to return to support his story? Or did he assume that Dick Marsh would back him whatever he said?

Simon was brought back to the present by Henslowe pounding his desk. 'But Marsh is in the middle of a major tour playing leading roles, and here you are saying I must find someone to go after him and fetch him back! Do you know what that means? I have to find a player, and not just any player but a good player, to take his place for anything up to a week or more. And I've already had to hire in another actor to play Spencer's roles, and he can hardly take on those of Marsh as well even if it were possible – which it's not because mostly they are in the same plays.'

He ran his hand through his bushy hair in exasperation. 'Anyway, how can you be so sure Spencer didn't do it? Have you any proof other than what you hope Marsh might swear?' It was clear that so far as Henslowe, noted for his ruthless business practices, was concerned, Charles Spencer was rapidly becoming expendable.

Simon did his best to be patient. 'No, not yet,' he admitted. 'But I truly do not believe he did it. Hot-headed and emotional he may be but a cold-blooded stabbing in the back is totally out of character. And no effort's been made to see if it could have been anyone else. It's only days since I was standing here in your office and we were both in agreement that Parsons might well have had something to do with Lane's death. I thought then that for all we knew a friend or relative of Lane's might have taken the law into their own hands and killed Parsons, believing he was responsible.'

That reminded him of his visitor. 'Talking of which, did you know that a man was found hiding in your theatre the other morning?'

'So I believe. The gatherer said something about it. But what's that got to do with anything?'

'The man was Lane's brother. He came to see me yesterday determined to get to the bottom of his brother's death. I think it unlikely it was him who took the law into his own hands,' he continued as Henslowe stared at him in surprise, 'not least because he is a man of some standing and repute, a customs commissioner from Gloucester, and he was locked in the theatre by accident. But we have only his word that he knew nothing of Jack Lane's death until he reached London, and if he could slip into the theatre in such a way unnoticed then why not another, why not Parsons's killer? I suppose,' he finished, thoughtfully, 'that while Commissioner Lane might not himself stoop to kill, it would not be hard for him to find someone prepared to do it for him. It has been known.'

For the first time Henslowe began to look doubtful. Seizing the advantage Simon continued, offering him Robert Greene's view that it might equally well have been a gaming-house creditor or a whore's jealous pimp, since Parsons frequently patronised both.

'Greene should know,' muttered Henslowe, 'he's so expert he's just published a pamphlet about it.'

'The fact that he is suggests that for once he might be talking sense,' agreed Simon. 'Then there are all those Parsons offended just by his manner and the men he drew on and fought with in public, not to mention the poets whose work they claimed he stole. And I suppose it's not beyond the bounds of possibility that his murderer was a woman. It takes little strength to stab someone unawares with a stiletto, just a knowledge of where to strike.

'Anyway, I propose to write to the clerk to the sessions pointing out that there are other suspects, and it would lend more weight if I could add that a member of your company is being brought to London to swear that Charles could not possibly have killed Parsons. I know that would be better coming from someone who wasn't a friend but as things stand it's the only hope we've got, unless we can find who really did do it before he's brought to court.'

'And that you are proposing to try and do?' Simon nodded. 'Very well,' said Henslowe finally. 'I suppose Marsh had better be fetched back, though who I'm going to send haring off after the company I can't imagine.'

'If you can't find anyone else, I'll go myself,' said Simon. 'It shouldn't take too long. Let's see, two days to get down to Southam or Coventry, possibly another to find where they are if they aren't at either, time to explain the position to Marsh and allow the company to make arrangements to cover for him without losing a performance, two days to get back to London – that means roughly a week or a little more, all told.'

Henslowe still looked far from happy but finally appeared to accept the situation. 'If you will go yourself, Dr Forman, then I suppose I must find a replacement actor to go with you. Lord Strange's Men don't appear to be doing very much at present. I'll see if they can spare us a man for a short while, preferably one with a good memory and the ability to learn lines fast.' He heaved a sigh. 'This is all going to prove very costly and touring is always a matter of risk. On one occasion the company took so little money they had to sell their own clothes in order to get back home. And you will need funds too, since I can hardly expect you to do it for nothing. What fee do you suggest?'

'Board and lodging for myself and my servant – John Bradedge is good at keeping his ear to the ground and might be useful – and stabling and fodder for our horses. I still have my own – though I can ill afford it – but I'll need to hire another two, one for Bradedge and the other for your actor. I'll keep a careful note of the reckoning and let you have it when I return. And, let's say, a further four guineas if I get Marsh back here safely and into court, whatever the outcome. After all, I can scarcely make any money doctoring during the time I'm away.'

'You drive a hard bargain, Dr Forman,' grumbled Henslowe. 'But I suppose I have no alternative but to agree. When do you propose setting off?'

'As soon as you find me an actor to take Marsh's place. They'll probably have left Southam by the time I get there but it's best I start with their first port of call.'

At first John Bradedge had exploded when Simon told him he was proposing to pursue the Lord Admiral's Men in order to bring Marsh to London, reminding him of the trouble he had got into the last time he had charged off on such a venture, though admittedly without him. Simon had taken it upon himself to confront a murderer, and had almost paid the price with his own life and might well have done so had not his servant, against orders, tracked him down to where his assailant was proposing to drown him. He was, however, somewhat mollified when Simon informed him that this time he was proposing to take John with him.

'At least you've learned some sense,' he growled. 'When do we start off then?'

'As soon as Henslowe's found an actor to go with us who can stand in for Marsh. Tell Anna we'll be away for about a week. And this time it's highly improbable there'll be any risk involved unless we're unfortunate enough to run into footpads on the way. We're not dealing with villains this time. By the way, has Mistress Allen been back for her horoscopes? Ask Anna, will you.'

He was thinking of what he had to do before leaving town, when John returned to say that Anna had told him no one had called while he'd been out, and should he see to the hiring of horses? Oh, and by the way, another letter had come for him sealed with the coat-of-arms seal.

Presumably Thomas Barton had recovered from the indisposition which had prevented his meeting his colleague in London, for he was threatening Simon with an immediate visit. He had now convinced himself he was being followed everywhere he went. For instance, when he'd crossed the river recently by ferry, now being afraid of using the ford in the light of his recent experiences, he had been deliberately jostled by two men and had nearly fallen out of the boat into the river and, moreover, he could almost swear that they were the two cut-throats from the previous attack.

If this is so, he wrote, *then it must needs be that someone is setting them on and that someone is my wife and her lover!* The strain of all this was proving too much and was affecting his heart. He was therefore coming to London within the next few days to ask for a remedy for palpitations, a further casting of a horoscope and, yet again, to request Dr Forman to return to Kent with him.

He ended his letter with a reference to Matthew Lane. *I have told a colleague of mine, a commissioner of Gloucester, of your skill for he is to come to London and I thought he might wish a consultation as to his future and the conduct of his wife, though he is not in like case to me, as he has been married these twenty years and so therefore it is unlikely Mistress Lane would stray, since she must be past having a taste for such things.*

If there was ever a good reason for getting out of town then this was it, thought Simon, and made a mental note to tell Anna to inform the lunatic customs commissioner when he arrived that Dr Forman was away in the country on urgent business, and that she was quite unable to say when he would return. He then penned a careful note to Avisa explaining that he had written out the horoscopes as requested and would she like to collect them, since he was about to leave London for a short while and would like to explain their meaning before he left. He sealed his letter carefully and gave it to John, asking him to take it over to Blackfriars and deliver it to the house of William Allen, silk merchant, before arranging for the hire of the horses.

He spent the rest of the day writing out in detail what he had told Henslowe as to Parsons having had numerous enemies, and notifying whoever it might concern that he would be bringing back from the country a person to stand witness for Charles Spencer. This he addressed to the clerk of the sessions, before making a copy to go to the relevant magistrate. He then left a note for Anna to give to Charles's father in the event that he arrived from Norwich while he was away. By the evening he was tired and depressed, and he was beginning to think that, after all, he was about to embark on a wild-goose chase. And when he got back he really would have to tackle the Royal College of Physicians again about his licence as there seemed no earthly reason now, he decided, why it should not be restored to him. Then he could once again put all this investigative nonsense behind him and confine himself to what he did best: looking after the sick and predicting future events.

It was in the middle of the evening that Anna showed in Emilia. He was sitting reading in his little-used back sitting room, had not heard any knock at the door and could not disguise his surprise at seeing her. Somewhat at a loss, he asked her to sit down and told Anna to bring a bottle of wine and two glasses. Emilia immediately made herself at home, flinging her cloak over the back of a chair and sitting down in it as if she was likely to be there for some time. She was exquisitely dressed in a flame-coloured gown which showed off her dark looks to their greatest advantage. She flashed him her most brilliant smile. 'Well, Dr Forman – Simon – since the mountain won't come to Mohammed, Mohammed must come to the mountain. Did you not receive my note telling you I was alone and wished for company?'

Simon had a feeling of foreboding. 'I did, Emilia, but I've had a great deal on my mind and much to do,' he said loudly as Anna brought in the wine before leaving them together.

'And what is it that you find more important than coming to see me?'

'A man's life,' he retorted. 'No doubt you'll have heard of the murder at the Rose. A young man who I believe is innocent is to be tried for it and, unless something is done, is likely to be hanged.'

'So what are you proposing to do about it? I presume you intend doing something, since you are so busy.'

'Ride down to the midlands to find the Lord Admiral's Men, and then bring back with me a witness who can swear Charles Spencer was nowhere near the Rose Theatre or the victim at any time that night.'

'I see.' She toyed with the embroidery on her skirt. 'Aren't you going to offer me some wine?' Simon poured out a glass for each of them and she drained hers as if she was a young gallant. She reached forward and poured another. 'As well as finding out for myself why you never replied to me, I've also come to tell you that you're a better lover than you are an astrologer and possibly a better physician than either.'

Simon was irritated at the slur on his professional competence. 'Why do you say that?'

'You cast for me and told me I was not with child nor likely to be in the immediate future. I already had doubts about whether you were right, though I desperately wished to believe you for the reasons you already know. Now I'm sure I'm with child and have been to a midwife who tells me I'm right. No,' she said as he started to speak, 'it cannot possibly be yours, it is much too soon. I'll admit I didn't tell you the exact truth when you asked me if my courses were regular, as I'd already missed one moon month when I came to you, though that doesn't always signify. Now I have missed another. No, the child will be Henry's and that means my time of ease is over,' she continued, bitterly. 'I can keep my secret for a little while longer, after which I'll be married off. Oh, Henry has had a husband marked out for me for a long time, a pathetic fool by the name of Alfonso Lanier, a court musician like my father. He'll do what my lord of Hunsdon says and take me with a bag of money as if I were a prize heifer at a country fair.'

Simon sighed inwardly with relief. For one horrible moment he had thought she was blaming her pregnancy on him. If she had then he thought he'd have received short shrift at the hands of the Lord Chamberlain. A forced marriage to Emilia would have been the most civilised option open to Henry Carey, since here was a better match for Emilia with a man who had no wife.

No doubt too his lordship would enjoy teaching a lowly physician a lesson he'd never forget for toying with his personal property. It didn't bear thinking of. The situation seemed to be becoming rapidly out of hand. He moved towards Emilia intending to suggest that it was getting late and time she went home but she misconstrued his move, pressing herself against him, her arms round his neck, putting her mouth up to be kissed. He kissed her and she hung on to him.

'Don't send me away,' she murmured, 'surely we should take our pleasure when there's an opportunity? It hardly matters what I do now since within months I shall find myself wife to Alfonso Lanier, instead of being the mistress of a great man.'

He hesitated a moment and then was lost. What's the odds, he thought, you might as well take what's offered. It's not every day so attractive a woman walks into your house and throws herself at you! He considered how best to get her upstairs to his bedroom without the rest of the household being aware but it seemed Emilia had other plans.

'Why not here?' she asked. 'You've a daybed over there. Lock your door if the idea worries you.'

'It doesn't lock,' he told her. 'I've never thought it necessary.'

'Well, what does it matter?' she responded. 'Surely you're master in your own house?' She unlaced her gown and stepped out of it, then divested herself of her petticoats so that she stood before him in her shift. He took off his doublet and his shirt and began to pull off his breeches as she removed her shift as well. Then she picked up her cloak, tossed it across the daybed, sprawled herself out on it and opened her arms to him. He made love to her as she had wished but felt curiously detached, as if he were an actor in a play, though he thought it unlikely such an indecorous activity would ever be simulated on stage. As on the previous occasion Emilia responded voraciously but without true warmth. They lay apart for a moment, then he abruptly left her and began pulling on his breeches.

'What are you doing that for?' she asked. 'Do you want to leave me so soon?'

It was at that point that footsteps sounded across the hall, the door was suddenly flung open and Avisa Allen entered the room. She took one look at the scene in front of her and stepped back, her mouth open with astonishment. Then she recovered herself. 'My apologies, Dr Forman. It seems I've arrived at an inopportune moment. Perhaps you'll be so kind as to send the horoscopes to my house by one of your servants with a note of the reckoning.' Then she turned, closing the door behind her.

'Avisa, for God's sake!' he shouted, frantically fastening the belt to his breeches as he raced after her, aware that he must present a ludicrous spectacle, shirtless and with bare feet and with a naked woman behind him on the daybed. 'Avisa, come back!' The noise brought Anna into the hall. She gave one startled look at her master then said, her accent becoming stronger in her distress, 'Mistress Allen called for the horoscopes as you asked, and so I saw no harm in asking her to go in to you seeing as you are likely to be soon travelling. I thought she'd gone into your study.' Then the true awfulness of the situation dawned on her. 'Also I thought the other lady must have left long ago and . . .' her voice trailed away.

'The fault is mine, Anna,' said Avisa. 'I opened the wrong door.'

'Don't fret, Anna,' Simon intervened, 'it's not your fault. Go back to the kitchen.' He grabbed Avisa by the arm. 'Avisa, *will* you listen to me!'

'Why? What have you to say?' Her eyes brimmed with tears and her voice quavered. 'You have the right to take your pleasure where and when you will. It was just that . . . I was surprised, that was all. I'm sorry to have disturbed you. You'd best get back to your mistress.'

'She's not my mistress,' he said, wretchedly. 'She's, oh, she's a woman with whom I spent a night some time ago.'

'So you share the lady with those in high places, do you?' countered Avisa. 'I had thought her the mistress of Lord Hunsdon; her face is well known in Blackfriars. You must move in high circles.'

'You may believe me or not as you choose but I never invited her here, nor would I except if she wished to consult me. She came of her own accord, in part to tell me that she's likely soon to be married off by Hunsdon to a court musician as she's almost certainly with child – and no, it is not mine, it's Hunsdon's. Or so she claims. Then one thing led to another and—'

'You owe me no explanation, Simon,' said Avisa. 'After all, we aren't anything to each other, are we?' And never likely to be now, he thought, raging at himself. 'And now, my horoscopes?'

He went into his study and found them for her. 'I really should explain the charts to you,' he said weakly, but she took them from him. 'I'll make shift to understand what you've written out,' she said. 'I won't take up any more of your valuable time.' She felt in the purse hanging from her belt. 'You generally charge a guinea for a major cast, do you not? Well here are two, one for William's and the other for myself. I'll let myself out.'

He went miserably back into his sitting room. Emilia lay on the daybed much as he had left her and was now reading the book he had put down when she arrived. She flung it aside when he entered and stretched her arms above her head. 'You finally got rid of the good citizen's wife, then? By Our Lady, her face was something to be seen when she came through that door! No doubt it will provide her with food for gossip with her friends for weeks. What are you doing?' she asked as he gathered up her clothes and threw them across to her.

'Get dressed, will you, Emilia. Then you'd best get back home.'

Why?' she asked, sitting up, 'what's the matter? We have the whole night in front of us.'

'This was a mistake, that's all. I was a fool to take such a chance. I'm sorry, but I'm no longer in the mood for dalliance. You must forgive me.'

Emilia stood up. 'Must I?' she raged. 'What do you think I am? A common trull who hawks her wares in St Paul's churchyard and takes her clients for sixpence, with her skirts hitched up and her back against a wall? I can take my pick of men. It's they who come and plead with me, not the other way round.'

'I've said I'm sorry. I'm – honoured – that you should have chosen me but as I told you, this is not the right time with a man's life at stake. Please believe me, the fault lies with me, not you.' She still looked unconvinced but sullenly began to dress herself.

'What is that woman to you?' she asked as she laced up her bodice.

'Nothing. She's married to a silk merchant and came to collect the horoscopes I'd cast for them. I knew her mother slightly, that's all.'

Emilia stepped into her shoes and picked up her cloak. 'You didn't look at her as if that was all,' she said.

'You're mistaken.' He took her hand which she angrily tried to pull away. 'I'm truly sorry, Emilia. You're a woman who would set any man on fire. The loss is mine.' He walked her towards the front door. 'I'll send to you when I return to London. Hopefully by then I'll have resolved this sad business one way or another and will have time for other things.'

'Send if you like,' she retorted. 'I can't promise I'll answer. There are other fish in the sea and I've no longer anything to lose. The young actor in my lord's company who wrote *The Comedy of Errors* has taken to sending me sonnets; he likens my eyes to black coals of fire. There is much passion there, I think. I'll bid you goodnight, Simon Forman.'

He returned to the sitting room, picked up the rest of his clothes and sat on the bed. Oh my God, he thought, what have I done? By what awful mischance did Avisa, of all people, come here tonight? I've lost both ways. Had Emilia not been here, then Avisa and I could have talked and who knows what that might have led to, if not this time then perhaps some other. And had she only come for her horoscope tomorrow, I wouldn't have mortally offended Emilia either – what other fool would pass up the chance of a night with so experienced a wanton, and without fear of the lady falling in love either? He did not envy what was in store for the unfortunate Alfonso Lanier.

Sweet Jesu, it had all been too much. Given the events of the night, leaving London was the best thing that could happen to him and it couldn't come soon enough. It wasn't until he was in bed staring sleepless at the ceiling that he was suddenly struck by the fact that Avisa Allen had chosen a very strange time indeed to call to collect her horoscopes.

Chapter 12

A Race Against Time

Once Henslowe had decided on a course of action, however reluctantly, then he would waste no time. Within two days of his discussion with Simon he had hired a young actor to take the place of Dick Marsh for as long as necessary and, if he proved useful, possibly beyond. 'I take it you'll leave tomorrow,' he told Simon after he had introduced him to young Antony Hunt, the substitute actor.

'I'll have to, it's less than three weeks now until the trial. I'll go and see Spencer this afternoon and tell him what's happening; it might give him some heart,' Simon replied, also wondering how Dick would take being told that appeals to Mistress Goodman and Fair Iseult had not only been in vain but had compounded the matter still further, both having been adamant that Charles had never been there on the evening in question.

After further discussion with Henslowe as to the likely reckoning for board and lodgings, he arranged for Antony Hunt to be at his house by six o'clock sharp the next morning, where their horses would be waiting for them.

'Which route do you propose to take?' asked Hunt as they clattered down the wooden stairs from Henslowe's office.

'That's something I'll have to make my mind up about tonight,' said Simon. 'They'll almost certainly have left Southam by now but just in case for some reason they haven't, I'd best at least pass through. We can either take Watling Street north and then go west for Southam, or go down through Oxford and Banbury and then north-east. Whichever route we take it's the best part of two days' ride. And this is going to be a race against time.'

He then went back to his house, saw to the two patients who had called round in his absence and checked with John Bradedge that all the arrangements were in place for the following day. There was no further word from Avisa Allen, and he would now have to leave making his peace with her, if that were possible, until he returned. After he had dined he went once more to the Clink and told Charles he would be leaving in the morning to fetch Dick Marsh back to stand witness for him. 'Thank heaven,' said Charles with relief. 'You've actually persuaded Henslowe to let you bring him back from tour? But how will they manage now with two short?'

'Philip Henslowe was persuaded because he realises it is almost our only hope,' replied Simon, realising as he said it that his response must sound brutal. 'As to being two short, he'd already sent another actor off in your place and I'm taking a second down with me to stand in for Marsh while he returns to London.'

Charles was looking brighter. 'It'll be so good to see Dick again. I do realise he mightn't be believed as we're such good friends but surely it will sow some seeds of doubt.' Then he paused. 'But you say nothing of Mary Goodman and Audrey. Did Jenny think better of it in the end and not seek them out? What's the matter?' he added, as Simon began to look acutely uncomfortable. 'Did one or the other refuse to see her?'

'Oh, both of them saw her all right,' said Simon. 'As luck would have it your Audrey was visiting her friend when Jenny called on her. But what they had to say was hardly helpful. They were quite definite that you were never there that evening, and that being the case they were unable to be of any help at all. Nor, to be frank with you, do I think they'd have been any more use if they *had* admitted to your being there that night.'

Charles tried to put a brave face on it. 'I can understand it. I've put both of them in a very difficult position.'

'Nothing like as difficult as the position *you're* in,' commented Simon.

'But you don't understand,' Charles insisted. 'It could ruin their reputations if it was known that they entertained two young men on their own late at night. I can quite see why they won't have anything to do with us.'

'I'm afraid it's not even as simple as that. They were both quite prepared to say that Dick Marsh was there – although they ran a mile at the suggestion they might be asked to swear to it – but insisted that you were not. They said they waited supper for you until after ten o'clock, and that when you still hadn't arrived they started without you. According to them, Dick Marsh left on his own around midnight.'

'Jenny must have misheard it,' protested Charles. 'I can see why they wouldn't want to get mixed up in all this but why would they support only half a story when it isn't true?'

'I was hoping you might be able to tell me,' responded Simon.

'Well I can't. If that really is what they both said, then . . . then I don't know what to say, or think. I can't thank you enough for going to find Dick for me, Dr Forman. At least he'll stand up for me. And when he gets back with you I'll also ask him to go and see Mary Goodman to find out what has made them claim such an extraordinary thing. There's no sense in it. If they're frightened of being found out then it hardly looks much better for them if there was only one young man present rather than two, does it? It would be better, if they were going to take such a stand, that they swore neither of us were there!'

It was impossible to refute the logic of such an argument and Simon did not attempt to do so. He left Charles trying to comfort him with the knowledge that, if all went as planned, he would be back with Marsh in a week.

After much thought Simon decided to take the Oxford road, simply because he had travelled on it before and knew nothing of the other one. It was dark when the three horsemen left, only the earliest risers stirring as they made their way out of the city, first west, then north. John Bradedge had insisted on standing over his master to ensure he took his sword, before buckling on his own. He also took with him a dagger and a pistol in case of footpads. 'And not only because of highway robbers and cut-throats,' he warned, 'but also because you never know what kind of people you're going to find in these foreign parts!'

The weather was still fine and the road a good one. By the end of the morning, they were riding through the great red and golden beech woods of Burnham on their way to High Wycombe where they stopped to break their fast, after which they made such good time to Oxford that Simon decided they should press their tired horses a little further to clear the city so that they could push on more easily the next day. They stopped overnight in the village of Kidlington and Simon felt content with the first day's journeying. He could only hope the rest of the trip would go as smoothly. Antony Hunt had turned out to be a pleasant enough companion, though he was neither as handsome nor as engaging as Dick Marsh. The actor was also worried as to what he would find himself playing when they finally caught up with the Lord Admiral's Men. He had played Hieronimo's son in *The Spanish Tragedy*, and hoped that he wasn't going to be presented with plays totally unknown to him and parts that he would, therefore, have to learn from scratch. The three men bedded down together in a shared room in the only decent-sized inn and, after supper, tired from the long day's ride, slept heavily until the morning.

They were up betimes making first for Banbury, then on to the straight road to Southam but it was well into the afternoon before they reached the small market town. Hunt had already told Simon, in answer to his query as to why it was worth while for a company to play in such a small place, that two great drovers' roads crossed at Southam and that at this time of year it was likely to be very busy, with plenty of people about with money in their pockets looking for entertainment. The last part of their journey was through gently rolling countryside and scattered villages and hamlets.

Just before riding into Southam they crossed one of the drovers' roads, the one from Wales, at which there stood a milestone marking the distances to Priors Marston and Byfield. The name Byfield rang a bell with Simon but for the life of him he could not remember what it signified, and with more important matters on his mind he soon ceased trying to recollect where he'd heard it before. Once in Southam, however, they drew a blank. Yes, they were told, certainly the players had been there and had stayed on longer than they first intended, but now they had moved on to Coventry, seventeen miles further north.

'We must press on,' Simon told his two companions. 'We can't risk losing another day. If we can reach Coventry this evening I'll be able to see Marsh and we can arrange how soon I can get him back. I seem to remember being told they'd be lodging at the Old Wall Inn but even if they aren't, surely we'll be able to discover from the landlord where they are putting up.'

It was dark when they finally reached the city, and even later by the time they had picked their way past the fine cathedral and through the narrow streets to the Old Wall. Leaving their horses with an ostler they entered the taproom where, to Simon's great relief, they found half a dozen members of the company, including Tom Pope and William Miller. Their arrival caused an immediate cessation of all conversation.

'What on earth are you doing here, Simon?' demanded Tom, voicing the feelings of them all.

'It's a long story,' Simon began.

'Then you'd best tell it over some ale,' he said, and called to the tapster to see to the needs of the three new arrivals.

William Miller looked even more puzzled as he regarded the third of the trio. 'You're Antony Hunt of Lord Strange's Men, aren't you?' he said to the young actor. 'Why have you come?'

'Put bluntly,' Simon intervened, 'and to be as brief as possible, we're here because Spencer's trial is set for the middle of next month.'

Tom whistled. 'Jesu save us! That's close.'

'It's very close. And they seem determined to look no further for Parsons's killer. Therefore I've come to fetch Dick Marsh back to London, with Henslowe's permission, to stand witness that they spent all that evening and the rest of the night in each other's company. It's about the only chance there is. And Antony's come with us to take over Dick's roles while he's away. He says he knows a good many parts,' he added as the bookman turned his eyes theatrically up to heaven and groaned.

'How am I to be punished next?' he asked, presumably of the gods.

'I'm a quick learner,' replied Hunt.

'You'll need to be the quickest learner that's ever set foot on stage!' retorted Miller. 'We're presenting five plays on this tour:

143

The Spanish Tragedy, Crack Me This Nut, Arden of Faversham, Friar Bacon and Friar Bungay and—'

'I've played all of them,' broke in the young actor confidently, 'excepting that I'm told you're doing the play of *Henry VI*, of which I know nothing.'

The bookman looked relieved. 'Well, that's something. As for *Henry VI*, it seems our bad luck continues for somehow on our journey we found we'd lost all the parts and since hardly anyone could remember any of it, there seemed little point in going on. So it was decided, since the same costumes would do, that we would replace it with the old play of *Harry the Fifth*. Do you know that?'

Hunt said that he did and Miller appeared somewhat mollified. 'Well, I'll give you your parts tonight. Have you ever played King Harry?' The actor shook his head. He had, he told Miller, played the Dauphin of France and, when a boy, the Princess Katherine, but never the leading role.

'Well if Marsh is to leave us for any length of time, you'd best apply yourself to learning it since he's playing the King for us. He at least has benefited from our losing the scripts. Did Master Henslowe say how long you would be with us?' The young man shook his head. 'Well, if you prove your worth it might be that you can stay on for the rest of the tour after Dick joins us again. I could use another actor, especially if people are going to come and go in such a fashion. Now, if you'll excuse us,' he said to Simon and Tom, 'I'll take this young man away and give him some lines to learn!'

'Is there room for us to stay here tonight, do you think?' Simon asked Tom.

'I doubt it. I think there's a spare bed in one of the bigger rooms where young Hunt could shake down but that's all. There's the Nag's Head, though, over the road. Some of the company including Ned Alleyn are lodged there.'

Simon looked round. 'I must find Dick Marsh at once.'

'That was what I was about to tell you,' said Tom. 'He's not here tonight.'

Simon's heart sank. 'Why not? What's wrong?'

'Nothing at all. It's only that he and Luke have been going ahead to all the towns in which we are to play to find lodgings and arrange where we'll set up when we reach them, as they did in Southam before we left London. Don't worry, they'll be back first thing in the morning. They'll have to be, since we're playing outside the Guildhall tomorrow afternoon and we'll be here for a couple of days yet. I think I told you that Sir Thomas Lucy of Charlecote who has a great house near Stratford has sent over to see if we would play there for his son's birthday, and we thought it only courteous to send Dick and Luke to confirm that we will, ask him which of our plays he would like and also to see where we'll be be performing. Setting up in advance has meant the tour's going more smoothly than they often do – at least in that respect.'

Something in his tone made Simon curious. 'Am I to take it that things are not too good in other ways?'

'It's hard to pin down,' Tom replied, 'but there's been a succession of irritating mishaps of which the losing of the *Henry VI* parts is but one. Usually on tour, because of the difficulties, we all pull together but this time – oh, it's hard to explain – there have been differences between actors, lost and broken props, a general feeling of tension.'

'Has someone stolen the *Henry VI* play to give to someone else?'

'There'd be no point. Will Shakespeare, who wrote it with Kit Marlowe, had every right to take it with him to Burbage and he did. And no one would benefit from us doing *King Harry* instead, as no one can remember now who wrote it; most likely a group of actors getting together. It's a good story but the script is of about the same standard as that of *King Mark*!'

Simon looked around for John Bradedge who was already on his second quart of ale. 'Finish that,' he told him, 'then go down to the Nag's Head and find us lodgings. Take the horses with you. Then come back and dine here with us. No doubt the landlord will be able to find us something to eat.'

Within half an hour John had returned, grumpily informing his master that he had procured a room for them, left the horses to be rubbed down and fed and that he himself was starving. He was in good time, for the landlord's wife came into the taproom at that moment and said the long table was set in the back room for all who wanted to eat. Nearly all the company was present – apart from Ned Alleyn – including those lodging elsewhere, as well as three apprentices who sat together at the far end of the table, whispering and giggling among themselves. As they all sat down they were joined by William Miller and a somewhat daunted Antony Hunt, who was clutching a great bundle of rolls. Simon and Tom joined the rest as the landlord's wife busily ladled out bowls of stew for each of them.

'Dr Forman's here to take Dick back to London,' Tom told the assembled company as they ate. 'For those who don't already know, Charles Spencer comes up for trial the middle of next month.'

There were general sounds of concern. 'Jesu preserve us!' exclaimed Jack Washfield, the oldest actor and he who'd played the Old Wife. 'We thought that was a while off yet and that we'd be back in London long before. And there is no question of its being any other killed Parsons?'

'Not in the minds of the authorities,' said Simon, 'though I've yet to be convinced he did. As to the trial, well, it seems they've decided to bring it forward in a hurry. There are plenty of puritanical magistrates and judges with low opinions of players who'd be quite happy to hang one of you.'

'But why are you taking Dick back to London?' called young Daniel from the other end of the table.

'Because he's the only person – or at least the only person willing – who can prove Charles never went near the Rose Theatre on the night Parsons died.'

Tom looked round. 'Most of us are here, aren't we?'

'More or less,' said Washfield. 'Dick and Luke are visiting the Lucys as you know, and Ned Alleyn's dining in state with the mayor tonight.' He looked round the table. 'I think a couple of the younger lads have disappeared out on the town in search, I imagine, of complacent young women.'

'I thought you might want to say something to them, Simon,' said Tom quietly, 'since the matter is so deadly serious. You never know, someone might come up with something they've remembered now it's actually come to it.'

Simon explained how what was needed was confirmation of any

kind that Charles could not have got into the Rose and killed Parsons that night. It might be that if they racked their memories they might come up with something that had been forgotten and that might help. He also rehearsed again the argument that Parsons could well have been killed by some member of the local lowlife who he'd offended or owed money to, or in revenge by some friend of Lane's who believed he'd tampered with the trapdoor.

'And regarding that last possibility, did you know that the man found inside the Rose the morning before you left London was Lane's older brother?'

There was a noisy reaction.

'I told you the gatherer's a complete fool,' fumed Tom. 'Anyone other than a boneheaded clown would at least have stopped to find out who the man was. Do you think he had some hand in it then?'

Simon thought for a moment, then addressed his remarks to the whole company. 'He came to see me, having been recommended for other reasons, although he had learned that I knew something of Lane's death. It seems he spent some time in taverns asking questions.' There was an outburst of noise as everyone denied ever having spoken to such a person. Simon waited for it to quieten, then continued. 'I find it hard to believe he would directly have murdered Parsons, not only because he says he didn't even know his brother was dead until he arrived in London after Parsons was killed—'

'He could easily be lying,' interrupted one of the actors.

'He could. It's not that so much, it's who he is. He's a commissioner of customs for the port of Gloucester and the son of a substantial landowner near to that city. While that doesn't preclude him from avenging his brother with murder, I think it more likely, had he murder in mind, that he would have paid some cut-throat to do it for him rather than soil his own hands. Though I doubt such a one would have gone to the trouble of arranging him as we found him, but stranger things have been known. However it might be worth giving thought to the fact that if he could slip into the Rose and remain there overnight – though he claims it was quite accidental and he was not seeking to do so – then so might others.'

'I hope you're not still pointing the finger of suspicion at me,' growled Gabriel Tanner. 'Because if you are, I've the perfect excuse. I was picked up by the watch that night and locked up in the Counter gaol for being drunk and disorderly in the street. I didn't say anything when the constable came to the Rose that day as Henslowe told me that if he had to bail me out of gaol for being drunk one more time, he'd throw me out of the company. But you're welcome to go and see for yourself, it'll be there in the records. I was fined two shillings.'

'I'm not pointing the finger at anyone,' Simon replied, 'but I ask again, if any of you can think of anything that might throw light on the situation, please come forward and tell me. Any gossip you might have picked up: a quarrel over a woman, heavy threats from a collector of gambling debts, why Parsons and Lane, once so close, apparently, fell out. If only we can find some possible alternative that might persuade the authorities that they're wrong, they might at least set the trial back until the next sessions. So tell me. If you prefer it to be in confidence then I promise on my oath that no one else will know.'

'Has Dick talked to any of you here about Charles?' asked Tom.

No one answered at first, then Jack Washfield pointed out that the actor had had little to say to anyone as he'd been very busy, for not only was he playing numerous roles and had needed to learn several new ones, he and Luke were always dashing off making tour arrangements.

'I think it might well be that he's too upset to discuss it and so keeps it to himself, and like the rest of us must have assumed there was more time to catch the real culprit. Your news will come as a shock to him but I'm sure he'll move heaven and earth to save his friend.'

The actors finished their meal and drifted away, silenced by what they had been told. 'And what do you want me to do?' demanded John Bradedge as he wiped the last traces of stew out of his bowl with a chunk of bread.

'Go back to the Nag's Head and mingle with any of the actors who have gone over there. You've heard what I need to know: names of people who had it in for Parsons, anything they might have recollected that they haven't thought important enough to mention until now.' Mollified somewhat, John did as he was told. There were worse ways of earning his wages than sitting drinking the night away.

As Simon and Tom were now left alone, they found a quiet corner of a small room off the taproom and Simon told his friend of the reaction of the two women to Jenny's plea for help. Like Simon, the actor was nonplussed.

'Well, Jenny did say that Audrey was a flaxen-haired simpleton, though her friend seemed much sharper. But there's no getting round the fact that it's a considerable setback. I didn't tell Henslowe as I thought he might refuse point-blank to let me bring Dick back to London.'

'And Charles is sticking to his story?'

'Absolutely. He says that as soon as Dick gets back to London he'll be able to back him up. If that's the case, then perhaps it might be possible to persuade the women to change their minds. Anything's worth trying, Tom. While I've only been too happy to do what I can and make sure Dick gets back to London in time, I fear even his testimony won't be enough to save Charles without support from elsewhere. It's a fearful prospect.'

'And what of Lane's brother?'

Simon shrugged. 'Who knows? Anyway, you're likely to have a chance to question him yourself since he's threatening to come upon you somewhere on your tour and get to the truth at all costs!' Tom groaned. 'He said something else too: he asked if it was true there was a young boy called Daniel Lee in your company. He didn't say why but seemed to have a low opinion of him, calling him a bastard and a thief.'

'I told you, I found the boy living with tinkers outside Gloucester and they were a pretty unsavoury crew. Perhaps young Dan got across the Lanes in some way long before he joined the company. I'll see what I can find out, but discreetly. The boy's still not himself and I've no wish to upset him further because of the prejudice of a customs man.'

They talked a little while longer, then Simon, suddenly weary with two days' travelling, yawned and said he'd make his way to the Nag's Head and go to bed but would return in good time the following morning to talk to Dick Marsh as soon as he was back.

He was just leaving the tavern when he heard a voice call his name. Looking round he saw it was young Daniel himself. 'What is it, lad?' he asked.

'You said you wanted us to tell you anything that might help.'

'Yes,' replied Simon encouragingly, 'have you something to tell me then?'

The boy looked greatly distressed. 'It's about Parsons . . .' then he stopped. 'No, I didn't mean to bother you. It's probably nothing.'

'Let me be the judge of that,' said Simon.

'No, no, I can't,' said the boy, 'I can't, I mustn't . . .' and he disappeared into the darkness.

Unsure where he had gone, Simon went out of the inn yard and looked around but there was no sign of him. What on earth was that all about? he thought. Does he really know something of moment, or was he just trying to show off and then thought better of it? He yawned prodigiously and rubbed his sore backside. Well, whatever it was, it'd have to wait until morning.

He spent a restless night, his limbs stiff and with spasms of cramp in his calves, and so was down to break his fast unrefreshed, his temper not of the best. John Bradedge was there before him but had little to report, except that none of the actors he had spoken to thought Charles Spencer would have killed Parsons with malice aforethought but were of the opinion that he, like most other men, might have done if driven beyond endurance, especially if drink was involved and Parsons had challenged him to a fight. There was general agreement that Parsons had been adept at making people lose their tempers.

Jack Washfield was so concerned that he'd offered to go back to London as well, if he could be spared, as he was quite prepared to tell the court that Parsons's behaviour was enough to drive a saint to fight with him, if Charles would only admit that was what had happened. 'That way,' Jack had told John, 'he'd probably cool his heels in gaol for a few months to teach him a lesson, even get himself branded as a felon, but it'd save him from the gallows.' Simon had to admit that was one way out of it, though he doubted

Charles would be prepared to admit to something he swore he'd never done even in such desperate circumstances.

'At least we'll have Marsh,' he told John. 'Let's hear what he has to say. I suppose he'll have to play a couple more days in the circumstances but then I see no reason why we shouldn't all set off home then without further delay.'

The two men made their way back to the Old Wall and were just greeting Tom in the inn yard when Luke and Dick came riding in.

'All's well, Tom,' said Dick, swinging himself down off his horse. 'Sir Thomas Lucy was most civil and is looking forward greatly to our playing for him.' He was flushed with his morning ride and glowing with health and strength, a sharp contrast to the state of his friend left behind in gaol. He really was exceptionally handsome, thought Simon: he must leave a trail of broken hearts wherever he goes.

'And wait until you see the great house at Charlecote,' Luke broke in as he joined them. 'It's the most magnificent place, with gardens right down to the river. And as for the great hall—'

'Why, whatever are you doing here, Dr Forman?' asked Dick, suddenly realising who Tom's companion was.

'I've come to see you,' he replied, 'and without delay.'

'You'd best come through into the taproom,' Tom told him. 'Luke, you go and find Ned Alleyn and Will Miller, they're somewhere about, possibly over at the Nag's Head, and tell them what you've arranged. Ned will be delighted to play for the Lucys. Did Sir Thomas express any preference?'

'He wants *The Spanish Tragedy*,' Luke replied.

'That should please him then,' Tom remarked as the actor left. 'Hieronimo's one of his most favourite roles.'

'So why have you come all this way to see me, Dr Forman?' Dick asked as they all sat down together.

'Because Charles is to be tried in the middle of next month, not much over a fortnight away.'

The young man went pale. 'God save us!' he exclaimed.

'You'd best pray he saves your friend,' responded Simon grimly. 'I've come to ask you to return to London with me as soon as is practicable – it's all right, arrangements have been made and I've brought an actor down to play your roles while you're away.'

Dick looked puzzled. 'But why do you want me to go to London? What can I do?'

'We need you to swear a statement as to where you and Charles were on the night of the murder. How you were both at supper with Mistress Goodman and young Audrey, how you then walked back to your lodgings together and spent the night in the same room and that therefore Charles could not possibly have killed Parsons. It might still not be enough, and your testimony might be discounted on the grounds that you would swear anything to save your friend but it's the only chance we have, unless by a miracle the real murderer is discovered. And as a man of science I do not, on the whole, believe in miracles.'

'Have you spoken to Mary and Audrey?' asked Dick.

Simon explained how Jenny had done so and that the young women, presumably fearful of having their indiscretion discovered, had not denied the supper party altogether but that Charles had actually attended it.

There was a long, long silence. 'So if you can arrange with your colleagues how soon you can leave, Dick, we can have you swear a statement before a magistrate by the end of the week and listed as a witness for the trial.' Still the young man said nothing.

'I take it you're willing?' demanded Simon, beginning to feel alarmed. 'I mean, there's no reason why you shouldn't, is there?'

Dick Marsh looked at him, his face full of misery. 'But there *is*, Dr Forman. The women are telling the truth. Charles was supposed to have met me at Mary Goodman's house that evening but he never came. I was very surprised as he's so reliable, and I've never known him do such a thing before. In the end I went back to my lodgings on my own. I didn't hear him come in but he was asleep in his bed when I woke in the morning. I asked him where he'd been and why he hadn't come to supper, but he refused to tell me. That's not like him either.'

Simon broke out in a cold sweat. 'But he was so certain that you were together. He's never deviated from his story from the very first, not even when I told him what the women had said.'

'If I could lie for him I would,' said Dick wretchedly, his eyes filling with tears. 'But not on oath, not on the Bible. Even if I wasn't a parson's son I couldn't lie before God. And on my solemn honour, I never saw Charles until the following morning, I never saw him at all.'

Chapter 13

Dead End

Simon rocked back in his chair feeling as if he had been winded in a fight. He had been so sure Charles Spencer was telling the truth – the man seemed without guile, had been so credible in his declarations of innocence. For the second time he was assailed by doubt but this time on an even bigger scale. He recalled how vehemently Charles had pleaded with him not to ask either Audrey or Mary Goodman to support his story, insisting he did not want to risk sullying their reputations even at the cost of his life, and how he had accused him of romantic chivalry carried to an absurd degree. Yet supposing there had been another reason? That he was fearful the women would tell the truth, that truth being that he had never been there?

'You're absolutely certain of this, Dick?' Tom sounded as astounded as Simon felt. 'You couldn't have mistaken the night?'

Dick gave a wan smile. 'Hardly. It's not often one gets invited by two pretty young women to a secret supper party while the hostess's husband is away from home.'

'In God's good name, what do I do now?' asked Simon helplessly. 'Everything depended on your coming back to London with me to be his only witness.'

'I'd come back with you if I thought it would do any good,' said Dick, 'but I can't swear to what I know isn't true.' A look of anguish crossed his face. 'And how can I possibly face my friend and tell him I can't do it? That I can't stand up in a court of law and lie for him?'

Simon looked across at Tom. 'What do you make of it?'

'As you do. I could also swear from all I know of the lad that he was telling you the truth. I simply can't accept his involvement in stealthy murder.' He turned to Dick. 'I seem to remember you saying much the same thing when the constable came to arrest him.'

'I meant it too,' the young man responded.

'Perhaps Jack Washfield's right,' said Simon. 'I asked them all last night if they could think of anything that might prove helpful, however trivial, however unlikely – in fact my words obviously made someone think,' he continued, digressing a little. 'Young Daniel waylaid me as I was leaving the tavern, saying there was something he wanted to tell me.'

'What was that?' asked Dick.

'In the end he didn't say. Mumbled something about it possibly being wrong, or that it was probably nothing, then he disappeared before I could question him any further. I couldn't decide whether he genuinely had something he was frightened to tell me, or if he was trying to make himself important in the way boys do. I've asked John Bradedge to have a word with him and see if he can find out, he's good with young lads.' He looked across to Tom. 'Perhaps Jack Washfield's right and we now have to get Charles to change his mind.'

Dick looked mystified and Tom explained to him what had passed the night before, and that Jack Washfield had offered to return to London with Simon and that, if Charles could be persuaded to admit he killed Parsons, but in a fair fight, then he'd be prepared to act as a character witness, swearing Charles would never kill in cold blood and that Parsons was notorious for provoking violence. 'And outside the Rose, few people would know how the body was found: even the constable took little heed of it,' he concluded.

For the first time Dick began to look more cheerful. 'He could tell the court too how Parsons set on Gabriel Tanner, couldn't he?' He began to warm to the idea. 'Don't you see, Dr Forman? It might work, and there could be other people back in London who'd be prepared to back him up.'

'Like Robert Greene and Emma Ball,' Tom agreed. 'Simon told us last night that Robert's suggested Parsons might well have owed money in a gaming house or stolen someone's mistress.'

'A drunken poet and a whore?' Dick sounded doubtful. 'That's how the court would see them.'

'Then there's Lane's older brother. You missed that too, Dick. Apparently the man's a customs officer from Gloucester and he's been in London making enquiries about his brother's death, vowing to discover whether or not it really was an accident. But I don't see it helping Charles, at least not in time, do you, Simon?' He put his hand on Dick Marsh's arm. 'Tell us truly, Dick, for this is a matter of life and death: do you think it possible in your heart of hearts that Charles did kill Nathan Parsons?'

Dick said nothing for a little while, then he slowly nodded his head. 'I think, if driven to extremes and in a highly emotional state . . .' He paused again. 'Then I suppose the answer has to be "yes". In certain circumstances. If he was drunk. If provoked beyond endurance.'

'Did he drink a good deal when he was with you?' Tom asked Simon.

'No. After I'd prevented him trying to go back into the Theatre, we went into a tavern and he had a quart of ale, as did I. Then we walked down to St Paul's and across London Bridge, by which time he was almost back to normal and what seemed uppermost in his mind was his assignation with his Fair Iseult. He'd agreed to leave any dealings with Parsons until the next day.'

Dick gave this some thought before answering. 'But suppose Charles went off by himself after you left him, Dr Forman, and began brooding on it all over again, and started drinking until his temper was roused and then decided to seek out Parsons at all costs and settle with him once and for all. Possibly he even thought he could resolve the matter and still come to the supper party. But time went on and he didn't find Parsons until late in the evening.'

Simon looked at him in surprise. 'But he told me that he met you before that on the Bankside on the way to change his clothes and that as time was getting on, you told him you'd see him at Mary Goodman's house and that's what he did. Are you saying now that you didn't see him earlier either?'

'Certainly I saw him *then*,' replied Dick without hesitation, 'but surely that's of little use? He seemed in an odd and bitter mood, said little of what had happened that afternoon other than that he wanted to get his own back on Parsons. I told him to shake himself out of it and come and enjoy the supper party he had looked forward to so eagerly.'

'But why on earth should Parsons be at the Rose that night?'

'I don't know,' Dick admitted, 'but for one reason or another he was there and the two met.'

Tom looked exasperated. 'But if they'd fought over the stolen script then there would have been clear evidence of a fight; so we're back again to a stab in the back!'

'Suppose Parsons said something a great deal worse than merely denying he'd stolen Charles's play,' Dick insisted. 'Suppose he told Charles the idea for the play wasn't the only thing they had in common, that the inspiration for them both had been the same Fair Iseult? That Audrey was now his mistress, and how they'd laughed at him and his play even as they lay together in bed. I think that would have been enough to drive Charles over the edge.'

Dick's words were very persuasive; the theory had the awful ring of truth. 'Would he have suspected her of such a thing?' asked Simon.

'I think he might have done. He was mad for love of her and desperately jealous. She meant more to him even than his play, and certainly more than me!' Dick sounded rueful. 'Whether or not she was worthy of such a grand passion I can't say, as I'd no opportunity to find out.'

'I shouldn't imagine so,' responded Simon drily. 'From what Jenny said she's an empty-headed doll who thrives on flattery.'

'What are you going to do now?' Tom asked Simon.

Simon shook his head. 'Leave as soon as we can. Accept Jack Washfield's offer and take him back to London with me, though what Ned Alleyn and Will Miller will say when I tell them I want to remove a different actor I can't think, or what I do if Charles persists in sticking to his story and refuses to admit he killed Parsons even under provocation.'

'And if he agrees to what you say?' asked Tom.

'Then he will have to throw himself on the mercy of the court, and hope the judge will accept benefit of clergy and the neck verse.[1]

---

[1]Those sentenced to be hanged could sometimes get off by pleading 'benefit of clergy' and reciting what was known as 'the neck verse', the first verse of Psalm 51 in Latin, as it was thought that pretenders to learning might well be in holy orders and therefore could not go to the gallows. It certainly did not always work but it gave the judge an opportunity to allow a more lenient sentence at a time when so many offences carried the death penalty.

Though if the judge is determined to make an example of him, then even that won't save him from the rope.'

Dick sighed deeply and stood up. 'I must leave you. I've much to do having been away yesterday, and I'm playing King Harry this afternoon. I must thank you for all you're trying to do for Charles, Dr Forman. I don't suppose Ned and Will will let Jack go with you until after we've played at Charlecote Park, as we need everyone for *The Spanish Tragedy* and he plays a crucial role in it, but in the meantime I'll try and think of something, anything, that might help.'

He flung the door open wide and strode out, leaving them looking after him in silence, still hardly able to grasp the fact that what had seemed their only hope had come to nothing.

Meanwhile John Bradedge had done as his master asked and gone out looking for young Daniel, having been told he and a fellow apprentice had been seen walking towards a piece of common land not far from the tavern. Merry shouts led him to them, for they were busy trying their hand at archery with two ramshackle bows they had made themselves. They had also set up a rough target but were having little luck, their arrows falling far short of it. Daniel, seeing John watching, waved and called over to him. 'Do you think you could help us, Master Bradedge? We don't seem to be doing very well.'

He went over and joined them and Daniel introduced his companion as Humphrey. 'Tom took us out the other morning to the great butts on the Fletchampstead to see an archery competition,' Humphrey told John. 'It was really exciting and the archers were very good, though the old men were saying it wasn't like it used to be when every able-bodied lad had to practise archery but Tom says that was a long, long time ago, in the days of the French wars.'

'I'm afraid it's arquebuses and shot now,' John agreed. 'The old men are right, though. If you'd been a lad way back you'd not only have had to practise with the bow, I'm told young boys used to have to stand still for twenty minutes at a time with their right arms extended – so,' he said, demonstrating it, 'and holding a weight in their hands; that was to strengthen their drawing arms.'

'I'd have loved to go off and fight in the French wars,' responded Humphrey. 'Wouldn't you?' he added, turning to his companion, 'like in the play of *King Harry*.'

Daniel looked thoughtful. 'Not really. I think I like it better pretending to be doing daring things on the stage.' He grinned at John. 'What I want to be most of all is a great actor.'

'He plans to be the second Ned Alleyn!' broke in his friend, mockingly.

Daniel disagreed. 'He's too . . . too *grand*. No, I'd like to be as good as Dick Marsh. He can play anything, not just great heroes and villains, but comic parts too.'

'Dick can do no wrong where Daniel's concerned,' Humphrey told John, then returned to his previous theme. 'But it must be very exciting to be in a foreign war and come back a hero.'

'That's if you're lucky enough to come back at all,' commented John, 'and as for heroics, I fought in the wars in the Low Countries and it was a dirty, nasty business. At the end of it all you can find yourself turned off with no trade and no money even to keep yourself fed. It teaches you how to look after yourself, though, and I can still use a sword or a pistol if need be.'

The two boys were obviously deeply impressed by this military expertise and bombarded him with questions which he answered happily enough, since on the whole he liked lively young lads and was looking forward to the time when his own son would be old enough to take an interest in such things. He cast a critical eye over the two bows which the boys had made out of hazel cut from a hedge, even they not wanting to risk being caught purloining yew from a churchyard, then went and fetched some wax with which to make the thin cord they had used to string them more flexible.

After that he sat down, took out his knife and did his best to remake their primitive arrows. Finally, having done all that he could, he positioned the boys opposite their target and helped each of them to draw their bow and aim at it. This time, to the boys' delight, both arrows actually hit it and on their second attempt Humphrey, more by good luck than judgement, landed one almost in the centre.

In this relaxed mood he took them both back to the tavern and paid for bread and cheese all round. Conversation soon turned to the previous day's play in which Humphrey played a small role but Daniel had not, his part in the proceedings being to assist in making sure the props and costumes were in the right place at the right time and to help Jack Washfield into his costume and paint him with stage blood in his role as the ghost of Andrea in *The Spanish Tragedy*.

The mention of ghosts seemed to bring Daniel up short. 'Do you believe in them, Master Bradedge?' he asked.

'Well, I've never seen one myself,' answered John, cautiously, 'though there are those who say they have.'

'Do the dead walk then?' demanded Humphrey, eager to join in so ghoulish a discussion.

John had no idea where all this was leading but decided it might be useful to go on with it. 'I don't know what to make of it all,' he told them truthfully. 'We're told that when we die we go to heaven or hell, depending on how good we've been in this life, but then some say we go there straight off, while others tell us we'll sleep fast in our graves until the Day of Judgement and the Last Trump sounds to raise us up. Where that leaves those folk cut up on the battlefield or drowned at sea, I don't know.

'But as to coming back to haunt us, if the dead do walk then it must be because they can't rest as they've something important to say; like they were murdered and wanted the murderer caught, or that they did some wrong for which they want to make recompense. Then there's those who take their own lives, they're supposed to walk too which is why they're staked down and buried at the crossroads. But this is a matter for a parson, not me. Let's think of something more cheerful to talk about, shall we?'

'But suppose someone had been killed by mistake,' insisted Daniel. 'Would his ghost come back then? Suppose whoever killed them hadn't meant to, would they still want their death to be avenged?' The boy was becoming distressed, and John began to wonder if he had some real-life example in mind.

'Have you heard of such a thing, then?' he asked.

Daniel had gone pale. It seemed for a moment as if he would answer but then he shook his head miserably. 'Only in a story. It's of no matter. But it would be a fearful thing if it was true.'

A church clock struck the hour as he spoke and he jumped up immediately from the table where they had been sitting, for he was to play the part of King Harry's page that afternoon. He thanked

John for his help with the archery and for the bread and cheese and rushed off in search of Dick. Humphrey, with more time at his disposal, finished his cheese and started on an apple.

'What ails your friend?' asked John.

The boy shrugged. 'I don't know, Master Bradedge, only that ever since we left London and even before that he's not been like he used to be, all full of jokes and game for anything. I think it goes back to when Jack Lane died.'

'Did he hero-worship Jack Lane, then, as he seems to do Dick Marsh?' asked John.

'I don't think so,' the boy replied. 'He wasn't particularly nice to any of us lads. But something must have happened about that time, though I don't know what, because afterwards Daniel became terrified of that awful Nathan Parsons. Charles Spencer actually had to rescue him once when Nathan was beating him.'

John pricked up his ears. 'Did he indeed. Perhaps you'd like to tell me all about it.'

So Humphrey did. Then, having finished his apple, he got up from the bench on which he had been sitting. 'I have to go now, though I only come on in the French court and I've nothing to say, but they'll be cross if I'm not there in good time. But it's not the first time Dan's talked of ghosts and haunting and revenge. Perhaps you should ask Dick Marsh if he knows anything, since Dan talks to him more than anyone else, these days.'

John had no idea what it all added up to, as he told his master later. With time hanging on their hands, both thought they might as well see the performance of *King Harry the Fifth* and, well wrapped against a chilly wind, they were sitting on raised benches in a space outside the Guildhall where a rough stage had been erected with room in front of it for the groundlings.

Simon thanked John, telling him he'd done very well and that he'd see if Tom Pope could throw any light on the matter. The staging for the play was very primitive compared to what he was used to at the Rose, and he could see why the actors found touring so exhausting. Finally it came time to start and the audience, still chattering and winding their scarves around them, settled down for the afternoon's entertainment.

Simon was amused to see that Antony Hunt was already being made to work for his living and was playing the part he knew, that of the French dauphin. There was a round of applause and a few 'oohs' and 'aahs' when Dick Marsh strode on in the full glory of his King Harry costume, followed by his retinue of lords. In spite of all the drawbacks inherent in putting on a production virtually in the street, Simon had to admit himself enthralled by Dick's performance. Like Ned Alleyn, he had that rare ability to appear actually to become the character he was playing, so convincing the onlooker he was seeing real events. His speech to his army the night before the battle of Agincourt when he reminded them of the glories of the English bowmen at Crécy and Poitiers had the crowd roaring their approval.

It was clear the young actor had a brilliant future before him. In spite of the cold and the length of the play, he held the audience in his hand right up until the end, even though Simon thought Tom right: so grand a story deserved a better script. Particularly touching was the episode where King Harry finds his page, cruelly slaughtered by the fleeing, perfidious French. As Dick picked Daniel up in his arms and cried vengeance on the perpetrators of the crime, Simon could have sworn he had wept real tears. That particular episode always went down well with the groundlings.

Later that evening Simon and Tom were sitting together in a corner of the taproom of the Old Wall when Ned Alleyn erupted through the door followed by the bookman. His presence had an immediate effect as everyone turned and looked at him. It had been decided, he told them, that there was little point in giving another performance in Coventry the following day. Therefore, as Sir Thomas Lucy had generously offered them accommodation at Charlecote Park, they would pack up in the morning and journey the twelve or so miles in leisurely fashion. This would give them time to set up properly and possibly rehearse in the room where they were actually to play the day after. Then he looked around until his eyes lit on Simon.

'Ah, Dr Forman,' he said. 'I've a letter for you here. It was enclosed with one sent to me by Master Henslowe, who asks what you're doing and when you are to return. I'm told you now want to take Jack Washfield back with you.' He sighed with the skill he usually brought to sad roles. 'I suppose in the circumstances we must agree, though it is most unwonted.'

He handed Simon the letter, adding that he presumed that if he was intending to return to London after the performance at Charlecote, then he could explain his actions to Henslowe himself. So saying he swept out.

The letter was from Robert Greene. *I've been asking around as promised*, it began without any preamble

> at first with no great success but then Emma brought one of the Bankside whores to me who says that on the night Parsons died she saw him and another entering the Rose very late. The other man had his hat pulled well down over his face but she recognised him as an actor she'd seen at the playhouse not long before. When you are come back she is agreeable to go to the Clink with you to see if it was your young friend or another, but is not willing to do so beforehand for fear of being clapped up for whoring and thieving. She says also she saw a young lad standing close by who saw them too.
>
> I'd thought you'd be returned by now so went to your house where I found Mistress Anna in talk with a man of Kent, a customs man, desperate for your whereabouts, claiming it was a matter of life or death.

Simon groaned before going on to the final paragraph.

> If you wish for gossip they say Carey's trull, Emilia Bassano, is with child by him and to be married off. I've heard it whispered you also tickled trout in that pond. As for me, Simon, I'm in ill shape and begin to dwell on the prospect of mortality. I trust this letter will stand payment for your skills when you return.

'Well that's something, I suppose,' he said, throwing the letter across to Tom. 'Possibly this young woman can prove either way whether or not Charles was with Parsons late that night though, again, a judge might well not believe her.'

Gradually the taproom emptied until they were alone, and Simon was just preparing to leave for the Nag's Head and his bed when the door opened and a man entered. With a sinking heart, Simon saw that it was Matthew Lane.

Lane looked at him with some surprise. 'I hardly expected to find you here, Dr Forman,' he said, without any other greeting. 'You said nothing of it to me.'

'There was no reason I should,' Simon returned in some annoyance, 'not least because I had not decided then whether to leave London.' As Lane showed no sign of moving he had then, perforce, to introduce him to Tom Pope, whereupon the customs commissioner sat down and called for the sleepy tapster to bring him a glass of wine.

He was, he told the two men, lodging with a friend in Coventry and since seeing Simon had returned home to Gloucester to tell the family what he had discovered before setting forth once more in search of the Lord Admiral's Men.

Tom, ever the peacemaker, expressed his sympathy with Lane on the loss of his brother in so tragic an accident.

'If it was an accident,' he barked. 'Dr Forman already knows my views.'

'Then he will also have told you that there is no proof it was anything else but that if mischief was involved, then the most likely perpetrator was the man, Parsons, who is now himself dead.'

'And I told Dr Forman that that appeared suspiciously convenient and that I wasn't convinced. I must tell you now that, after talking the matter over with my family, I have become certain that there are those in your company who know a good deal more than they claim, and that you have among you one who could well have brought it about.'

So remarkable a statement left both men silent for a minute. Tom asked Lane what in the name of all the saints he meant by such a remark.

'I told Dr Forman that I thought I recognised, coming out of your theatre, a tinker's bastard known as Daniel Lee. One of a crew

165

of thieving ne'er-do-wells I regularly have whipped out of town, though they always seem to return. The Lees have long hated our family – we've twice laid information against them which has seen two of them hanged – and would do anything to harm us. I must insist I see him now and question him.'

'That's quite impossible. He's not here in this tavern but in other lodgings,' he lied smoothly. 'He will also be asleep as are most of our company, and I will not have him roused until the morning. No,' he continued as Lane started to interrupt, 'I'm not prepared to bandy any more words with you about it.

'I rescued Daniel myself from the hands of his tribe from whom he'd received nothing but cruelty and abuse, and he has repaid his debt by working hard and behaving well. He is most trustworthy and honest. However, if you persist in your belief and wish to question him, then come here tomorrow morning at nine o'clock.'

Lane was obviously far from satisfied but there was little else he could do in the circumstances but accept. He swallowed off his wine, grunted goodnight and left.

'What happens now?' asked Simon. 'Are you going to let him question the boy?'

'Not if I can help it. The man obviously wants to pin his brother's death on someone and it would suit him for it to be Daniel, prejudiced as he is against his family. I'll have a word with Will Miller but I know he and Ned wanted Dick to go on ahead early tomorrow morning, first to Bidford Manor to see what the owners wish us to perform for them there, then back to Stratford to the White Swan to make sure we can play in the yard, and then to see to finding lodgings for us all in the town.

'That will certainly take until it is dark, and it was already decided he could stay overnight in Stratford and come to meet us at Charlecote the following morning. I see no reason therefore why he shouldn't take Daniel with him.'

Chapter 14

The Drovers' Road

The day's events were still going round and round in his head when Simon finally went to bed, preventing him from sleeping. There seemed nowhere else to go, he thought. Single-handed and in the time available, how could he possibly come up with an alternative to Charles as the murderer of Parsons? Most damning of all now was Dick Marsh's sad refusal to perjure himself. He heard him again, his voice shaking, explaining how he couldn't lie on oath even for so dear a friend, not least because of his being a vicar's son.

A vicar's son! Simon sat bolt upright in his bed, oblivious of the snoring John Bradedge on the other side of the room. Of course! That was why the name 'Byfield' on the milestone in Southam had struck a chord in his memory as he rode past. Surely Dick had told him in the Anchor after Lane's funeral that his father was a poor parson there. It could be, of course, that Dick's family had disowned him but surely if his father was a man of God he would understand his son's dilemma and, perhaps, suggest some way round it which would not involve either outright lying or jeopardising his immortal soul. While Simon recognised that some men of the cloth led lives of blameless holiness, he was cynical enough to know that many others were less nice and were prepared to bend the rules when it suited them.

First thing in the morning he'd ask Dick if he'd mind his going to Byfield to see his father to ask him if there was some way round the impasse, some form of words Dick could swear to without perjuring himself on oath. Yes. That's what he'd do. Having made his decision he fell into a deep sleep, so deep that he awoke much later than he had intended.

But the cold light of morning brought doubts. He recalled how entertainingly Dick had spoken that day of the horror of his family when he had told them he was going to be a player, and how they had done everything in their power to prevent it. That being so, it might well be that he was now completely estranged from them and would insist Simon did no such thing. Yet some instinct drove him on. It would surely be obvious how the land lay once he had spoken to Dick's father, and it could be that by this time he was only too happy to welcome home the prodigal son, even to be proud of his talent, and so would listen sympathetically to what Simon had to say.

As it turned out the decision was out of his hands for, after stumbling out of bed and making his way over to the Old Wall, he found a scene of frantic activity as costumes were packed in baskets and props in boxes. As Tom had proposed last night, Dick had already left, bound first for Bidford, then Stratford, taking Daniel with him.

Both Ned and the bookman had been more than happy to see him go as the very last thing either wanted was more trouble dogging the Lord Admiral's Men, not least the possibility of Commissioner Lane laying a complaint against Daniel and getting the boy arrested. 'By the time Lane gets here,' affirmed Tom Pope, 'I can tell him with truth that Daniel is no longer in the town, having been sent off elsewhere without my knowledge and that I understand he has gone into, oh, Northamptonshire. I'll be quite convincing. Don't look so shocked! I am, after all, an actor!'

Simon made up his mind. He would go to Byfield. He did not, however, want to raise hopes unnecessarily and decided against telling Tom. Therefore he said only that he had bethought him of some business he might see to while in the area, and that as he could do nothing profitable that day he would take the opportunity of riding over again to Southam and that because of the distance and the now short days, he would probably put up at an inn overnight and join the company at Charlecote the following day. If Tom had any suspicions that he was not being told everything, he gave no indication of it, merely explaining to Simon exactly where Charlecote was and pointing out that he had two possible routes to it, one back through Warwick and the other west along the old Roman Fosse Way.

It was a fine crisp morning with a hint of frost in the air as Simon rode out of Coventry. He rode easily through lush farming country and woodland where the sun turned the falling leaves to bright gold. Small villages and hamlets dotted the landscape, while set back from the road lodge gates led up to fine timbered or brick mansions, the homes of the landed gentry. As he drew nearer to Southam the land opened out under wider skies and the cottages by the roadside changed under their thatched roofs from limewashed lath and plaster to honey-coloured stone. It was a countryside at peace.

In Southam he stopped for refreshment, enquired the way to Byfield and was directed to the old drovers' road from Wales where it snaked its way through the outskirts of the town on its way east. He followed its track, straight as a die until it reached the village of Priors Marston, where it coiled around the church and a group of cottages, congratulating himself on the ease of his journey. It was about a mile the other side of the village that his horse suddenly went lame. Swearing, he got down to inspect the damage: the mare had cast a shoe. He had seen no smithy in Priors Marston and had no way of knowing whether or not he would find one in Byfield. As he stood helplessly by the side of the road wondering what to do next, he heard the sound of cartwheels and from a narrow lane a cart rumbled out driven by a red-faced man who, from his dress, was likely to be a farmer.

The man pulled up on seeing Simon. 'Trouble?' he enquired.

'My mare's cast a shoe,' Simon told him. 'I'm on my way to Byfield, is there a smithy there?'

'There is,' the man replied, much to Simon's relief. 'And I'm bound for Byfield. If you'd like to hitch your mare to the cart you can travel with me. It'll save you having to walk her the best part of four miles. Joe Jenkins'll see you right, he's a good smith.' Thankfully Simon joined the farmer in his cart and the two chatted comfortably together as they went along. The farmer expressed some surprise at finding a London doctor on the drovers' road, so Simon explained that he had been on business in Coventry and was on his way to Byfield to pay his respects to the local parson on behalf of mutual friends. 'I hear he's a good man,' the farmer commented, 'though we go to church back there in the village ourselves.'

They trundled into Byfield down a narrow road which led past a substantial stone church, then along a lane of stone cottages and an attractive inn to the smithy, where the farmer helped Simon unhitch his horse. Simon was surprised at both the size of the church and the comfortable dwellings having imagined, from Dick's description of the poverty of his family, that Byfield would have been no more than a collection of hovels with a small and run-down church. His rescuer seemed in no great hurry to leave, greeted the smith as an old friend and explained what had happened. They were fortunate, for the smith had no immediately pressing business and agreed to shoe the mare straight away.

'It's as well you met with Harry there,' he said, motioning towards the farmer. 'This way at least she hasn't gone permanently lame on you.' He seemed a merry fellow, whistling while he worked, and he soon had the forge glowing red and the metal ready for the shoe. Popular mythology would have it that all smiths were good-natured and all millers mean and dismal and Simon, watching him working expertly at his trade, wondered if it was indeed true and if so, whether the reason for it was because smiths worked in the warmth and had a steady stream of grateful customers, while millers lived and worked in the damp, never out of the sound of water, permanently covered in dust and with customers who endlessly complained about the cost of flour and its milling. Perhaps the fact that smiths could hammer their bad temper out on pieces of metal also helped keep them equable.

'Dr Forman here has come to see the parson,' the farmer informed the smith.

The smith began hammering the red-hot shoe. 'Is that right? And what do you want with him?'

'I've come to see him about his son,' Simon replied. The smith stopped what he was doing and both he and the farmer stared at Simon open-mouthed. Simon, aware that he appeared to have said something startling, enquired what was strange about that.

The farmer began to laugh heartily. 'A *son*, you say? How about that, Joe Jenkins?' he guffawed.

The smith, also creased with mirth, wiped his eyes before returning to his hammering. 'Parson Jonas Chalenor's got six girls,' he said when he finally drew breath, 'the youngest only a babe, and a sad trial to him it's been; but never no son.'

Simon was mystified. 'Parson Chalenor? But I thought your parson's name was Marsh.' Then a thought struck him. Possibly Dick's father had retired or gone on to another living and this man had only recently come to Byfield. He cursed himself for not finding out before leaving Coventry how long it was since Dick had left home. 'So Parson Marsh was your previous parson?' he suggested.

'Parson Chalenor's been here, let's see, close on fifteen years now,' said the smith. 'The living's in the gift of the Knightleys – they're the big landowners hereabouts – and a good many of them have been rectors here, the younger sons that is. Though the last two rectors have been from outside but always gentlemen, mind. But so far as I know there's never been no Parson Marsh hereabouts, has there, Harry?'

'My family's been in these parts since before Bosworth Field when they killed King Richard,' the farmer responded, 'and I'd know if there'd ever been a Parson Marsh. I hope you've not come all this way from London expecting to find him here,' he added.

The smith fetched Simon's horse over and began to put on the shoe. Simon was once more at a loss about what to think. 'I must have misheard what was I told,' he said finally, 'but I met a young man in London by the name of Marsh and I could've sworn he told me he was the son of the parson of Byfield in Northamptonshire. Is there another village of that name?'

The men shook their heads, and then a sudden thought struck the farmer. 'Marsh, you say? What's the lad's name?'

'Richard,' said Simon, 'Richard or Dick Marsh. He's a player in the acting company of the Lord Admiral's Men.'

The smith looked up from what he was doing. 'Dick Marsh? I wonder . . . what's he like?'

'Very handsome. Dark hair, blue eyes, most lively. And talented. A good voice, too.'

The smith finished his task, stood up and wiped his brow. 'Could it be now . . . Harry, didn't Sara Marsh call one of her children

Dick? You know, Sara out on the Boddington Road.'

'She might well've done,' replied Harry with a laugh. 'She's enough of them, and like as not every one by a different father. Come to think of it, you're right. I reckon the first or second boy was called Dick. But, dang me, I doubt as his father was a Byfield parson or anyone else's parson for that matter! Sara's always gone with the drovers, ever since her old father died and left her alone in that cottage. She never married,' he explained. 'You see, she'd never got no looks even before she got marked by the smallpox, and she was ever a slattern.

'But then the men from Wales and Hereford aren't particularly fussy when they get up here for a couple of days' rest with money in their pockets and ale in their bellies. Yes, I reckon that might well be her boy. Like as not he didn't want to say he was a bastard who doesn't know who his own father was, and I doubt Sara can remember. He's had you on, Doctor.'

'Can't say as I blame him,' said the smith as he checked the fit of the shoe. 'Did he know you were coming out this way looking for his supposed dad?'

'No, he didn't.' Simon was beginning to feel tired. It was now well into the afternoon and would soon be dark. 'No,' he repeated, 'it's my own fault. I'm a fool for not checking with him first. But he sounded so convincing.'

'Well you said he was a player and a good one at that,' commented the smith. 'Reckon he could play the parson's son as well as anything else.' He stopped short. 'Is he in any trouble?'

'Not that I'm aware of. A friend of his is, though, and it was on his behalf that I came seeking Dick's supposed father. I've obviously wasted my time and that's something I'm very short of.' Simon felt in his pocket, brought out some coins, asked the smith the cost of his labour and then thanked him gratefully as he paid him. The smith took the money. 'Now you've come all this way, why don't you go and see Sara yourself? She's only a mile or two the other side of the drovers' road.' Why not, thought Simon, I've nothing to lose now.

He left the farmer and the smith still deep in conversation. No doubt they would amuse their friends for weeks with the story of the London doctor who came all the way to Byfield in search of a parson who didn't exist. Twenty minutes later he was outside Sara Marsh's cottage, which lived up to the graphic description of it the two men had given him before he rode away. There were holes in the thatch and what passed for a garden outside was covered in rubbish of various sorts. A pig scratched at the back, churning the ground into mud, and an evil-smelling midden stood almost on top of the front step. He alighted from his horse, tied it to a tree and knocked on the door.

The woman who opened must have been in her forties as she was suckling a baby, though she looked older. She was, to say the least, unprepossessing. Her greying hair was lank and straggly; her face, as he'd been told, pock-marked. She had lost many of her teeth. She looked Simon up and down. 'Well?' she asked. 'What do you want?'

Simon hoped she didn't take him for a prospective customer. From what he could see of the interior of the cottage it was both dark and filthy.

'Do you have a son called Richard?' he enquired. 'A player with the Lord Admiral's Men?'

'What do you want to know for?' she asked, belligerently.

'Well, have you?' he reiterated.

She swapped the baby to the other breast. 'I might have. What's he done?'

'Nothing wrong. I came here on behalf of a friend of his.'

She motioned towards the room behind her. 'You'd best come in then, though I'm not saying your man's any son of mine.' The inside of the single-roomed dwelling was in an appalling state. A cooking pot simmered over a hearth scattered with turnip peelings and bits of old bones which were being gnawed by a mangy dog. A noise from a corner of the room made him turn his head to see a child of about three sitting on the floor. She was undersized, pale-faced and dirty. Sweet Jesus, thought Simon, no wonder Dick Marsh wanted to forget about all this. In another corner of the room was a rough bed heaped with old blankets. The drovers must be desperate indeed if this was what they spent their money on after trudging all the way from the Welsh marches.

She followed his glance as if she knew what he was thinking. 'It wasn't always like this,' she said shortly, 'and I was younger then. This,' she joggled the baby, 'was a mishap when old Todger Banks from Byfield called in here on his way home from the Mop Fair, and she's my daughter's child,' she said, pointing to the little girl. 'So what's he like, this lad you say's my son, and why are you here?'

'He's a very good-looking young man,' Simon told her, 'dark-haired and blue-eyed. He's also quick-witted and has a way with words.'

'That sounds like Dick,' she agreed.

'As to why I'm here, it's to do with a friend of his.' He wasn't quite sure how to broach the subject but finally plunged in. She heard it out in silence. 'From what your son said I had thought him to be the local parson's son – his legitimate son, that is,' he concluded.

The woman broke into a peal of laughter. 'The parson, come to me? Dick must be all of twenty-four by now and that'd make the parson back then one of the Knightleys. Landed gentry, they are. They'd have me turned out for a whore or a witch if they could. So that's what Dick told you, was it? Well, I can't say as I'm surprised. He always was a liar, right from a little child. Could convince anyone. I used to think that in the end he actually believed what he was saying was true. I might not be much to look at, never was,' she continued, 'but I'm not stupid. It caused much trouble in the end – folks never knew where they were with him.

'It was the same when he went to be a player. One of the playing companies came to Daventry and he and a friend went to see if they might be taken on. It seems they wanted his friend but at the end of the day it was Dick that went. I've never found out why, as he's not been home since.'

'Didn't you see him when the company was in Southam last week then?' asked Simon.

'I didn't know they were. Living out here I don't hear much. So he was with them, was he? Fancy that – and never came to see his own mother. Well, that's Dick for you. Now are you going to tell me what you want or not? I don't feel like standing here all day.'

So Simon explained to her how Charles's life hung on Dick's confirming that the two young men had been together when a murder was committed, and how Dick swore that this hadn't been the case and that the other two possible witnesses said the same.

'If that's so and there's two other people saying the same thing then he might well be telling the truth,' she said after giving it some thought. 'Further than that I can't help you. But bear in mind what I've said. Unless he's changed a good deal since he left here, he's one of the best liars you'll ever come across – just like his father before him.'

'Who *was* his father?' asked Simon, somewhat surprised she knew in view of her reputation.

'Hywel Ap Evans, he called himself. A drover from Wales. He was handsome too, a lovely man and generous with it. He came here every time he was passing through for going on four years. He kept promising me he'd marry me, told me he was really landed gentry fallen on hard times and that he'd a great house somewhere on the border and that I'd be mistress of it one day.' For the first time her face softened. 'When he knew I was with child and it was most likely his, he said he'd marry me as soon as the child was born and take me back to Wales with him. I never saw him again. Later one of the other drovers told me he'd a wife and four children back home and was in prison for killing a man in a drunken brawl, and that it was a miracle he'd escaped hanging. Is that enough for you?'

Simon thanked her and pressed a coin into her hand. 'That's for your help.' He looked again at the small child who was struggling round the room on unsteady, bandy legs. 'If I'd the remedy on me, I'd give you something for the rickets,' he told her. 'But if you've any skill at all in these matters, take three handfuls of the hart's tongue plant from a hedgerow and mix it with a small handful of bugloss, some capers (if you have them) and a good handful of hops.' He gave her another coin. 'Use that to buy some honey. Then boil it all up in water until you have a syrup and give the child a spoonful each day. It's too late now to stop it altogether, but it might help.'

'Who are you?' she asked, now curious.

'My name's Simon Forman. I'm a physician. Thank you again. I must be on my way, I need to find lodgings before nightfall.'

On the way back to Southam he had to make way for a drover driving a small number of cattle before him. Simon greeted him, calling out and asking him where he came from. The man replied that he was from Monnington near the English border and that they were on their way south.

'Is it worth your while to travel such a long way?' Simon queried, looking at the cattle who were lean from their journey. The drover assured him that it was, and that when they reached the villages on the outskirts of London he would pasture the animals for a short while to fatten them up before taking them in to sell as there was always good money for cattle midwinter; and with that he strode off after wishing Simon Godspeed. The brightness had gone from the sky and already it was growing towards dusk. Simon watched the drover disappear into the distance in search of a place to camp out with his cattle for the night. Such a one had been father to Dick Marsh.

Chapter 15

Lucy's Mill

Commissioner of Customs Matthew Lane arrived promptly at the Old Wall Tavern at nine o'clock, shortly after Simon had left for Byfield. As Tom had warned all the senior members of the company of his previous visit, and that there was the possibility of trouble, both Ned Alleyn and Will Miller were present when the news was broken to Lane that Daniel Lee was no longer in Coventry. He exploded with rage, accusing Tom of deliberately setting out to deceive him.

Will Miller intervened. 'The rest of us knew nothing of the arrangement, Master Lane,' he said, 'since most of us were abed when you paid your visit last night.' This was strictly true, although Tom had in fact roused the bookman who had agreed Daniel was best got out of the way.

'So where is he?' demanded Lane.

'Out with one of our company making arrangements for the rest of our tour. They could be in any one of a number of places,' the bookman replied, 'with instructions to cover the ground as quickly as possible since we are playing at the home of Sir Thomas Lucy of Charlecote tomorrow evening.' Miller felt fairly safe in saying this as it was unlikely even a customs commissioner with a grievance would insist on marching into such a house and seizing the boy in front of the wealthy and influential Sir Thomas and his guests.

'We are thinking of going into Oxfordshire,' added Tom, carefully avoiding the eyes of his colleagues, 'possibly even as far as Banbury.' Reflection had caused him to conclude that Northampton, which was in the opposite direction to where the company were to play the following day, might seem too unlikely a destination.

'I see,' raged Lane, 'that I've been made a gull by a crew of common players!'

Alleyn had been standing looking on in his usual aloof fashion, saying nothing – no doubt, thought Tom, considering himself to be above such unpleasantness but Lane's comment was as a red rag to a bull to a man who considered himself head and shoulders above the usual run of actors. It was fair to say that this was a view shared by most of his public (which explained his enormous popularity), even those who thought young Dick Burbage was rapidly catching up. Off stage, Alleyn lived like a gentleman and behaved like one.

'You demean your calling, Master Lane,' he boomed in his grandest voice. 'The days are long gone when those who professed the craft of acting were considered no better than rogues and sturdy beggars. We are the Lord Admiral's Men, the company of the Lord Admiral of England. The death of your brother, for which members of our company have already expressed regret, was considered by a properly convened coroner's inquest to be the result of a tragic accident. I am prepared to go so far as to say that it might have included carelessness on the part of some unknown person but that is by no means certain.

'However, sad as your loss is, it does not give you the right to demand that we hand over to you one of our properly bound apprentices for whom we are responsible. We are well aware of the boy's background, and no doubt the tribe from which he came is everything you have described to Thomas Pope. But Daniel is with us because he wished to put his previous life behind him and we are glad to have been able to give him the opportunity to do so,' he continued, blandly ignoring his own original opposition to taking the boy. 'Since when he's given us no cause for concern. The fact that he is apprenticed to the company and was in the performance during which your brother died is no more than a coincidence.'

Lane's face went an even darker shade of red than could be thought possible. 'I am,' he said through clenched teeth, 'one of the most respected men in the city of Gloucester; my family owns much land in and around the city. I am not prepared to let the matter lie.'

'Then you must seek to take it further by proper means,' replied Alleyn in his most autocratic manner. 'You will need to lay information before a magistrate, which means you must offer some proof to support your claim that the boy was involved in your brother's death before you bring in the law. In the meantime no doubt you have much to attend to regarding the import of goods at the port of Gloucester, and I suggest you return there and see to it. I know nothing of such things.' Alleyn then turned and walked out in the manner of one who has decided an audience is at an end.

Lane turned on Tom. 'Don't think I don't know when I've been made a fool of,' he threatened. 'I'll see you sorry or I'll see you in hell!'

He pushed past them and strode off out of the inn and across the yard, so blind with rage that he almost knocked over young Humphrey who was coming from the opposite direction, struggling under a pile of costumes. The two collided, Lane swore an oath and was about to knock the boy out of his way when he had an idea. Humphrey, expecting a blow any minute from so obviously enraged a gentleman, automatically ducked to one side as he apologised.

'Never mind that,' said Lane. 'Are you an apprentice with this company?' Humphrey admitted he was, apprehensive as to what his admission would bring down on him. Lane forced himself to calm down. 'You are bound for Charlecote Park, I hear.' Humphrey agreed this too. 'I see they keep you busy,' Lane continued, eyeing the pile of costumes. 'Are there no other boys to help you?'

Humphrey told him there were two and that one of them, Paul, was even now helping to pack props into boxes but his friend Dan was fortunate, indeed had all the luck, as he'd been sent off with one of the actors to see to setting up in the other places where they were to play after Charlecote.

'So where are they off to?' asked Lane. 'Banbury?'

'Oh no, that's much too far,' the boy replied confidently. 'They're going first to the manor of Bidford as we have been invited to play there, and then on to Stratford-upon-Avon to the White Swan Inn where we give our next public performances and where they're to spend the night.' Humphrey, who had been somewhat fearful of the gentleman, was very surprised to find himself warmly thanked, and even more amazed to be given a shilling.

Matthew Lane watched him depart with his pile of doublets and kirtles and rubbed his hands in satisfaction. Stratford-upon-Avon, was it? An easy day's riding with a good repast in Kenilworth or Warwick should bring him there comfortably by the evening.

Simon rode away from Byfield deep in thought. He would have to tackle Dick Marsh as to his origins but it would need some care. Would he himself, in similar circumstances, have been prepared to be honest with all and sundry had his own background been similar? Indeed, while his parents had been properly married – so far as he knew – and his family respectable if poor, he had on a number of occasions given the impression that they were other than they were, that he was a gentleman by birth not by profession.

What then must it be like to know that your mother's the village whore and your putative father a Welsh drover now sitting in a Monmouth gaol? And did this one lie throw any doubts on Dick Marsh's truthfulness in other respects? It was unlikely his mother took an unbiased view of her wandering son. Perhaps he should talk to Tom Pope first.

Enquiring in Southam as to the best way to reach Charlecote, and having been informed it would have been quicker to avoid the town altogether, his informant sent Simon off, swearing his was the shortest route. As he rode for what seemed endless hours along back lanes and byroads, the night drew in and he was thankful when the moon rose that it was full enough to light his way. None of the scattered villages through which he passed boasted any kind of hostelry, and he was seriously beginning to wonder if he would have to sleep under a hedge for the night when he saw dim lights glowing ahead. It was the village of Kineton and, praise the Lord, it had an inn. The innkeeper was hospitable and, after showing him a decent chamber in which he could spend the night, told him that Charlecote was less than two hours' ride away and he would put him on the right road the following morning.

A splendid dinner of pigeon pie washed down with good red wine and followed by cheese and fruit did much to lift his spirits. A cosy fire burned in the taproom and it was with difficulty that, tired as he was, he finally forced himself to leave its warm glow and go to bed.

He fell asleep almost at once but his dreams were uneasy. He dreamed that he was standing outside a huge maze made out of box hedges, holding Robert Greene's letter in his hand, haunted by the notion that he had been told something of note but that its significance had escaped him. It was night but the moon was full and shone as brightly as it had during his long ride from Byfield, bathing the strange, dream landscape in a harsh white light.

Then somehow, as is the way of dreams, he found himself in the middle of the maze, unable to find his way out while, always ahead of him, rode Dick Marsh on a white horse with Daniel up before him on the saddle. He kept calling out to them to wait for him but every time he tried to reach them, a new piece of hedge appeared which prevented it. Finally he found his way to the exit only to find it blocked by the figure of a man with his back to him, clad all in black.

He begged the man to turn round, and Simon saw that his face was covered by the mask used by Revenge in the company's production of *The Spanish Tragedy*. 'Who are you?' he asked in desperation, and the man pulled the mask off and it was Tom Pope, who leered at him and said as he had the previous evening: 'I am, after all, an actor, you know . . . an actor, you know . . . an actor, you know . . .'

Simon woke up with a start, his heart pounding, and gazed into the darkness as an appalling thought struck him.

The ride over to Bidford had been a most pleasant one in the fine, crisp weather. Dick, with Daniel riding pillion, easily reached the town of Kenilworth by the forenoon, splashing through the ford which ran across the narrow lane past the castle, once home to Robert Dudley, Earl of Leicester, cousin to the Queen; even, some said, her lover. Here they broke their journey at a tavern where Dick bought them pieces of pie, apples and ale.

For Daniel the trip was an unalloyed delight, coming as it did after weeks of anxiety, depression and guilt over the matter he had been unable to discuss with anyone other than Dick. That this had been compounded by subsequent events had driven him near to the edge of total despair but Dick had even been comforting about that too. Dick was unlike anyone he'd ever met. You could tell him anything, he was so understanding, and one of the reasons he was so pleased at being offered the chance of this unexpected treat was that it might give the two of them a chance properly to discuss the problem that evening well away from the rest of the company.

It therefore came as a dreadful shock when Dick, over their lunch, told him that he felt he should know, now they were safely away from Coventry, that Commissioner of Customs Matthew Lane had been asking about him, first in London, then, only the previous evening, in Coventry.

Daniel paled and almost choked on his apple.

'Don't fret,' Dick assured him cheerfully. 'He knows nothing, and while he might say much he can do little. He won't even be chasing after us since he will have been told this morning that we are elsewhere altogether. There's no need to worry about it.'

At first Daniel was doubtful but by the time they passed through Warwick, close to the lowering walls of an even greater castle, he had regained his spirits and listened with relish while Dick told him tales of the Wars of the Roses and how those who had held this very castle had been mighty men, the mightiest of them all being that Earl known as 'the Kingmaker' because of the power he had held in his own hand over the whole land. He spoke about it in such a way that Daniel could almost imagine he had been there.

They continued on, skirting Stratford, until they turned off to cross the bridge leading into the village of Welford and so along a country lane which brought them finally to Bidford and its manor. They were warmly received by the owner who, after some discussion, decided he wished for a comedy and so they settled on *Crack Me This Nut*.

Dusk was falling as they rode back over the bridge at Welford, and by the time they reached the outskirts of Stratford it was dark, a huge full moon lighting their way like a giant lamp. They mistook their road slightly, for instead of arriving in the centre of the town they found themselves riding along a road close beside the river. A rushing noise suggested a weir or a millstream and there indeed was a mill with a fine house beside it. A board outside proclaimed it 'Lucy's Mill'. Presumably, said Dick as they stopped to watch the mighty wheel turning, this must also be part of Sir Thomas Lucy's property. Next they passed the church, then a scatter of cottages before turning into a street with houses each side which led them, slightly uphill, into the market square, their horse now tired with the long ride.

Dick pointed with his whip. 'The White Swan's on the corner there. I'll settle you in the taproom, see if they can find us beds for the night and, if so, leave the horse in the stables to be fed.'

They rode into the inn yard and Dick dismounted, handed the boy down and sent him, with a pat on his backside, into the taproom telling him to order them some ale. He reappeared as the tapster set two foaming tankards on the table and they both sat in a corner and drank gratefully.

'That's settled then,' he told the boy. 'There are beds for us tonight and the inn yard is ours to use for performances for three days.' He looked round and, seeing a serving boy, asked what was for supper. Informed that there was a good rabbit stew, he ordered two portions and some more ale.

'What do you think Matthew Lane will do?' asked Daniel, remembering what had brought him there.

'There's little or nothing he can do. Rest easy. You know what I've kept telling you about what happened and your part in it. It's all in the past. Put it behind you. No one knows now except me. There's no need to go on fretting about it.'

Daniel did not seem entirely convinced but it seemed he also had another cause for concern. 'Charles Spencer, Dick. Do you think they'll really hang him?'

The actor looked grave. 'I fear so, Daniel. I think little can save him now from what he did, unless Jack Washfield manages to persuade him to change his story and plead self-defence. But I would guess that might well be a forlorn hope after so long a time pleading innocence.'

'But Charles is a good person, a *kind* person,' Daniel insisted. 'Not the sort that would strike in the dark. And Parsons was awful, you know he was.' He became quite passionate. 'You know how he threatened to tell everyone about the trapdoor even though . . .' He stopped and shuddered. 'And how Charles looked after me and would've fought Parsons when he beat me if he hadn't been stopped.'

'Did you never talk to Charles at all?' asked Dick, as the tapster put two steaming plates of rabbit stew before them.

Daniel shook his head. 'I was much too ashamed to tell him,' he replied, then, his troubles temporarily forgotten, applied himself to his supper. He was only eleven years old and it was a long time since he had eaten his piece of pie.

Dick put his hand lightly on his shoulder. 'Don't put Charles on too high a pedestal,' he told the boy. 'He's charming and amusing, I agree, and I counted myself his good friend. But I got to know him better than most and it's no good blinding yourself to the fact that he has flaws, possibly a fatal flaw. I'm afraid poor Charles was a sad liar. This is by no means the first time I've known him not to tell the truth, though before it's not been so vital.'

'You mean about where he was that night when Nathan Parsons was killed? When he said you were together all the time?'

Like most boys, information tended to go in one ear and out the other and what was retained was often muddled. The niceties of supper parties and who attended them had passed him by. What Daniel did know, however, was that there was much muttering within the company about Dick's stance on refusing to testify in court for his friend. While not dismissing the perils of committing perjury (which could mean the perjurer himself ending on the gallows if found out), the general view was that Dick could have stretched a point on this occasion with the blessing and backing of the whole company if it meant Charles's life was saved, especially as Nathan Parsons's death was considered no loss.

As if he knew what the boy was thinking, Dick sighed. 'Indeed. That's why, although my heart bleeds for him, I can't go back to London with Dr Forman and swear in court to what I know is a lie.'

'Perhaps he'll get off by reciting the neck verse,' suggested Daniel, who was well aware of such an avenue of escape, not least because his own illiterate relatives had been unable to make use of it.

'Not, I think, for premeditated murder,' Dick replied seriously. 'Killing in a rage or during a quarrel, possibly, but not in cold blood. And as I say I don't see the judge believing him now if he suddenly changes his story, not after they've heard how Parsons was found, laid out as if for a scene in a play. That must have taken a cool head and some imagination.' He finished his stew, remarked that it was good, sat back and smiled.

'So,' he continued, 'there's nothing else fretting you, apart from that old business and the fate of poor Charles? Nothing else you think I should know about?'

Daniel came to a decision. He would tell his friend the piece of information he had been holding back, fearing it might be used to send Charles to Tyburn. But if there was no help for it anyway, then he would remain silent no longer. He owed Dick Marsh that much.

'Just one thing I've known all along but didn't say anything about it before, since I thought it might make things worse but if you really think there's nothing to be done, then I'll tell you as it proves what you say: that Charles wasn't with you all that evening. He couldn't have been.'

He launched into his tale and Dick heard him out in astonishment. 'You're quite sure of that?'

'Oh yes. Quite sure. Are you pleased?' he asked anxiously.

Dick's face glowed. 'Delighted. That should stop any further talk about me – oh, yes,' he continued, 'I'm well aware what's been said.'

Happy to have been of assistance, Daniel prattled on for some time about the journey, the prospect of the performance at Charlecote the next day and a host of other things, and Dick let it flow over his head. After a few minutes he said there was something he had forgotten to tell the landlord and he would be back shortly.

Daniel sat in his corner, tired, replete and happy. Now, satisfied in the knowledge that he had truly helped his friend, he regarded the scene before him with interest. The room was busy, filled mainly with local worthies. One man, seeing the boy, asked if he and 'his brother' were staying long, as he had seen them ride in together.

'Dick's not my brother,' Daniel told him, though he was proud to be considered so close a relation. 'He's my friend and an actor in the company of the Lord Admiral's Men. I'm apprenticed to them,' he told them, adding with no small pride, 'tomorrow we are to

185

present *The Spanish Tragedy* for Sir Thomas Lucy at Charlecote, then we will play here for three days.'

From the response it was clear the company had been expected and eagerly awaited, at least by some of those present, and soon Daniel was answering questions about Edward Alleyn (was he as good as they said?), the repertoire likely to be offered and if it was true that in London there were special playhouses built for performances which held hundreds, nay, thousands of people, which gave him the opportunity to extol the glories of these wonders, especially the Rose.

'Well now,' said one of his inquisitors, 'one of our local lads – his father has a tanner's business in Henley Street – left here of a sudden some two or three years back to be a player, 'tis said with one of the travelling companies who were passing through.'

'Aye,' agreed another, 'and the town wasn't the only thing he left either. He'd a wife and three children, the youngest two of them twins barely out of long clothes. It's all fallen on his family. You don't happen to have a Will Shakespeare in your company, do you?'

Daniel shook his head. 'No. But I think there was before I was apprenticed, for we've two plays in our book chest by an actor of that name. I don't know if it is the same man but if so, then I think he's now with the Burbages' company, the Lord Chamberlain's Men,' he explained. 'Perhaps his family should send to seek him there. They're at the playhouse called the Theatre, near to Finsbury Fields.' They chatted on a little longer, then both men rose to go.

Dick seemed a long time returning, so long that Daniel finally left his seat and went out into the hallway outside to look for him. As he did so Dick came striding towards him.

'Matthew Lane is here!' he told him brusquely. 'He must somehow have found out where we are.'

'What shall I do, hide in my room?' whispered Daniel, looking round, expecting Lane to appear at any moment.

'Not yet. He's threatening to search the inn from top to bottom. Make yourself scarce outside somewhere for a little while then come round the back into the yard. I'll wait for you there and tell you when it's safe to come back in. Go on now,' he urged, and pushed him towards the inn door.

Daniel ran out into the square not knowing what to do or where to go in a town strange to him. The moon was now hidden by clouds and it was very dark. He turned blindly down into a street which had a chapel of some kind on its corner and a fine house on the other. It was then that he became convinced he was being followed. Very faintly behind he could hear footsteps. He stopped, panting for breath, and the footsteps stopped as well. When he began to run again, at a brisk trot, the footsteps also gathered speed but when he turned round he could see no one.

Quite suddenly he found himself back by the river and turned towards the church, remembering in his fear some tale he had been told that one could seek sanctuary there. The moon came out again briefly and a chill wind began to blow. He raced to the church door and clawed at it with his hands but found himself unable to open it. He looked round in desperation but could see no one; the gravestones cast shadows in the moonlight, any one of which might conceal his pursuer. He began to sob with fear.

He ran on out of the graveyard and along a path beside the river, then paused for a moment. He could no longer hear the footsteps. Perhaps they'd never existed, he thought, except in his own head. He leaned back against a tree, panting for breath, wondering whether he could safely return to the White Swan. Surely Dick would have satisfied Lane by now that he was not there. But what about the tapster, the customers in the taproom and the landlord who was giving him a bed for the night? They all knew he'd been at the inn.

He looked back at the path down which he had run and thought he saw a slight movement. No, Matthew Lane would not be waiting for him at the inn. He must have seen him leave and had followed him here. He moved away from the tree, still looking backwards down the path when, without warning, he was caught from behind and hands of iron closed round his neck. He began to choke, gasping for breath as a voice hissed in his ear: 'You tinker's bastard!'

Summoning up all his tumbling skills Daniel struggled to free himself and succeeded, by dint of kicking out behind him, to loosen the grip on his neck. As his assailant tried to regain his hold, the boy used every trick he had ever learned in frantic attempts to break loose, while all the time they were moving closer and closer to the water's edge. The moon was again behind ever-thickening cloud and it was no longer possible to see where he was. He made one final attempt, with failing strength, to wrench himself free but his legs began to slip on the wet bank and his captor, realising what was happening, kicked them from under him and before he could regain his balance, pushed him into the river with sufficient force to ensure he went into the water well away from the bank and out towards midstream.

At first the water closed over his head, then he rose to the surface. As he did so the moon suddenly came out from behind the clouds, bathing the bank in a bright white light as if it were a stage and Daniel saw his attacker's face looking down on him, not contorted with rage and vengeance but smiling as if with satisfaction.

Then, the river being full from recent rains, he was carried away downstream. He tried to swim against it but it was too strong; his legs hurt from where he had been savagely kicked and he struggled for breath as the cold water closed again over his head. He bobbed up briefly, struggling now to keep from sinking, aware of the sound of rushing water ahead of him as he was swept inexorably towards the mill-race at Lucy's Mill.

Some half an hour or so later, Dick Marsh found the inn yard empty. There was no sign of Daniel. He went through to the taproom again which was not as busy as when he had left it but there was no sign of the boy.

'Have any of you seen the lad I left in here some time ago?' Dick asked. 'The small boy dressed in green. We ate here together.'

The handful of men who had been there earlier shook their heads. One told him that the boy had got up and left a while ago. 'He said you're with the players who are coming to town the day after tomorrow.'

'That's right,' said Dick. 'Tomorrow we play for Sir Thomas Lucy at Charlecote and must make an early start. I'd best go outside and see if I can find him.' He went out of the front door of the inn and walked round the square calling out to him but there was no response and so he returned to the inn.

'I should get yourself a quart of ale and let it be,' suggested one of the taproom regulars. 'You know what boys are like, especially boys of that age. Can't sit still for five minutes and always going off when they shouldn't. It's getting late. He'll be back when he's tired and wants his bed. There's not much harm could come to him here. Tell the innkeeper, he'll keep his eyes open for him.'

So, after having a word with the innkeeper, Dick took the man's advice and sat in the taproom a while longer but then, as there was still no sign of the boy, he told the last few stragglers that he'd decided he'd best go to bed. If Daniel was still missing in the morning, then at least he would be able to look for him in the light.

But by morning Daniel still had not returned. In spite of comments from the innkeeper and the tapster that the boy had either wandered off and got lost and would eventually make his way back, or that he'd run away and there was therefore no point in looking, Dick made a sufficient fuss for the innkeeper to send the potboy and an ostler with him to scour the streets surrounding the inn but to no avail. By the time they finished it was after nine o'clock and the company would be expecting him at Sir Thomas Lucy's.

So, after asking the landlord to keep Daniel safe with him until the following day should he turn up, Dick got on his horse and set off for Charlecote.

Chapter 16

Missing

As Simon rode over to Charlecote after an early breakfast, he was still undecided as to how to proceed. If the startling notion that had come to him in the middle of the night was correct, then the only way of resolving it that he could see was to try to force the issue. Yet, now he had thought the unthinkable, he could see that there had been possible pointers all along the way. As soon as he arrived at his destination, there were questions he must ask and measures to be taken without delay.

He reached the great gates of Charlecote Park sometime after ten o'clock and, passing a servant on the drive, was directed round to the side of the house and its outbuildings where he expected to find a scene of great activity. The actors, apart from Alleyn, had been accommodated in the servants' quarters, and had been offered a large storeroom as a tiring house. But the costume baskets and prop boxes remained unpacked, stacked up immediately inside the door, while far from rehearsing for the evening's performance in the great hall, the actors stood in small groups talking dispiritedly among themselves. As Simon dismounted, John Bradedge came running up to him and took his horse.

It was clear there was something wrong. 'What's the matter?' he asked John. Before his servant could answer, a tall, important-looking personage came out of the house and went over to a knot of actors standing in the corner by the storehouse. He had the air of one who enjoys breaking bad news.

John motioned towards the man with his head. 'Sir Thomas's steward. No doubt come to tell us to pack up again. It seems we've all wasted our time coming here.'

'Why?' asked Simon, his immediate concerns put on one side for the moment.

'Because there's complete turmoil in there,' John told him. 'It seems young Master Tom, that's Sir Thomas's eldest son, has an abscess on his neck and is roaring and screaming fit to bring the house down, while the maids run round like headless chickens. No one can comfort him, not even his mother. So it's likely that Sir Thomas will say there can be no play tonight even though the performance was for the boy's birthday. It seems he's one of those spoiled lads who stay tied to their mother's apron strings and act as if they're still in long clothes!'

'Then I must see if I can help,' said Simon. 'Go and find a groom to see to my horse, will you? He had a long weary journey yesterday. Then come back here, for I've much to tell you.'

The steward was about to walk away from the dismal group of actors when Simon intervened. 'I've heard of the trouble with the boy. Is there no doctor in Stratford that can be brought in to see to the lad?'

The steward looked him up and down as if his comment was an impertinence. 'There is indeed a doctor in the town. But the boy won't have him sent for. So you will all have to pack up and go. Sir Thomas will see you're properly remunerated. I bid you good day.' It was clear he considered that to be the end of the matter.

'I am myself a physician and surgeon,' Simon insisted. 'My name is Dr Simon Forman and I practise in London. I am here because I have business with the players. Can I not look at the boy?'

The steward was somewhat mollified but remained doubtful. 'He says no doctor's going anywhere near him with a knife. Since he always gets his way, it looks as if there's nothing to be done.'

'If the boy has an abscess then it's best the poison's let out as soon as maybe, whatever the boy might do or say. If it isn't lanced, the infection will spill into the blood and then anything can happen. I've known some die of it. Is it not possible to speak to Sir Thomas Lucy himself on the matter?'

The steward thought for a moment, then grudgingly stated that he'd go and ask the master. 'Your name again is . . . ?

'Forman. Dr Simon Forman.'

The steward processed out of sight in stately fashion but within minutes was back at a brisker pace, followed a few steps behind by a florid-faced gentleman who, from his agitation, must almost certainly be Sir Thomas Lucy. He came up to Simon and, after they had greeted each other, shook his hand.

'Dr Forman? Come with me if you will, sir, and let's see if we can make the foolish boy see sense.' He looked at the actors and the carts which were still standing in the yard. 'And see these good men get refreshments,' he instructed the steward. 'It may be that the doctor here can settle matters.'

He took Simon with him into the house and by back ways brought him to a handsome chamber overlooking the park, through the door of which Simon saw a woman, presumably Lady Lucy, sniffing into her handkerchief while trying to apply herself to her embroidery frame.

'This is Dr Forman from London,' he told her. 'He came with the players and asks if he might see our son.'

Lady Lucy put down her needle. 'That's kind of you, sir, but Tom won't hear of seeing a doctor. He is quite adamant about it.'

'For that I blame you,' retorted her husband, 'You've always indulged him and danced to his every tune.' The lady shook her head and sniffed afresh.

Simon thought it time to intervene. 'As I explained to your steward, should the abscess not be properly lanced or poulticed, then it might well be that the poison within it enters the blood with unknown consequences. Let me at least try what I can. I have an instrument with me which will do the trick but could do with my usual salves and herbs.'

'We have herbs in the stillroom,' Lady Lucy told him, 'and some syrups. Oh, and some pots of a salve made with marigolds.'

'Excellent!' Simon responded. 'The very thing. Shall we see the boy then?'

They could hear the noise made by Master Tom Lucy before they reached the door of his room. He was a not unattractive child of about ten or eleven, lying on his bed and still in his nightshirt. When he saw his parents and Simon he roared loudly.

'Now, Tom, enough of that,' said his father, firmly. 'This is Dr Forman from London, who will make you better.'

'I don't want a doctor. I don't want to see any doctor,' he yelled. 'I told you I wouldn't see a doctor. I won't have it lanced.'

Simon went over to him. The abscess could clearly be seen behind his ear. He gave it a cursory glance. 'Quite right too, if you prefer to suffer.' He turned to the Lucys and caught Sir Thomas's eye. 'So that's that, sir,' he said, briskly. 'He's made his mind up. But even if he doesn't want to see the play and the great Edward Alleyn, who has come especially for his birthday, there's no reason why the rest of you shouldn't. Edward Alleyn is truly splendid in *The Spanish Tragedy*, indeed people in London flock to see him in their thousands.'

Lady Lucy was about to protest when her husband checked her. 'Of course,' said Simon, winking at Sir Thomas over his son's head, 'the poison will spread to the ear and it might well become mortified and drop off but then who needs two ears?' At this Master Tom stopped roaring and looked at Simon open-mouthed.

'What do you want to do when you're of age, young man?' Simon asked him, turning as he made for the door as if he were about to leave.

The boy sniffed. 'I want to be a great soldier.'

Simon burst out laughing. 'A soldier? *You*? Oh no, I think not. Soldiers don't make a fuss every time they take a wound. I've been one, I should know. No, no, you'd best think of some other career. A parson, perhaps?'

The boy was obviously not at all used to being spoken to in such a fashion. He ceased his crying and looked at Simon in some surprise, then asked: 'Is Ned Alleyn really as good as they say?'

'Better!' Simon confirmed.

'And the play exciting?'

'Very. There are sword fights and hangings and shootings and much mayhem.'

Master Tom came to a decision. 'Very well, Dr Forman,' he said. 'You can lance my abscess.'

'Now that's more like the way a great soldier would talk,' Simon told him, adding to his mother: 'Can you find the child's nurse or a servant to fetch the calendula[1] salve, also a bowl with water and a cloth? Meanwhile I'll go down to my pack and fetch . . . er . . . what's necessary.'

Ten minutes later the abscess was lanced with only the most modest of yells from Master Tom, the pus squeezed out and the wound dressed with calendula salve. 'Keep it open to the air,' Simon told Lady Lucy, 'and let it drain and then dry out of its own accord. You'd best get dressed, young man,' he said to the boy, 'and start to enjoy your birthday. Perhaps your parents will let you watch the actors setting up and then you can actually meet Ned Alleyn.'

He left the room and went downstairs feeling well pleased with himself, the thanks of the Lucys ringing in his ears. Then he looked grim. What was to come would be far from pleasant.

John Bradedge had been waiting for him below, and as they left the house Simon told him of the various discoveries he had made the previous day, not least the fact that Dick Marsh was no parson's son. As he himself had thought, John, when told of the actor's true parentage, opined that he could hardly be blamed for being less than frank about his origins and that it wasn't as if there was any harm in it.

'Are you going to say anything to Tom Pope?' he enquired.

Simon slowly shook his head. 'No. At least, not yet. An idea came to me in the night about which I'll tell you later. But now there are things I need to ask members of the company.'

The scene was now a busy one. A rope had been strung along the length of the storeroom and the costumes were being unpacked, shaken out and hung on it. Young Humphrey was busy unpacking props and two actors were practising a sword fight outside. Simon was looking round considering who to speak to first, when he saw Tom and hailed him.

'So,' he called out, 'all is now well. You can play tonight.'

But Tom looked far from happy. 'It seems that no sooner are we over one crisis then we find ourselves in another. It's nearly noon and Dick and Daniel haven't yet returned.'

Simon felt cold. 'When did they leave?'

[1] Marigold.

'Yesterday morning as planned. Matthew Lane returned, as he promised, but they had long gone. We told him they'd gone into Oxfordshire and could be anywhere. He knows we are to play here tonight but I thought it unlikely even he would come roaring in here demanding we hand Daniel over to him.'

'How did he take it?'

'Not well. Ned was at his grandest, especially after Lane had called us mere common players! He left making all kinds of dire threats.'

'Is it possible he's carried them out? That somehow he discovered where they were going and followed them?'

'I don't see how he could,' replied Tom, but he looked less than happy. He was about to say more when a horseman came clattering round the side of the house.

'It's Dick!' cried Tom in relief, then he saw the actor was riding alone. 'But where's Daniel?'

The sound of the horse brought the actors out from both the store and the back of the house and there was soon a hubbub at the sight of Dick on his own.

'The boy's missing,' answered Dick, gasping for breath, for he had ridden hard.

There were immediate cries of 'How?' 'Where?' 'Why?' through which cut the voice of the bookman.

'Get your breath back and tell us what happened,' he said.

'I don't know what's happened,' replied Dick, looking wretched. 'He disappeared yesterday evening. We'd eaten our supper and I left him in the taproom while I went to have a further word with the landlord. Our journey had been quite free of trouble. But as I left the room, I saw Matthew Lane. He was threatening to search the inn for Daniel, so I returned to him and told him to go outside and make himself scarce for a while.'

'But how did Matthew Lane know you would be at the White Swan?' asked Tom. 'I told him myself that you were bound for Banbury.'

There was a startled cry from behind him. 'Sweet Jesu!' said young Humphrey, his face going red. 'I think I told him. At least I told a big angry gentleman in a puce doublet where they were going.'

196

The reaction was such that Simon thought he had better do something before the assembled company fell on the hapless boy and administered summary justice. 'Tell us exactly what happened, young man. No one will be angry with you if you tell the truth.'

So Humphrey told him how he had almost run into the gentleman who had then asked him about the other apprentices, and how he had told him that Daniel was lucky to have a chance to go off in such a fashion. 'No one had said anything to me,' he said in an injured tone. 'I didn't know it was supposed to be a secret.'

'And what did he do then?' asked Simon.

'He thanked me and gave me a shilling.' Humphrey took it out of his pocket and showed it to them.

'I don't like the sound of this,' said Tom, 'I don't like it at all.' Then, to Dick, 'And did he do as you asked?'

'I saw him leave through the front door, then I went to the chamber he and I were to share together. Presumably, the innkeeper must have got rid of Lane because he never came and sought me there, and when I went back downstairs there was no sign of him. I'd told Daniel to come back and meet me in the yard but I waited and waited and he never came, so I looked again in the taproom but no one had seen him return. Then I searched the streets nearby for some time but to no avail. Eventually I considered it better to look again when it was light and so went to bed.'

'And sought him again this morning,' said Miller.

'Of course. Which is why I'm so late. The innkeeper sent an ostler and a potboy to help me but there was still no sign of him. Finally I left it with the innkeeper that if he should return to the Swan after I'd gone, he should keep him there until we arrive tomorrow. I can't see what else I could have done.'

Tom agreed. 'We can't call a halt to everything because one boy's gone off somewhere, even though the fact that Lane caught up with you is worrying. But he's an independent lad. He probably decided to go as far away from the inn as he could, then became lost in the dark and so found himself somewhere to sleep for the night, an outhouse or a barn. He'd have been tired after a long day and quite possibly slept on well into the morning, and awoke to realise you must already have gone.' But he sounded doubtful.

Dick, too, was still concerned. 'I keep thinking it's my fault,' he said.

'You did the best you could,' returned Miller. He addressed the other actors: 'We've wasted enough time already. I want everything made shipshape here, then you can begin to set up in the hall. We have the use of it until this evening.' He looked at the clock over the stables. 'It's nearly noon. We'll all meet there at half past the hour.'

The actors started to disperse. Dick, however, remained where he was.

'I suppose you're right,' he said to Tom. 'Possibly I've made too much of it. After all, Lane's hardly likely to harm him, is he? Not a man in his position.' He looked at them both.

'It has been known,' said Simon.

'I have wondered,' Dick continued, 'if he was beginning to have second thoughts about being an actor.'

'He does seem to have had something on his mind recently,' Tom agreed. 'I've had no luck in finding out what it is.'

Simon, saying John Bradedge had talked to the boy a day or so previously, called him over.

'He talked of ghosts and walking spectres,' John told them. 'Old wives' nonsense, most of it. You know how boys like to scare themselves. Nothing that made any sense.' He turned to Dick. 'The other boy said that if anyone knew what the matter was, then you would. That he talked to you more than anyone else.'

Dick shook his head. 'He talked to me of small mischiefs and how frightened he'd been of Nathan Parsons. Perhaps he thought his ghost would return, seeing as it's said that those who are murdered cannot rest until avenged. The play we are about to perform has that very plot! Oh, it's probably some small thing that only seems important: something left undone that should not have been, a wrong word here or there, perhaps being tempted into taking something he ought not to.'

Tom and the bookman agreed. It all sounded most reasonable but Simon wondered why he had a strange sense of watching a scene in a play, of having heard it all before. He wondered then whether he should voice his own misgivings but before he could decide, Humphrey came out of the house to tell the actors that the rehearsal was about to start.

'Well,' said Tom, 'I can't stand here talking any longer. I must go and rehearse. We'll talk about it later, Simon.' And with that he went away.

Dick agreed. 'That goes for me too. And I must have something to drink before I start, my throat's as dry as a desert.' He put his hand on Simon's shoulder. 'Don't worry, Dr Forman. Tom's right. I'm sure Daniel hasn't really come to any harm, you'll see. I'm making too much of it.'

They disappeared through the door and Simon stood where he was, staring after them. He'd had no opportunity to tackle Dick about his parentage but in view of what had happened it no longer seemed so pressing. He looked round for John Bradedge, who had left when the actors went into the house and after a few minutes found him in the brewery, leaning against a wall, tankard in hand, discussing the finer points of the art of brewing with the maltster.

Simon took him on one side. 'I want you to go into Stratford now and search the town for the boy, starting at the White Swan. Tell any tale you like if you think it'll help; discover if you can what Lane's movements were. I don't share Marsh's views. He must be found, if it's not already too late,' he added darkly.

'But why should anyone harm him?' asked John.

'Perhaps because he knew something he shouldn't, or because someone decided to take the law into their own hands. Either way he could be in danger.'

'And where will you be?' asked John.

'Here. I'm not going to let any of them out of my sight. And it's here too that Lane will come if he hasn't found the boy in Stratford, or wishes to cover his tracks!'

John rode into Stratford within half an hour of leaving Simon and wasted no time in setting about his search. He began by walking briskly round the middle of the town, then made his way to the White Swan.

It was market day and the taprooms and private dining rooms were crowded with people. Red-faced farmers bargained with each other loudly, banging down their quarts of ale on the table tops; old men reminisced in chimney corners, while in the smaller rooms, the farmers' wives and daughters, dressed at the very least in their second-best, chatted to each other about the ways of their menfolk and gossiped about the goings-on of their neighbours.

The tapsters were run off their feet. John bought a quart of ale and asked one of them if he remembered a young man and a boy coming in the previous evening, both of whom were members of the company of the Lord Admiral's Men but the lad shook his head. He had not worked the previous day and was interested only in trying to remember the orders shouted at him from all directions. John was just about to search out the innkeeper when a burly fellow standing behind him tapped him on the shoulder.

'A man and a boy, you say?'

John replied that was so.

The man took a swig from his tankard. 'Well there were two such in here last night. Man youngish, with black hair and blue eyes? Looks Welsh? We get many through here from the border. Lad small, with dark curly hair and brown eyes?' John nodded. 'Sounds like the two of them. You remember the two lads from the players' company, don't you, Master Quinney?' he asked the man standing crushed beside him.

Master Quinney agreed and recalled how the boy had boasted of being apprenticed to the Lord Admiral's Men. 'We asked if they knew neighbour Shakespeare's son, Will, who went off to be a player, and the boy told us he'd most likely be with – now what was the name? – Barber, Burridge? Something like that.'

'Burbage?' suggested John.

'That's it. Richard Burbage. We'd a family of Burbages once hereabouts but—'

'Well the boy's missing,' broke in John, stemming the flow of irrelevancies. 'Dick Marsh, that's the young man who was with him, says he must have run off somewhere. He spent half the night trying to find him, it seems.'

'That's boys for you,' nodded Quinney, 'always playing pranks and getting lost. He'll turn up when he's good and hungry. Now I remember once when I was but a little tacker—'

'No, wait a moment,' another man broke in. 'That's right. That young man did come back in here looking for a boy. After I'd been home, I came back for a while as old Tom Lupton from over Snitterfield brought me in a fleece for the wife, and I bought him a drink before he went home. The player came in and asked if we'd seen the lad, then went out looking for him. Not half the night, but for a while. Then he came back and said there was no point and he'd search in the morning when it was light. Talk to Sam Barber, the innkeeper. He must know about it.'

Barber, mopping his brow, was out in the kitchen directing the cook and potboys as the tapsters and serving wenches rushed in and out with orders for pies, soup, capons and bread and cheese. Yes, he told John irritably, the player had asked him to watch out for the boy and keep him there if he returned but he'd seen no sign of him. However there were now so many people coming and going he might be here for all he knew, somewhere in the crowd.

John thanked him and said there was one more thing.

'What now?' The innkeeper was rapidly losing his patience.

'Did you have a man here, a customs commissioner from Gloucester, also searching for the boy?'

'Has the world run mad?' Barber exploded. 'How many of you does it take to find one boy? As to who came looking for him last night, I don't know. I forget,' he said firmly. 'And if this is leading to some kind of trouble, then my memory's failed me altogether.' Then, calming down a little, he added, 'Come back at the end of the afternoon if you've had no luck and we'll talk of it again.'

John left him swearing at a potboy and shouting to the cook to hurry up with the capons. He left the inn and wondered where to go next, and finally turned to his left and walked down the street towards the river. He stopped a woman coming the other way and on the off chance, asked her if she'd seen a young boy on his own. 'Small, dark, dressed in green.'

She shook her head.

'What's down there?' he asked, pointing towards the river.

'A lane going back into the town and a path that goes along the river bank to Lucy's Mill. When did you lose the boy?'

201

'Last night. He was here with one of the players from the acting company.'

'Well, 'tis to be hoped he didn't wander off down there in the dark. Though it's fine and dry now, we've had much rain here lately and the path's still slippery. It's always bad down there this time of year. After the rain the river floods and leaves the banks awash with mud.'

He thanked her and continued on his way. As she said, there was a well-trodden path along the river bank and in places it was extremely muddy, flattened grass beside it showing where the river had risen above the bank. It was then he saw a splash of colour.

It was a short piece of yellow, tinselled material, the kind of thing out of which costumes were made and he could have sworn he had seen Daniel wearing it as a scarf. As he bent down to pick it up, he saw that the path had been churned up all around it by two pairs of feet, as if there had been a struggle. Worse still, there were clear marks which appeared to show that something, or someone, had gone over the bank into the river. Seriously worried now, he looked downstream, noticing how strong the current ran. He remembered the woman had mentioned there was a mill nearby.

With a sinking heart, he continued along the path and within a few minutes saw the mill, its great wheel turning, and next to it a substantial timbered dwelling. He put the scarf in his pocket, made his way to the house and knocked on the door.

It was opened to him by a pleasant-looking, youngish woman, neatly dressed in a russet gown with a white linen cap on her head. She did not have the look of a servant and was presumably the miller's wife. She looked him up and down and asked what she might do for him.

John explained that he was searching for a missing boy, having found his scarf on the river bank. He pulled it from his pocket. He was fearful, he told them, that the lad might have slipped and fallen into the river. The woman heard him out, looked at him levelly, then said only that he should wait where he was while she fetched her husband. She returned a few minutes later with a tall man who, from his dusty appearance, could only be the miller. He looked at John with deep suspicion.

'Looking for a boy, are you then? And who might you be?'

'John Bradedge. Servant to the famous Dr Simon Forman of London,' replied John promptly. 'My master's at Charlecote even now with Sir Thomas Lucy having just treated his boy for an abscess behind the ear,' he added for good measure.

'With Sir Thomas, is he?' returned the miller, scratching his head. 'Well it shouldn't be too difficult to see if that's true or not.' He turned to his wife. 'What do you think, love?'

'He doesn't fit the description, Hugh,' she said, eyeing John again. 'Reckon we might take a chance on it. You'd best come in, sir.' She opened the door to him and he followed them both into the house, down a corridor, and into a pleasant kitchen not unlike the domain of Anna back at home. A fire burned cheerfully in the large open fireplace and beside it, lying on a settle and wrapped in a blanket, was Daniel. The boy was white-faced and had a cut over his eye which had obviously only recently stopped bleeding.

'Why, Master Bradedge,' he called out in a hoarse voice. 'What are you doing here? Have you come to fetch me?'

John looked at the miller and his wife. 'How did you find him?' he asked.

'You mean *where* did we find him,' retorted the miller. 'I'd gone out the back door early to go to the mill when I saw what I thought was a bundle of wet rags lying by the gate. When I saw what it was I called to my wife and we carried him in and did our best to bring him back to life. He's quite a tale to tell.'

'What happened to you, Daniel?' John enquired, gently enough.

'He tried to kill me!' he began to sob. 'I struggled to get away and fell into the river. I thought I'd drown.' He began to shake. 'I never could swim well and the water was roaring down to the mill. I was sure I'd be swept over.'

He did his best to control the tears, then continued. At the last moment, he told John, when he'd thought all was lost, he'd been pushed up against a willow branch and had grabbed it and hung on for dear life. With great difficulty he'd managed to haul himself up, hand over hand, until he was out of the current, terrified all the time that it would tear away and break. Finally he reached shallower water and managed to crawl up the bank and on to dry land.

He'd seen the lights of the mill-house and tried to walk towards them but was so weak and cold that he'd kept falling over, on one occasion hitting his head on a large stone. He didn't remember much of what happened next but thought he'd reached a gateway. Then he knew nothing until he woke up in the warm kitchen with the miller's wife trying to force sips of cordial down him.

It seemed an almost unbelievable tale. 'You're quite sure of all this?' asked John when he came to the end of it.

'He's telling the truth all right,' said the miller's wife. 'Look at this.' Gently she pulled the blanket away from the boy's throat. Purple bruises, the width of fingers, stood out on each side of his swollen neck.

'God's blood!' roared John. 'What a scoundrel!'

'Indeed,' the miller agreed. 'The boy was as nearly killed as makes no matter. Whoever did this deserves to be hanged.'

'And possibly for more than that,' responded John, grimly. It was now well into the afternoon. The performance of *The Spanish Tragedy* was due to take place in the early evening, followed by a festive meal. And tomorrow, Simon had planned to leave for London at first light.

'If you're agreeable,' said John, 'I'd be grateful if we could remain with you a little while longer to rest the boy. Then I'll take him back to Charlecote and we'll see if we can get justice done.'

'Sir Thomas is himself a Justice of the Peace,' said the miller, 'and so you can turn to him. I must get back to work but you're welcome to stay as long as necessary. My wife will give you hospitality. Perhaps you can tell her what this has all been about. But it seems the lad crossed a rare villain!'

Chapter 17

Trapped

'I set the trap, he breaks the worthless twigs . . .
                    The Spanish Tragedy, Act III sc. 4

Dusk had fallen by the time John and Daniel left Lucy's Mill, the miller's wife reluctant to let the boy go. She too, she told them, would have had a boy of that age but he'd died of the plague when he was five, and although she had two small daughters she did not know if God would bless her with another son. It was, therefore, dark when they reached Charlecote, which was what John had planned. Lifting the boy down from the horse, he bade him stand out of sight behind a bush while he found out what was happening.

A busy servant rushing hither and thither with dishes of dainties told him the play was soon to start, and that Dr Forman was in the hall with the actors. He asked her if she would kindly ask him to step outside as his servant had an urgent message for him.

'Well?' asked Simon, as he came out to him. 'Did you find him?'

'I did,' replied John.

'I'll go and tell Tom Pope,' said Simon.

John grabbed his arm. 'I think you'd better come with me and find out what happened first. There's been real evil afoot, it's a mercy the boy isn't dead!' Without saying any more he led Simon to where he had left Daniel, still shivering with shock and fear, his face very white.

'He needs to be put somewhere warm, where he can be concealed and is safe,' John told him, and after some discussion they decided to take the boy to the stillroom where Simon had found the calendula salve. The boy was then sat on a stool, still wrapped in the blanket given him by the miller's wife.

'What happened, lad?' asked Simon, gently.

Daniel pulled back his collar and showed him the livid marks on his neck. 'God's blood!' exclaimed Simon. 'Who did this?'

John told him. 'That bastard,' he raged, 'first he tried to strangle the boy and when that didn't succeed, he pushed him into the river above the mill-race assuming he'd drown. It's a miracle the boy managed to hang on to the branch of a tree and then crawl up the bank. By the time the miller found him he was almost gone.'

'But why?' asked Simon. 'Why did he do this to you?'

'I don't know,' Daniel replied. 'I've gone over and over it again in my head. *I don't know*! As he pushed me in he called me a "tinker's bastard". Surely that can't have been the reason, can it?' Then he stopped and his eyes filled with tears. 'Perhaps he thought I deserved it, that it was right I was punished. I've thought about it for weeks, I know what I did was wrong.'

'What do you mean, what are you talking about?' asked Simon.

Daniel swallowed. 'You see,' he began, starting to cry, 'you see, *I* killed Jack Lane.'

The two men looked at him open-mouthed. Simon took a deep breath. 'I think you'd better tell us everything,' he said. 'Nobody's going to hurt you, just tell us the truth. I think there must be more to it than that.'

So Daniel embarked on his story. How the actor had lost no opportunity to be unpleasant to him when he realised that he was a member of the notorious tinkers' tribe from Gloucester, finding fault with everything he did and slapping and cuffing him when nobody was by.

'He also called me "the tinker's bastard". He'd come into the theatre and shout out, "Where's the thieving tinker's bastard?"' Daniel hadn't liked Nathan Parsons much either when he'd been in the company but had kept out of his way and had little to do with him. At first Parsons and Lane had appeared the best of friends but later they'd quarrelled, Parsons blaming Lane for getting him dismissed from the company.

But before he left, Parsons had somehow managed to get hold of the key to the door of the Rose and have it copied. So it was that on the day of the first performance of *The Old Wife's Tale* he entered the theatre without difficulty during the morning and watched with interest as the company practised using the new trapdoor.

'He found me on my own and said he wanted to play a trick on Jack Lane and would I help him. Then he said what it was. He asked me if I thought I could let the trapdoor down before Jack jumped into his grave so that he'd fall much further than he thought he would.' He sighed, heavily. 'I know now that it was foolish and wrong but he made me think it was only a jest. He said the drop wouldn't be enough to do any real harm but it would teach him a lesson.'

Simon looked grave. 'So you let the trapdoor down. What about the mattress?'

'I left it on when I let the door down, I'll swear to that. Someone else must have moved it.' He paused. 'That means someone else must have know what was going to happen, doesn't it? And made it worse.' He started to cry again. 'No one's going to believe me, are they?'

'What happened next?'

'You know most of it. I did what Nathan Parsons asked – there was no one about – and then went back where I was supposed to be. I really thought it was funny when he leaped backwards into the hole like he did. I never thought . . . Oh, Jesu, I *killed* him!'

'And afterwards?'

'I said to Parsons we must tell someone what we did, that it was only intended to be a jest but it went wrong. I thought he'd agree but he told me I was mad! Then he said that if I told anyone at all, he'd say he knew nothing of it, that it must have been my idea and that he was being falsely accused. He told me that I'd be *hanged*.' But in spite of that, he'd tried several times to make Parsons change his mind, the last occasion being that on which he had been rescued from a beating by Charles Spencer.

'So no one knew of this?'

'Only Dick. He said he'd keep it a secret and that no one need ever know; that it was an accident and I should think no more about it. He's always been so kind to me.'

After asking Daniel several more searching questions, Simon did his best to reassure him that matters might yet turn out for the best. Then he turned to John. 'Stay here with the boy, keep him concealed, Don't let anyone in the company know he's been found and don't let him out of your sight, whatever you do. I can take no action until after the performance.'

'You act as if you expected it all,' grumbled John. 'You might have told me.'

'I certainly didn't expect the revelation about the trapdoor. In an awful way Matthew Lane was actually right! But as for the rest, well, I began to have my suspicions some time back and by last night I was becoming certain. But I couldn't make up my mind how best to proceed, and by the time I'd reached a decision it was too late, nearly fatally too late.

'It must be time now for the play to begin and I must go, or people will become suspicious. After it's over I'll have a word with Sir Thomas and see what's best to be done. In the meantime I'll try playing the actor!'

The scene in the hall as he entered was an impressive one. A large space at one end had been cleared to become the stage and a curtain rigged across part of it to act as the discovery space, necessary for this play where a number of horrid scenes of death and torture had to be set up to be revealed as the curtain was pulled aside. In front of the acting area were glass globes containing candles. The richly dressed audience sat on chairs and benches facing the stage.

As Simon took his place at the rear of the seated guests, the noise of conversation ceased and Jack Washfield entered dressed in a shroud stained with stage blood, his face painted a greenish white, and announced himself to be the ghost of Andrea. He then proceeded to explain how he had met his death and what he wanted to do about it. Behind him stalked a figure draped in black who, at the end of Andrea's speech, turned to the audience revealing a hideous mask. It was Revenge, played, as in Simon's dream, by Tom Pope, who told the audience that he would see to it that those who caused Andrea's death would themselves die.

The grim saga of murder and revenge took its course through a succession of betrayals, hangings, stabbings, shootings and tortures, Ned Alleyn, as ever magnificent as the sorely tried Hieronimo.

Dick Marsh, however, did not seem to Simon to be as good as he usually was although the role he was playing, that of the Machiavellian Lorenzo, was one of his favourites. Presumably the events of the previous evening and the search for Daniel had affected him.

While at the Rose the play would run to its end uninterrupted, Sir Thomas had felt his guests should be offered some sustenance halfway through. Therefore, at the end of an appropriate scene, Humphrey, in his role as Lorenzo's page, came forward and informed the guests that wine and sweetmeats would now be served, after which the performance would continue.

While this was taking place, the actors retired to a small chamber which had been put aside for their use, there to wet their parched throats with ale or water, repair their make-up and, where necessary, change their costumes. As Simon entered he was hailed by both Dick and Tom.

'Any news?' asked Dick. 'Has your servant returned?'

Simon told him he had.

'And the boy? Has he found him? Or any sign of him?'

Simon heaved a sigh. 'No sign of Daniel *alive.*'

Tom looked appalled. 'Are you saying that he's dead?'

'We don't know,' said Simon. 'John went to the White Swan, of course, but he wasn't there, after which he looked all round the town and asked everyone he came across. Then, just as he was about to give up and return here, he heard a rumour that a boy's body had been taken from the river near to the mill just outside the town. He thought it too late to find out more tonight. It will fall to someone tomorrow to seek out where the body is laid and find out if it is indeed young Daniel. But I fear the worst.' At this Tom Pope gave him a most strange look, which Simon ignored. Dick, however, was quite distressed.

'How dreadful! What on earth can have happened to him? I did the best I could to keep him out of the way of Matthew Lane; he must have found him after all. I feel it's my fault, but I don't know what else I could have done.'

'Well there's nothing to be done now,' said Simon. 'We'll talk of it later. If I were you I'd say nothing until the play's over. There's nothing anyone can do now.' He rose and walked away. Tom was still staring at him, his ale almost untouched, as the actors began to line up by the door, ready to walk out to begin the second half of the play.

They swept back on to the stage, Dick and Tom with them, and Simon took up his original position again at the back of the room. For some reason, Dick seemed finally to rise to the occasion and truly shone in his role of Lorenzo. Having set up the murders of, among others, his supposed friend and the agent of one of his killings, he then turned to the audience and, with no little relish, explained what he proposed to do next. Simon had never seen him better than when he gloated to the audience afterwards at his success:

> 'I lay the plot, he prosecutes the point;
> I set the trap, he breaks the worthless twigs,
> And sees not that wherewith the bird was limed.
> Thus hopeful men that mean to hold their own,
> Must look like fowlers to their dearest friends.
> He runs to kill, who I have helped to catch,
> And no man knows it was *my* reaching fatch.[1]
> 'Tis hard to trust unto a multitude,
> Or anyone in my opinion,
> When men themselves their secrets will reveal!'

The play came to its bloody conclusion to tremendous applause. Sir Thomas Lucy rose and went over to Ned Alleyn to thank him personally for his magnificent performance. Alleyn, wiping the stage blood from his mouth on to a kerchief, thanked him as best he could as Sir Thomas told the actors that there would be food and drink for them in abundance, and that they were most welcome to mingle with his guests.

As soon as an opportunity presented itself Simon made his way towards Sir Thomas and then asked if he would be kind enough to spare him a few minutes in private. His genial host agreed, leaving his son subjecting Alleyn to an inquisition as to how he had appeared

[1] *fatch* – stratagem.

actually to tear out his own tongue and what he used for blood.

In as few words as possible Simon explained to Sir Thomas what had happened. 'But this is diabolical!' exclaimed the knight.

'And there's more evil still,' Simon told him, 'and that also of some concern. But I wonder if I question him a little later if you could be close by and listen to what he has to say? Presumably if he admits it, then he can be kept secure. I can assure you,' he added, 'that it is not usual for players to behave in such a fashion. I know many, and all decent and hard-working.'

Sir Thomas assured him there'd be no problem. 'And if it turns out to be true, I'll have him brought before me on the bench tomorrow morning and sent off to be tried at the assizes afterward,' he assured Simon. 'He can dwell on his sins in Warwick gaol.'

For a little while longer Simon possessed his soul in patience, joining in the general eating and drinking. Then he slipped out to the tiring house. He had arranged with Sir Thomas to take John and Daniel to a room away from the hall where they would be undisturbed and where Daniel could be concealed behind the long curtains that covered the window and where there was a door to an inner chamber in which Sir Thomas could conceal himself until needed. After seeing them safely bestowed, Simon waited until Sir Thomas was free for a moment then nodded at him to indicate that all had been set up. Then he went and sought out first Tom, then Dick, telling them that he had urgent business with them if they would come with him for a few minutes.

Daniel had been distressed and frightened at the prospect in store, but Simon had reassured him. 'You've nothing to fear. John and I will be there and Sir Thomas will be listening outside the door. It'll soon be over.'

Tom Pope still looked uneasy but Dick was glowing with a heady mixture of success, good red wine and the compliments, and overt glances of interest, from several of the good-looking young women present. But he sobered once they were alone in the room.

'Do you have firm news then?' asked Tom.

'It seems the boy somehow fell into the river,' replied Simon in his gravest manner. 'He was found by the miller early this morning.'

'Sweet Jesu!' exclaimed Dick. 'How could that be?'

'I was rather hoping you might be able to tell us that,' said Simon.

Dick looked bewildered. 'I don't see how I can help you. As I told you last night, I never saw him again after he left the White Swan. That's why I spent so long looking for him. I thought I'd looked everywhere; I even went as far as the river bank by the new bridge, though not as far along as the mill – we'd passed the mill on our way into town,' he explained. 'The path was quite slippery. I suppose he must have wandered down there and fallen in. Perhaps he was fooling about too near the water, as boys do.'

Tom gave Simon a startled look as realisation dawned.

'In the dark?' he demanded. 'And wandering so far afield in an unknown town? And with a special performance the next day?'

'I told you why he'd had to leave the Swan. Matthew Lane was there looking for him.'

'The innkeeper had no recollection of anyone of that name demanding to search the inn,' broke in John Bradedge. 'Or anyone else either, for that matter.'

'Then he has a poor memory,' returned Dick, heatedly. 'Or he wants no trouble. There can only be two reasons as to why Daniel ended up in the river: either he fell in by chance or he was followed down there by Lane who pushed him in.'

The other three looked at him, saying nothing.

'What is this?' he demanded. 'What are you all suggesting? That I knew all along that the boy had met with a mishap and never told you of it?'

'I think it's rather more than that,' said Simon.

'What do you mean?' Dick's face had paled. 'What I've told you is the truth.'

Simon looked at him and smiled. 'And you set great store by telling the truth, don't you? So much so that you'd let your best friend swing rather than tell a lie on his behalf. You being the son of the Byfield parson.'

'And what's that supposed to mean?'

Simon went over to him. 'I went to Byfield. I thought I might be able to persuade your "father" to help you find a way of saving your friend from the gallows without perjuring yourself. The rector of Byfield is one Jonas Chalenor and he has six daughters; but no son. I was, however, directed to your mother, Sara Marsh: the local whore who services the drovers. Your father, she told me, is in gaol somewhere on the Welsh marches, fortunate not to have been hanged.'

Dick laughed. 'So that's it! Well, do you blame me for being less than frank about my background? How many of you would like it known your mother's a whore and yourself a bastard?'

'That's quite understandable,' Simon agreed, 'but it does put something of a strain on our believing you to be the soul of honesty. And,' he continued, with a glance at Tom, 'you are, after all, *an actor*!'

'You can think what you like,' cried Dick wildly, 'but it *is* the truth. I know nothing of what happened to Daniel after he left the inn.'

Simon motioned to John who went, and, with a flourish, pulled aside the heavy curtain. As soon as the boy saw Dick he shrunk against John and hid his face in his sleeve.

'But I thought . . .' All the colour had drained from Dick's face. 'I thought . . . What kind of a black joke are you playing on me? You let me think the boy was dead when all the time he was alive. Have you run mad?'

'Tell us all again what happened, Daniel,' Simon asked the boy as gently as he could. With some sniffing and halting, his voice still hoarse from his ordeal, Daniel repeated what he had told them before. Then he turned his face to Dick, wet with tears.

'Why did you do it? Why? I admired you above all men. I'd have done anything for you.' He looked at the others. 'I'd even told him something which would help him, even though – Jesus, forgive me – it means Charles Spencer was lying.'

He was becoming desperate. 'I told you only last night that I knew you were telling the truth, Dick, when you said Charles wasn't with you all the night Parsons was killed. That he couldn't have been, for I saw you myself on the Bankside very late and you were on your own. It was after midnight for I'd heard the clock strike a good while before, and I know I should have been in bed but sometimes we boys do creep out after the old lady goes to sleep.' He turned to the other three.

'And before that I'd see Nathan Parsons outside the Rose. I didn't tell anyone I'd seen Dick because I thought it might look even worse for Charles, but Dick had been so kind to me and people were saying . . .' his voice broke. 'I thought you must have been looking for Charles so as to stop any trouble. I was only trying to help you. Why did you try to kill me? I thought you my friend.'

There was silence when he finished.

'What do you say now, Marsh?' demanded Tom.

'That the little rat's a born liar, bred as he was in a nest of liars and thieves. He's afraid of being whipped for running off and being disobedient. That's all there is to it. Drowned in the river indeed!'

'And you have no wish to change your story?' Simon enquired in a quiet voice.

'None at all. I should have left him to his fate and let Matthew Lane find him. What I've told you is the truth.'

'Ah, that word again.' Simon beckoned Daniel over, then pulled his doublet away from his neck to reveal the blue-black fingermarks. 'And these? Oh, and before you blame Matthew Lane, one of the guests here told Sir Thomas earlier this evening that they had come upon him by chance in an inn in Warwick. On his way over to Stratford yesterday a hound had run out in front of his horse and he was thrown, injuring his leg. He drew attention to himself by demanding to know the whereabouts of Charlecote Park, and whether or not he could hire a carriage to bring him over here tomorrow. I couldn't help but overhear it as I was standing close by.'

Marsh made a dive for the door. 'He did do it, he did do it!' shrieked Daniel. 'He tried to choke me to death, then he tried to drown me.'

John Bradedge jumped forward to stop Marsh leaving and the two men struggled with each other. There was the sudden flash of a knife but John was ready for it. Twisting Marsh's arm behind his back he forced him to drop it. Simon strode forward and picked it up. 'An Italian stiletto,' he remarked. 'How interesting. Later we'll see if it matches the others used in the play. But I rather think not.'

The inner door was flung open and Sir Thomas Lucy appeared with two lusty servants behind him. 'I think I've heard enough,' he said firmly. 'Bind that villain, will you. I'll deal with him in the morning.'

Dick looked from one to the other. 'You set a trap. You deliberately set out to trap me.' He seemed more concerned over the fact that he had been tricked than at the enormity of what he had done.

'If I can trespass on your patience once more,' Simon said to Sir Thomas. 'There is one other matter that must be settled and I think it best if the boy is now put somewhere comfortable, for there's no need for him to stay.'

'Let your man take him through to the kitchen,' replied Sir Thomas. 'Tell the cook to give him something to eat and drink and to have a bed found him for the night. Now,' he added as John and Daniel left, 'tell me of this other matter as briefly as you can, for I must get back to my guests. They'll be wondering what's happened to me.'

As succinctly as he could Simon explained why he had left London in the first place; of the plight of Charles Spencer and how he had journeyed to fetch Dick Marsh back to London to support his friend's claim that he could not have murdered Nathan Parsons, as the two had been in each other's company all night long. How Marsh had refused to do so on the grounds that he had not seen his friend at all that evening, and to say otherwise would be to perjure himself. That too was a lie. It seemed certain he'd killed Parsons himself and was perfectly prepared to see his friend go to the gallows for him.

'Trying to murder the boy because he saw you on your own late that night would have done you no good, Marsh, since there's now another witness who will swear she saw you outside the Rose with Parsons after midnight,' Simon informed him.

'Have you told Sir Thomas that little runt of a boy is also a killer?' sneered Marsh.

'I shall tell him that Parsons persuaded a young and naive lad to help him play a practical joke on Jack Lane, a joke that went tragically wrong, and that when the boy begged Parsons to come with him and tell the truth, Parsons refused, saying he would put all the blame on him. Daniel's guilty only of having played a part in someone else's mischief with consequences even Parsons, stupid and jealous as he was, couldn't have foreseen.'

Dick Marsh continued to smile. Simon looked at his handsome, confident face and felt anger rising within him. 'You can stand there so calmly, after trying to murder a child, and show so little feeling? Not to mention letting your best friend *hang* for you!'

It was then that Dick Marsh made a fatal mistake. 'It was better him than me. He's a run-of-the-mill actor and an excruciatingly bad playwright. His death would be no real loss to the theatre. But I have real talent, would have ranked equal with Alleyn and Burbage. And by killing Parsons I did you all a favour.'

He could say nothing more for Tom Pope, who had watched throughout almost in silence, strode over to him, grasped him by his doublet and shook him like a doll. He might have done worse had Sir Thomas not intervened.

'You're all fools, nothing but a pack of fools,' shouted Marsh, throwing all caution to the winds. 'How I've enjoyed playing with you all! It wasn't Parsons who stole the playscripts, it was me. I passed them on to him. It wasn't difficult as I stole one of the keys to the bookman's box. I could take out what I liked, when I liked and copy it. As you know, companies pay well for plays. It was easier still with the dreadful *Tragical History of King Mark*, of course – I could copy or steal pages of it while Charles was working on his mighty opus in our shared lodgings.

'Charles brought it all on himself, creating such a great fuss at the Theatre. Even Nathan Parsons wanted no more after that. After the performance, the Burbages told him that unless he could prove beyond a shadow of doubt that he was not responsible for stealing the script he'd brought them, he would be dismissed from the company and that they'd do their best to see he'd never work for anyone else ever again.'

'So he arranged to meet you later that night?' said Tom.

'I didn't intend to kill him,' Marsh continued as if he were discussing some minor matter. 'We met at the Rose and went in. You'd best see to your locks, Tom Pope, for *he* had a key to the theatre! I tried to pacify him, he refused to listen and then he went for me and we duelled there on the dark stage. It was him or me, so

I drew my knife and killed him.'

'And then laid him out in the obscene way you did?' asked Tom.

'Obscene? Hardly. I gave him what he wanted, centre stage in a tragedy of his own making.'

'There was no fight,' said Simon, wearily, 'no duel with knives. Parsons was unarmed.'

'Take him down to the cellars and keep him secure,' said Sir Thomas to his servants.

Tom still looked mystified. 'But *why* did you want to fool us? To make trouble by stealing scripts, to set one of us against another, do all that you did?' he asked as Marsh was dragged away.

Marsh flashed his brilliant smile, then shrugged. 'I am what I am. What you know, you know. You won't hang me,' he said. 'I'll claim benefit of clergy. I know the neck verse.'

'The neck verse will not save you,' responded Sir Thomas, sternly. 'In these parts we are without pity for those who seek to murder children. You'll not live to hang at Tyburn. You'll hang here in Warwick!'

'What is it the Bible tells us?' enquired Simon. 'That any who should cause offence to such little ones, it were better a millstone were hanged around his neck and he were drowned in the depth of the seas.'

Chapter 18

Dark Angel

Simon and John left Stratford mid-morning the next day, planning to stop overnight in the city of Oxford. Sir Thomas Lucy's man, bearing his letter to the relevant authorities clearing Charles Spencer of Parsons's murder and declaring himself a witness to the confession of Dick Marsh, had already gone on ahead; by changing horses on the way, he was expecting to arrive in London well before the other two. Marsh himself had duly been brought up before Sir Thomas in Stratford first thing in the morning, and was now in Stratford gaol waiting to be sent for trial at Warwick during the next sessions.

Left behind, the players were still in sombre mood. The crisp sunshine had gone and the weather had become overcast and cold. Shocked and saddened as they were by the recent dramatic events, it had been decided that the Lord Admiral's Men would play at Stratford, honour their obligations at Bidford Manor, then return home without further delay. Simon was taking with him a letter to Henslowe to that effect.

Once back in London they would still be expected to play at the Rose during December and January, weather permitting, but in the nature of things performances were likely to be few and far between. Surely, thought Tom Pope as, yet again, he oversaw the packing up of props and costumes before setting off for the White Swan, there must come a time and soon when there would be indoor playhouses, so that the companies might play in comfort in the winter. He was only too happy to be going home to his wife and family but while he was relieved that Dick Marsh's arrest and confession had saved Charles Spencer's life, it had left him full of unease: at one time he'd even thought Simon suspected *him* of some kind of wrongdoing.

Furthermore, standing as he was to some extent responsible for young Daniel, he had felt it keenly that it was he who had happily waved the boy off with the man who then attempted to kill him, believing he was actually keeping him out of trouble. Somehow he felt he should have known. As for Daniel himself, he was still deeply shocked, and Tom wondered if he would ever feel able to play again when everything in the Rose would remind him not only of his ordeal but of the part he played in Lane's death.

As to that matter, it had been necessary to be most circumspect where Sir Thomas was concerned, since no doubt his views on tinkers and gypsies were much in line with those of Customs Commissioner Matthew Lane. Lane, too, thought Tom, would have to be sought out and given a version of events which would persuade him not to pursue the incident any further.

The ride to Oxford gave Simon ample opportunity to go over the events of the last week. How different the outcome was from the one he'd imagined when he set off from London what seemed like weeks ago; when all he'd had to go on was his own instinct that Charles Spencer was innocent and that an injustice had been done. An evening in the city's fine Cross Inn gave him the opportunity to talk over the extraordinary series of events with John Bradedge, who had been grumbling ever since Marsh was unmasked, hurt that his master had not properly confided in him.

'I suppose you knew all along,' he groused, as they sat over their supper.

'That I did not,' Simon reassured him. 'I was enchanted the first time I met Marsh, he'd so much charm and talent. Then, it's hard to say really, he was almost too perfect, always so caring, always saying exactly the right thing. So I did wonder why he hadn't even attempted to go and see his best friend in gaol before leaving London, however urgent his business for the Lord Admiral's Men. All the way to Coventry I kept telling myself it must be because he was too upset to face seeing him in such a predicament.

'Whatever my misgivings, though, it never occurred to me that he wouldn't come back to London with us and it came as a dreadful shock when he supported the women's version of events.' He shook his head. 'He really did do it very well. He was so believable, not least his fear of perjury – which of course it would not be right to expect him to commit – but also his reiteration of it being particularly difficult for him to be anything but completely honest as he was a parson's son.

'But there were things he said that puzzled me. When we were discussing Charles's great love, Audrey, and how Jenny Pope had thought her unworthy of him and I asked Marsh what he thought about her, he claimed to have had no opportunity to find out. Yet on his own admission he'd spent an entire evening with the girl! And even though I half-accepted his denial that Charles had been at the supper party, it seemed most odd that he also claimed to have forgotten they'd met earlier that afternoon after Charles had returned from the Theatre. Especially as, if anything, it might help prove his story rather than disprove it.

'Then, in the guise of the sympathetic friend, he put up an extremely persuasive case for Charles having murdered Parsons, by coming up with a series of convincing excuses for him having done it. Yet even as my suspicions grew I kept telling myself I must be wrong.

'It was something Tom Pope said later that finally sealed it for me. It was when we were discussing how best to put Matthew Lane off pursuing Daniel. He told me frankly that he would lie to Lane as to where Marsh and the boy were going and when I looked doubtful that this would work, Tom said I needn't worry that he couldn't carry it off convincingly: that he was, after all, an actor!

'When you came to Charlecote I even thought you suspected Tom Pope,' said John. 'You seemed most strange with him.'

'Poor Tom. I must make my apologies again when next we meet. No, I never for one moment thought he had played any part in anything. It was just that I felt it best to keep everything to myself until I was ready to do something about it, and felt it better that Tom should not know what was intended rather than be forced again to make up a story.

'But right up until I reached Byfield I still believed Marsh to be the parson's son and that his father might at worst be persuaded to talk him into making some kind of statement to help his friend that didn't involve perjury, and at best make him confess to some involvement in Parsons's death. Yet even when I discovered his real parentage, I thought I must still give him the benefit of the doubt since it's likely many would lie in such circumstances. Then, that night, I had a strange dream.

'In it I heard Tom Pope once again telling me he could lie and be believed because he was, after all, an actor. I woke convinced Marsh was Parsons's murderer. If Tom could deceive anyone if he chose because, as an actor, it was his trade, then why not Marsh? Marsh could make anyone believe anything *because he was an actor*! Had there been time, I could have appealed to the stars to see if I was right, though they are not always willing to answer personal pleas,' he remembered, with feeling.

'Did you fear then for the boy?' asked John, as a wench removed their platters and offered them apple pie.

'No. There I nearly made a fatal mistake. I thought Marsh had a genuine affection for Daniel and in a strange, twisted way I think he probably did, and of course I'd no idea of the boy's involvement in Lane's death. I thought Matthew Lane prejudiced and deranged even for considering it to be a possibility. No, I don't think Dick intended to kill Daniel when they rode off to Stratford. He enjoyed the boy's adoration and the hold he had over him, being privy as he was to what the boy had done. It must have come as a dreadful shock when, in all innocence, Daniel told him he'd seen him alone late that night near the Rose when he'd sworn all along he was fast asleep in his lodgings all night, after returning from the supper party.'

Simon attacked his apple pie and sent for more wine. 'As I waited for you to return from searching for Daniel, other things occurred to me, such as the scripts of *Henry VI* that disappeared. It couldn't be Parsons this time because he was dead. And who was the beneficiary? Marsh, of course, who played King Harry. And finally, he condemned himself when he spoke of fighting with Parsons for his life. In his desire to mystify everyone and enjoy a macabre joke at our expense, he left no weapons there at all, which meant no one could believably accept self-defence, not even himself.

'I'm for my bed,' he said, sighing and rising from the table. 'Remind me, should I ever consider again being so foolish, that my mission in life is to heal the sick and seek advice from the stars and that from henceforth I should keep to it!'

They rode to London as swiftly as they could the next day, aware that Charles had been left in gaol until barely a week before his trial. As soon as he had seen that all was well at home, Simon would go to the authorities to collect the document which would exonerate Charles and release him from prison. No doubt he was now frantic as day followed day with no sign of Simon, his friend Dick or anyone else arriving to save him.

Anna, having welcomed her master and her husband home, had much to tell them. There had, she said, been a continual stream of visitors in their absence, by no means all patients. Charles Spencer's lawyer father had arrived from Norwich and called in several times hoping to see Dr Forman about his son. He was now deeply depressed as, barring a miracle, there seemed no way of convincing the judicial authorities of his son's innocence; it seemed they were determined to make an example of him.

Then there was Thomas Barton. Finding Simon out of town, he had returned to Kent with extreme reluctance, finally only leaving when Anna had insisted yet again that she had no idea when the doctor would be back. But he had refused to be put off entirely: a small stack of heavily sealed letters from him awaited Simon's attention. There had also, Anna told him primly, been two ladies to see him: the foreign-looking woman with the strange name to say she was married and, now being with child, desired him to cast as to the outcome; while the other was Mistress Allen, the silk-merchant's wife from over the river, who did not divulge the purpose of her visit. Then, that very morning, Master Henslowe had called by demanding to know what had become of the doctor as he had expected him back days ago.

Simon groaned at the amount of business with which he would have to deal but it was clear there were two priorities: first to extract Charles's release from the hands of the authorities that same day, and then to inform Henslowe of the outcome of his business and the imminent return of the company.

With regard to Charles, he found the task less arduous than he had feared. Sir Thomas's man was waiting for him when he went to seek the actor's release to ensure that all was in order, and Simon was handed an official letter to the governor of the gaol asking him to set free immediately one Charles Spencer, on the grounds that another man had now confessed to the crime in question. Simon took it at once to the Clink and, after a session with the governor and an argument with the head gaoler, Charles was finally unshackled and allowed his freedom.

The young man was hardly recognisable. He was gaunt and thin, his eyes enormous in his face. He now had several weeks' growth of beard, his clothes were ragged and filthy and he stank of the gaol for, as his trial drew nearer and the money collected by the company had run out, he had been forced to share a different cell, submerged below street level, with others expecting sentence of death. He said hardly anything, looking at Simon in wonder as he breathed in the sea smell of the incoming tide from the river.

'The first thing is to get you washed and into some clean clothes,' Simon told him. 'For the time being you can come back with me; there's a spare room in the attic.'

'Where's Dick?' asked Charles, looking round.

'He's not here,' Simon responded brusquely as they walked the short distance to his house. 'I'll tell you all you want to know later.'

As soon as they reached the house Simon sent John Bradedge off to fetch Charles's father, asking him to call in at the actor's old lodgings on his way back to see if his clothes and personal belongings were still with his landlady.

'It might well be that she knows nothing of your imprisonment and has assumed you were on tour with the others,' he told Charles, when the actor shook his head and said that she had probably sold them. He then asked Anna to heat water enough to fill his own bathtub so that Charles could wash, telling him that while he did so he himself must seek out Henslowe.

Henslowe looked up at first in some surprise when Simon entered his office, then snorted, laid down his pen and announced that it was about time too. He heard Simon out in silence, sighing heavily when he reached the end of his story. He raised his eyes to the ceiling and asked where it would all end; since although one actor was now to be returned to him, it seemed that another – and that his most promising – was almost certain to end on the gallows.

Simon had been deliberately vague on the subject of Lane's death, saying only that Parsons had involved young Daniel Lee in what had been intended merely as a particularly unpleasant practical joke. To his relief, Henslowe appeared to accept this, commenting only that Parsons always had been both a fool and a knave, whereas the boy was obviously only a fool.

Informed that the company would shortly be returning, at first he shook his head gloomily. 'No doubt by the time the news is put about that yet another Rose actor is destined for the gallows, the whole of London will consider indeed that we are made up entirely of felons and rogues. Therefore our run of ill luck will never end, and we shall play to empty houses.'

Simon was quick to reassure him. 'Who will know in London what's happened to Dick Marsh? He went off on tour and is now no longer with the company, that's all. If he hangs, as seems likely, then it will be in Warwick or Stratford for attempting to murder the boy, not at Tyburn for the murder at the Rose. Who will hear of it, it being so far away? And so far as Charles Spencer is concerned, then it must be made known that he's been proved innocent and another man charged with the offence. There need be no more said. Memories are short and the matter will be soon forgotten. It will be assumed he was hanged at Tyburn, and too many are turned off there each week for any one felon to be remarked.'

Henslowe saw the truth of this, and was also somewhat mollified to be informed that the tour, shocks and revelations apart, had been reasonably profitable. Then his face brightened. 'At least none of this had anything to do with the workings of my new trapdoor.' The thought seemed to cheer him up. 'Therefore we will be bold and resolute and ensure its use in our next performances.' He proffered his hand to Simon. 'You've done very well by me, Dr Forman. I recognise that. Shall we say ten guineas?'

Simon pocketed the money gratefully. There was still no sign of his expected letter from the Royal College of Physicians. That was something else he'd have to chase after.

After Simon left, Henslowe took up his diary and wrote in it:

Lent to Wm Atkynsone, leather dresser, in ready money forty shillings to be paid me again on the 13th day of next month. Paid to Percival Craffte, the fustian dyer by the sign of the Cross Keys in the Watling Street, three shillings for the dyeing of cloth. Today Dr Forman returned from Warwickshire and told me that my actor, Dick Marsh, was lying in gaol on a charge of seeking to murder the apprentice, Daniel Lee, and that he has confessed also to the killing of Nathan Parsons. Therefore my actor, Charles Spencer, is let out from the Clink. Also it is certain that there is *no fault to be found with the making of my trapdoor* and thus it can be used again when the company returns. That is *very good!* Paid, therefore, to Dr Forman the sum of ten guineas for his services, I say paid.

By the time John Bradedge arrived back with Master Spencer and a bundle of clothes, Simon had returned and Charles was sitting by the fireside in the kitchen wearing an old shirt and breeches belonging to the doctor, tucking into a large bowl of soup washed down with a quart of ale.

When he had finished his meal, Simon took father and son into his study and shut the door. 'Now,' he said, looking at Charles, 'I'd better tell you all about it. I fear you're going to find what I have to tell you very distressing but I'd prefer you said nothing until I come to the end of it.'

The Spencers heard him out in silence, although the older man had to restrain his son from interrupting on several occasions. 'So,' Simon finished, 'you owe your release in part to Sir Thomas Lucy of Charlecote, who sent his own man post-haste to London to inform the authorities of what had happened.'

'And you say this evil creature, this villain who would have seen my son hanged, is to stand trial in Warwick?' asked Spencer. 'Are you sure of that?'

'Quite. He is charged with the attempted murder of young Daniel and is likely to hang for that, irrespective of what he might have done in London so it's unlikely he will ever be brought to book here for the murder of Nathan Parsons.'

Charles looked numb. 'But *why*? Why did he act in such a way? Why try and blame it on me? Surely he could have claimed he acted in self-defence even if no knife was found at the scene; there'd have been plenty to speak up for him. Instead of which he let me be accused of murder, knowing full well that I was innocent, put to rot in gaol for weeks, and was quite prepared to stand by and see me hanged for his crime. No one in the gaol expected any other outcome.'

'That's true,' added his father gravely. 'I did everything I could, looked up old colleagues and pleaded with them to give the boy a chance, but all to no avail. It seems he was sent for trial by a magistrate who loathes actors, and was likely to be tried by a judge who detests them even more! Added to which there is much concern at present over easy knife and sword fights in public places, and word has gone out that those found guilty of such affrays without pressing reason must be made examples of.'

'And what of Daniel?' asked Charles. 'Is he now in jeopardy for what he did? It was very wrong but the responsibility surely lies with Parsons.'

Simon sought to allay his fears. 'Don't fret. Sir Thomas was told only what he needed to know and as to the rest, even Ned Alleyn concluded that the boy had suffered enough for his sins. I fear the boy's still far from having recovered from his dreadful experience, nor from discovering that his great idol was a thoroughly wicked man who'd been quite prepared to kill him.'

'I'm finding that hard to come to terms with as well,' said Charles, quietly. 'I thought him the best friend I'd ever had . . .' his voice broke and he struggled not to give way completely.

'What are you going to do?' his father asked him. 'Are you going to come back to Norwich with me, or rejoin your colleagues at the Rose?'

'I think he should sleep on it before any final decision is taken,' Simon intervened. He felt dog-tired himself. 'I intend going to bed early and I think Charles should too. It'll be the first night he's had in a comfortable bed in weeks. Though the thing Henslowe said,' he added, turning to Charles, 'was that you'd best be ready to rejoin the company as soon as they reach London as gaol or no gaol, there's work to do!'

Charles smiled, but somewhat bleakly. 'That sounds like him all right.'

'I must pray you come to your senses,' his father told him. 'Surely now you must see how pointless this acting business is? Come home with me, Charles, and we'll make a lawyer of you yet.'

Charles put his hand on his father's arm. 'I'm truly grateful for what you've done, Father, and, yes, I think you're probably right, I should return to Norwich and train for the law. But whatever I decide,' he added as his father sighed with relief, 'first I must honour my obligations to the Lord Admiral's Men. They've already had enough to contend with without losing me at a moment's notice as well.' And with that his father had to be content.

When Simon got up the next morning he found that Charles was already out. A brief note informed him that he was going to try to see Audrey. Simon sighed. He felt there would be little to be hoped for in that quarter, and indeed within half an hour Charles had returned saying that he must now go back to his old lodgings, after which he had arranged to meet his father. Before leaving he thanked Simon once again.

'You saved my life. What can I possibly offer you for that?'

'Nothing,' replied Simon. 'I'm grateful that at the last justice was done.' He hesitated, wondering how best to ask what had transpired between Charles and Audrey. Charles guessed his dilemma.

'I know what you want to ask me,' he said. 'I wasn't even allowed to see her; her father's servants turned me away at the door. So I went round to the house of her friend who deigned briefly to speak to me, once she'd got over the shock. I asked why they'd lied about my being there that night, even though what they said might well have hanged me.' For a moment he was unable to speak. 'She made light of it. It was of no importance to her compared to the risk of losing her good name. I am, after all, "merely an actor", and so of little account. You were right there too, Dr Forman, it *was* Dick who told them what to say. It seems I've been a lackwit and a trusting fool all round!'

'You could hardly be blamed for trusting your supposed best friend and the girl who claimed to love you,' Simon pointed out. 'But hard as it is, you must put it all behind you. Go off and join your friends and colleagues and good luck to you, whatever your decision!'

In spite of his brave words to Charles that he'd been grateful to see justice done, Simon's mood remained sombre and on the following Sunday morning he took himself off to the church of St Mary Overy. He did not consider himself a religious man, was not naturally devout and usually attended church only sufficiently to avoid paying the fines for non-attendance, but now he felt the need to make sense of what had happened.

Looking round the church halfway through the service he saw to his surprise (for this was not her parish church) Avisa Allen, with a man who must almost certainly be her husband. As the congregation filed out afterwards she came towards him and introduced the two men. The silk merchant seemed an austere man, though polite. Simon was just about to say farewell to them when an elderly man caught Allen's eye and waved to him. Allen excused himself, explaining that he had arranged to meet the man that morning, which is why they had attended St Mary's church, whereupon he left Simon and Avisa alone.

'I hear you've saved a young man from the gallows,' said Avisa. 'His father has been lodging with acquaintances of ours.'

Simon nodded, at a loss for words.

'That's a very fine thing to have done. You must feel proud. Perhaps one day you can tell me about it.' She looked across to where her husband was now deep in discussion. 'He came with the greatest reluctance but it was convenient as he needed to see Master Barnes: they are considering a joint venture.' She looked up into Simon's face. 'I confess I was hoping I might see you.

229

That night, the night I came to your house—'

'Don't remind me of it. That I could have been such a fool!'

She touched his arm. 'I've told you many times, we have no rights in each other.' Then she smiled and her whole face lit up. 'In retrospect, if I hadn't been so upset, it would have been very funny: seeing you like that, half out of your breeches!' Simon's face burned. 'But there is one thing I think you should know. William was away that night, and I'd finally summoned up the courage to call on you for . . .' she halted and the colour swept over her face, 'To call on you to see what might come of it.'

'That makes it even worse,' cried Simon, in anguish. He looked guiltily at Allen, who was now making his way back to them.

'Who knows,' whispered Avisa, 'there might yet be another time!'

He looked after them for a while after they left, then, on an impulse, returned to the empty church and sat down in one of the pews. He could see the parson at the end of the nave, tidying away the Bibles and psalters. What, he asked himself for the hundredth time, had made Dick Marsh what he was?

Sara Marsh was not the best of mothers but neither was she the worst, and anyway he had put all that behind him. He'd had so much in his favour: intelligence, good looks, great charm and, above all, a truly major acting talent. He could have achieved great things; his ranking of himself with Edward Alleyn and Richard Burbage had been no idle boast, and he was also popular and well-liked. Yet he had been prepared to squander everything. And for what?

Fame? Greed? No: he'd stolen playscripts not as Nathan Parsons and so many others had, to try and pass himself off as brilliant poet and dramatist (for he had not wished his name attached to them), nor simply to make himself easy money for that too seemed incidental, but for the arrogant enjoyment of the rows and ill feeling that followed.

But this was small stuff compared to what had come next. Personally, Simon thought Marsh had every intention that night of seeing to it that Parsons could make no more trouble for him but he had not been satisfied simply to leave it there. After arranging to meet him after the supper party and killing him, he'd then gleefully and coolly set about arranging the body in the most bizarre fashion before returning to the room he shared with Charles and going back to bed.

Going out had not been much of a risk. After such an exhausting day of anger and fury over his play, an evening of dalliance with his beloved and, no doubt, a copious amount of drink, Marsh could be almost certain Charles wouldn't wake and find he was alone. Perhaps he even added something to his friend's wine to guarantee it. It then followed that when Parsons's body was found, Charles would be the obvious suspect.

Presumably then, as soon as Charles had been arrested, he went round to Mary Goodman's house, warned her of what had happened and told her that the only way she and Audrey could ensure their not becoming involved in a prime scandal was for them to deny flatly that Charles had ever been with them. He had thought of everything.

After which he'd gone calmly off on tour with the Lord Admiral's Men, ensuring he was always on the move by offering to go ahead of them to make the tour run smoothly, while hypocritically refusing to perjure himself. Until Simon arrived, he must have considered himself home and dry.

Again, though, the question *Why?* Was it jealousy of Charles? Had Dick, unbeknown, been overwhelmed with desire for Audrey? Somehow Simon doubted it. If anything he felt that if Dick was capable of desire and affection at all then its object was more likely to have been Charles himself, for it had occurred to him some time back that perhaps Marsh favoured Kit Marlowe's preference for young men.

Then, most chilling of all had been the attempted murder of Daniel. Once the child had innocently informed him of what he knew, thinking it would only please, he had, coldly and without compunction, done his best to kill the child who had adored him. It was when he heard Marsh suggesting possible excuses for Daniel being missing that he realised he *had* heard it all before, for in just such a way had Marsh earlier thrown suspicion on Charles while offering only sympathy and help. His evident relief when he thought Daniel's body had been taken from the river was palpable and for that alone, thought Simon, there was scarcely sufficient punishment on earth – or elsewhere.

He sat in the church for so long that eventually the parson came over and asked him if there was anything amiss. Simon shook his head.

'Nothing and everything,' he replied. 'A dying woman, born into the Old Faith, once asked me to fetch her a Roman priest so she could confess her sins. I smiled at the time but now realise it might be useful to have such a one to turn to, rather than merely reciting out loud that we are sorry for what we've done.'

'Have you many, then?' asked the parson with a smile.

'Sins of commission and omission,' Simon responded. 'I have done those things I ought not to have done and left undone those things I should.'

The parson regarded him with sudden interest. 'Are you not Dr Forman?'

Simon admitted that he was. 'The great necromancer and practiser of black magic. That's what some say of me.'

'And do you so practise?' enquired the parson.

'No, nor am I ever likely to. But I read from the stars and that, I know, you forbid.'

The parson agreed this was so, though adding, 'But I also know you do much good for the poor folk of the Bankside.' He smiled. 'I think that will count in your favour on Judgement Day. Is there anything else?'

'It has been my good fortune to save a man from the gallows but in doing so I have met one the like of which I hope never to meet again, one for whom I can find no reason in God's universe.'

The parson seated himself beside Simon. 'Perhaps you'd better tell me about it,' he said. 'I have nothing more pressing to attend to.'

With an increasing feeling of relief, Simon did so. 'Yet when he was caught,' he ended, 'he showed not the slightest sign of remorse for what he had done – though he leaves behind at least one dead man, a child who suffered greatly and may never fully recover and the friend he betrayed, who is unlikely to trust so much in anyone ever again. Not to mention the petty spites and mischiefs which set his colleagues against one another. And all for what? So tell me, how can God let such creatures be?'

The parson did not answer straight away. Then he laid his hand on Simon's arm. 'I have no easy answer with which to satisfy you. All I can say is that it has been said of such men that they must be one of the band of dark angels that fell with Lucifer.'

Epilogue

Arden of Faversham

On a brisk, cold day in December Simon was returning from seeing a patient when he was hailed from across the road by Tom Pope. He had heard that the Lord Admiral's Men had returned a few days earlier, and Tom informed him that they were preparing to give a performance that afternoon even though they were weary from their tour. 'We do agree with Henslowe though,' he told Simon, 'There will be few opportunities to play much now until the spring, and we should seize this one while we can.'

'And Charles?' asked Simon.

Tom sighed. 'Still with us but not, I fear, for much longer. What happened seems to have taken all the enthusiasm out of him. Oh, he plays well enough but the drive is no longer there. It's a pity, for he would have done well. He hasn't yet quite made up his mind but I think he'll go. I suppose you heard what his father did before leaving London?'

Simon had. In spite of his son's protestations, Master Spencer had made it his business to call on Masters Newbold and Goodman, remaining closeted with both for some time. The result was that her parents informed Audrey immediately following his visit that it was high time she was married and that a suitable husband, most likely a man of mature years, would be selected for her. Until then she would not be allowed out of the house without a chaperone and that included visits to the home of Mistress Goodman, who had behaved with monstrous impropriety.

Mary Goodman, meanwhile, had faced a deeply unpleasant scene with her husband after which he informed her that he had decided his mother, a sour-faced puritanical woman, would visit them, as soon as this could be arranged, for a prolonged stay.

'And what of Daniel?' asked Simon.

'Altogether much quieter and more serious than he used to be. Possibly that's no bad thing but I find myself wishing back the merry imp he once was. The miller's wife from Lucy's Mill has written to me saying that, should he not wish to continue as apprentice, they will be happy to offer him a good home and bring him up as one of their own. For the time being we'll see how it goes but it might well be the best thing for him.'

Simon agreed, adding: 'Have you heard anything of Matthew Lane?'

'He arrived in a carriage just as we were leaving Charlecote. Sir Thomas had returned from Stratford and so explained to him what had transpired. Lane then spoke with Ned who told him that his brother's death had been the result of a malicious practical joke played by Parsons, who was not even a member of our company, and is now himself dead, murdered by Dick Marsh. It was made clear to Lane that the matter is now ended. I think the combination of Sir Thomas and Ned at his most eloquent will suffice to prevent his taking it any further.'

The actor looked round at the familiar street and gave a satisfied sigh. 'All I can say is that I've never been so glad to be back home with my wife and boys and all things decent. Now,' he said, changing the subject, 'will you come to see me in the play this afternoon? I think you owe me that!'

Simon was about to say he was too busy, then thought why not? He had no particularly pressing business that afternoon, and he felt he did owe his friend something for having kept him in the dark.

'Very well then,' he said with a smile. 'What is it?'

'*Arden of Faversham*. It's a strange piece about a woman who keeps trying to murder her husband. It should suit you very well!'

'I'll ignore that!' retorted Simon. 'Who wrote it?'

'Nobody remembers who wrote it: my own feeling is that it was half a dozen actors using the pamphlets and gallows' confessions of the time. It's based on a true story from some fifty years back which ended most grimly: Alice Arden went to the stake. But the play is in a lighter vein and much of it will make you laugh.'

So that afternoon, warmly dressed and with an extra cloak to put over his knees, Simon bought himself a seat in the first tier of the galleries and prepared to enjoy himself for an hour or two. As Tom said, it was an odd piece and very soon after it began Simon became convinced he knew what was going to happen next, even though he'd never seen the play before.

The plot was set up early on. Mistress Alice Arden had an old lover, Mosby, and wanted to be rid of her elderly husband, Thomas Arden, Customs Commissioner for the port of Faversham, who her family had forced her to marry. First she tried poisoned porridge, then a poisoned picture, then—'God's blood!' exclaimed Simon out loud, causing a score or so of people to turn round and stare at him. He quickly recovered himself. So this is what Thomas Barton, Customs Commissioner of Kent, had addled his brain with! The old buffoon had told him how he and his wife had gone to the theatre while on honeymoon, indeed had been about to bore him with details of the play they had seen, when he'd stopped him in his tracks.

Now it was clear what had happened. Suspicious that his young wife was playing him false, he had cast himself in the role of Thomas Arden, convincing himself that he too was having attempts made on his life. Simon had finally roused himself sufficiently to read the correspondence that had come from Barton in his absence and had found himself becoming more and more certain, as he read through yet more tales of attempted abduction, dark figures lurking in closets and shifty knaves who followed him wherever he went, that the man was mad and should be confined somewhere out of harm's way.

The realisation that he was right shifted a burden off his shoulders. He determined that after the play he would go home and write to Mistress Barton explaining the situation, saying that in his opinion her husband was suffering from delusions and that she should call in a local physician, adding that in future he should be kept away from playhouses at all costs. Simon pondered on what Barton might have got up to had the play he'd seen been *The Spanish Tragedy*!

Having made this decision he was able to enjoy the rest of the play, not least the inept hired assassins, Black Will and Shakebag.

Tom was a fine Thomas Arden, Antony Hunt not a bad Mosby, the part that had previously been played by Dick Marsh. Charles was the young artist from whom Mistress Arden obtained poison and it was clear that Tom was right; he played it well enough but the spark was no longer there.

The trapdoor, however, most definitely was there, for Henslowe, true to his word, had insisted on its use in the performance although there was no obvious place for it in the plot. In the end it was decided that, concealed behind a bush, it should become one of the hiding places in which the inept hired assassins lurked before making one of their failed attempts on Arden's life. Simon, along with those in the audience who recalled its notorious past, were amused to see how carefully the two actors playing the roles peered into its depths before stepping down into it to hide, and how quickly they bounded out of it as soon as the plot allowed.

As the performance drew towards its close, Simon reflected that it had caused laughter and shudders in almost equal proportions but that at the end of the play, had moved into a different and more chilling realm altogether when Arden, finally murdered by Mosby after all other attempts had failed, was carried by him and Alice Arden out into the fields. The idea was that when he was found it would be thought the dead man had been set upon by footpads. But it starts to snow (giving the apprentices much enjoyment throwing tiny pieces of white material down from the balcony), so that the footsteps of the murderous pair lead their pursuers straight to the body, at which point it bleeds anew, a sure sign that the murderer is close by. Would that it were so in real life, thought Simon, for Parsons would have bled when Marsh stood near him and so saved us all much grief.

He returned home late, having drunk long and deep in the Anchor with Tom and other members of the company, and this being the case he did not find time to write to Mistress Barton until the next day. He had just finished setting down his view of the matter when Anna came into the study bearing in her hand yet another letter with the familiar seal.

Well, thought Simon, at least it would be the last. He opened it, then exclaimed with surprise. It was from Mistress Barton. *Dear Dr Forman*, she wrote:

> It has become known to me that my husband, Thomas Barton, consulted you on several occasions claiming that he was the victim of attempts on his life. I fear his mind must have been turned by our visiting the playhouse while in London after our marriage, where we saw a drama in which a wife tried to murder her husband. It affected him profoundly – Thomas was always very suggestible to such tales.

Was? thought Simon. *Was*?

> You will, I'm sure, be sad to hear that he has indeed left this world for a better. He choked while eating some nuts after supper a sennight ago and died before I could fetch help. I do not know if he owed you any money for his consultations but if he did, please send me a note of it and I will see that you are recompensed. Your assured friend, Catherine Thomas.

Oh my God, thought Simon, sitting down in his chair with a thump. Was it all simply a fantasy? Or could it be that she really . . . ?

He made up his mind. Looking round his study, he gathered up all the missives he had received from Thomas Barton, adding to them the letter from the grieving widow. After which he went into the kitchen, stuffed them into the fire and watched them burn.

Author's Note

THE REAL DOCTOR SIMON FORMAN

Almost the only knowledge we had of him for a long time was the note in the *National Dictionary of Biography*, written by Sir Sydney Lee in the late 1870s, which is full of inaccuracies and described him as a charlatan and a quack, a view presumably he had taken after reading of the clashes Simon Forman had over a period of years with the Royal College of Physicians. Later research, for much of which we are indebted to Dr A. L. Rowse, shows he was very far from that and indeed that he had many new ideas gleaned from the Continent which were in advance of those prevailing in the England of his day. As an example, he did not believe in wholesale blood-letting, a common practice then and for centuries afterwards, as he considered it merely weakened the patient. Nor did the fact that he practised astrology, cast horoscopes and also used them for diagnoses make him a quack; most doctors did so then, including one of the earliest respected presidents of the Royal College of Physicians.

Simon Forman was born in Quidhampton, Wiltshire, probably in 1558, the youngest of five children. His father, who worked on the land, died when he was very young, leaving the family far from well off. After going to the village Dame school, he achieved a place at the local grammar school where he was considered a bright scholar. He was fascinated by the New Science and wanted to study medicine, and his teachers were eager that he should go to Oxford University, but, hardly surprising in her circumstances, his mother was unsympathetic towards his ambitions. The best he could manage was, when possible, to act as servant to a local parson's son who

241

was a student at Oxford and attend some lectures, but he was not allowed to become a student himself as he had no funds and had not been offered a scholarship.

After a year he returned to Wiltshire to find work locally. He soon upset the local landowner, Giles Estcourt, as a result of which he spent nearly a year in prison. There is then a great blank after which we find him working as a medical practitioner in Salisbury (during which time he fathered an illegitimate child) before moving on to London where he set up as a qualified physician formally recognised by the University of Cambridge. He may or may not have studied in Italy (or elsewhere on the Continent) but he certainly studied somewhere and I decided on Italy for the purposes of this story.

When he first set up in practice in London he was endlessly hauled up before the College of Physicians who refused to recognise him as a doctor, even when his status was confirmed by Cambridge. They disliked his attitude, considered him an upstart who had risen from the ranks of the poor, and were the most likely source for the rumour that he was a necromancer who practised the Black Arts.

Dr Rowse dates his setting up in London as around 1593–94, and it has been suggested that on one occasion Queen Elizabeth's great Spymaster, Sir Francis Walsingham, intervened on his behalf to prevent his being sent to prison by the Royal College of Physicians. If this is indeed the case, then he must have been practising in London as early as 1590 for Walsingham died in the spring of that year.

Certainly by the early 1590s Simon Forman was living in a good house near to the Bankside (outside the jurisdiction of the City of London) with a garden in which he grew herbs and flowers for his medicines. He treated patients both at his own home and by visiting them, and he almost uniquely crossed the entire social spectrum from the publicans, actors, writers and whores of the Bankside, through the City merchants to the aristocracy and the Court. He enjoyed the theatre, leaving us the first accounts of seeing Shakespeare's plays, and Shakespeare's Bankside landlady was one of his patients as was the wife of Richard Burbage. He had a tremendous weakness for women and was candid about sex. He had a code word (*halek*) for those ladies who paid him in kind rather than in cash. He also had a brief, if stormy, affair with the strongest contender for the role of Shakespeare's Dark Lady, Emilia Lanier, née Bassano.

The long-term love of his life was, however, Avisa Allen who was married to a merchant older than she was and who also 'distilled', that is made medicines from herbs. Since he outlived her and divorce was out of the question there was no possibility of marriage. She became his mistress and their relationship continued until she died. Many years later he married Jane Baker, the daughter of a Kentish knight. He was an expert on poisons and death, and would have been a witness in the trial of Lady Howard for the murder of Sir Thomas Overbury, but he died suddenly just before the trial, from what might well have been appendicitis.

Simon Forman, like many doctors of his age including Shakespeare's son-in-law, John Hall, kept a meticulous Casebook of his patients and their maladies, and also of the horoscopes he cast. Forman also wrote books both on medicine and astrology. While my portrayal of Simon Forman owes much to poetic licence it is clear that the original was lively, clever and energetic and never ceased to have an enquiring mind.

OTHER PEOPLE IN THIS STORY

The people listed below really did exist, although the part they play in this novel is purely fictional.

Philip Henslowe, theatrical entrepreneur and owner of the Rose Theatre, was a most remarkable character and it is thanks to his habit of keeping a diary and writing up inventories that we know as much as we do about life in the Elizabethan theatre. The diaries, inventories, recipes for medicines and details of card games were among papers concerning the importing of timber, which finally came into the possession of Dulwich College along with letters he wrote to **Edward Alleyn**, when the latter was on tour, and letters from Alleyn to his wife Joan (known as 'mouse'), and to Henslowe in return. Would that Richard Burbage had left a similar treasure. I hope I will not be shot by purists for adding my fictional diary entries to genuine ones.

Edward Alleyn was one of the two greatest actors of his day (the other being Richard Burbage). He was not as versatile as Burbage but was considered to be unsurpassed in some of the great roles, especially the mighty overreachers of Christopher Marlowe like *Tamburlaine* and *Dr Faustus*. Most unusually for a player of his day, he lived a life of exemplary rectitude (his portrait makes him look like a wealthy City merchant), gave up the stage at the end of the 1590s and when he died left enough money to endow Dulwich College. In a later era he would surely have been a knight.

Robert Greene, rakehell, gambler, poet and pamphleteer, was a popular dramatist of the day and he did indeed have a mistress, **Emma Ball**, sister to a notorious highwayman, Cutting Ball Jack. **George Peele**, poet, dramatist and drinker, was his boon companion. **Thomas Kyd** is best known as the writer who shared a workroom with **Christopher Marlowe** and so became caught up in the events leading to Marlowe's death, suffering torture to compel him to betray the writer as a blasphemer and traitor. His play, *The Spanish Tragedy*, was, however, the single most popular play of its day.

Thomas Pope was an actor who worked with a number of companies, including the Lord Admiral's Men, eventually moving to the Lord Chamberlain's Men and becoming, with Shakespeare, a sharer in the Globe Theatre.

Emilia Lanier, née Bassano, the orphaned daughter of a court musician, was the mistress of the Lord Chamberlain for some years. She first appears in Simon Forman's diaries in the mid-1590s but it is clear they already knew each other and he is quite frank that, from time to time, he 'haleked' her.

Avisa Allen was the real love of Forman's life and we shall hear more of her in future.

The Reverend Jonas Chalenor was the vicar of Byfield in 1591 but I have no idea whether he had sons or daughters. **Sir Thomas Lucy** owned Charlecote Park at the end of the sixteenth century and had a son, also called **Thomas**. The Elizabethan house known as **Lucy's Mill** still stood where the mill had been until about thirty years ago – indeed Sir Peter Hall lived in it when he was artistic director of the Royal Shakespeare Theatre. As soon as he vacated it, it was mysteriously destroyed and block of 'luxury flats' built in its place.

PLAYS AND PLAYERS

The stealing, poaching and pirating of original playscripts was a real problem in the early days of the playhouses, and it was not until playwrights were able to register their scripts at Stationers' Hall that matters began to improve. In some cases dramatists took their ideas from older texts; there are, for instance, previous versions of plays later rewritten by Shakespeare including *Richard III*, *King John* and *Henry V*. There was also an earlier play of *Hamlet* before Shakespeare's, the text of which has long since disappeared but it is usually attributed to Thomas Kyd. Robert Greene found himself in trouble after selling his adaptation of *Orlando Furioso* to several companies at twenty nobles a time, assuring each of them that they had the sole rights. Of the plays referred to in this book *The Spanish Tragedy*, as noted, is by Thomas Kyd and *The Old Wife's Tale* by George Peele. Scholars disagree on *Henry VI*, one view being that the three parts were co-written by Marlowe and Shakespeare.

Shakespeare did write for Henslowe early in his career but by the date of this story had joined Burbage's company which he never left. The author or authors of *Arden of Faversham*, *Fair Em* and *Crack Me This Nut* are unknown. So far as I am aware neither *The Tragical History of King Mark of Cornwall* nor *The True Tale of Sir Tristram and the Tragic Iseult* have ever existed!

THE TRAPDOOR

Stage trapdoors were in use from the 1590s onwards as there are contemporary references to them and we know that when Burbage's playhouse, known as the Theatre, was moved to the Bankside to become The Globe, it had a stage trap big enough to take at least two grown men. Trapdoors were used in all kinds of plays such as those involving demons coming from hell. There's no proof there was one at the Rose – or that there wasn't. There seems to be no definite consensus as to what they were like and how they worked.

The trapdoor at the present-day Globe Theatre in London is a simple hole with two hinged flaps which are secured in place by timbers. But as Henslowe extended and refurbished his Rose Theatre at about the time this story is set, I decided to give him a more sophisticated version as he would have wanted the newest inventions. My apologies if it was installed too early.